DARK E

A Brad Willis Adventure

Tom Boles

This is a work of fiction. All characters and events in this publication, other than those clearly in the public domain, are fictitious and any resemblance to real persons, living or dead, is purely co-incidental. Businesses, places, and events are either the product of the author's imagination or used in a fictitious manner.

ISBN-9798512080726

For Rita.

Author's Note

Dark energy was introduced after 1998 to explain the acceleration of the expansion of the universe. Supernovae, exploding stars, were used to make the discovery. The Higgs boson was discovered in 2012 using the Large Hadron Collider at CERN. Peter Higgs and Francois Englert, who first proposed the mechanism, were awarded the Nobel Prize for Physics in 2013. The inflaton is a hypothetical particle used to explain the expansion of the universe. The Hubble constant is a measure of the rate of expansion of the universe.

PROLOGUE

It was a day for skulduggery. Leaden clouds hugged the landscape and bathed the ground in depressing gloom. Distant daytime streetlights illuminated the underside of the low cloud with an indistinct orange glow.

Before him stood the biggest and most expensive experiment in human history, the Large Hadron Collider at CERN in Switzerland. He made his way towards the freight lift, a lone figure. He looked like any of the other maintenance personnel; his red boiler suit, white hard hat and orange metal toolbox made him inconspicuous. His only challenge so far had been the security card he had to proffer to the card reader in the lift. Vladislav Yerkin had no problem with security systems; they were easy to fool. He had chosen his time with care to avoid engineers coming off shift; they might have recognised him as an intruder had it been a normal workday.

From a leafless branch, a solitary bird chirped. A weak wind hissed, interrupting his solitude. There was only a skeleton staff on duty, chosen from anyone willing to work on the holiday Thursday of Jeûne genevois. Those who had volunteered were busying themselves with routine safety tasks. The sooner they had finished, the sooner they could head home to their families.

Two men in red boiler suits approached Yerkin from the opposite direction. He mumbled a greeting. They parted to let him pass. A narrow service track stretched in front of him and along the tunnel that ran under the Swiss-French border. His destination was in sight – there was not far to go now. A small electric vehicle stood outside a door leading to electrical switchgear. Its owner had disappeared inside the room amidst a tangle of wiring harnesses that would keep him and his two companions occupied for some time. These tiny yellow three-wheeled cars were used to speed engineers along the tunnel, and this was a godsend – there was no way he could have hoped to find a car here. At this stage, speed was not important, but it would be after he had completed his task. He slid into the car and touched the switch. The car moved off, the soft sound of rubber wheels on concrete echoing off the tunnel walls.

Within minutes, a huge metal structure towered over him, its jumble of red, white and green wires providing the only colour in the greyness of the tunnel. His employer had described it to him in detail. He knew what he had to do, for he had practised every move again and again until he was perfect. From his toolbox, he took three small packages. He placed each in the exact locations he had rehearsed. Three lengths of coiled wire trailed down from each package. Yerkin smiled. The ends of the wires snapped onto a connector inside the toolbox. This was easy. He pushed a button. A four-digit display burst into life. The red LEDs illuminated Yerkin's complexion, making his sallow complexion look almost healthy.

I can shorten the sequence, he thought, thanks to my luck in finding the electric buggy. He pressed another few buttons. The number 5 flashed in the minute row on the display.

Yerkin checked along the tunnel to see if anyone was nearby. There was no reason to hurt anyone; no one was close. He pressed another button. The display changed to 4 minutes 59 seconds and continued to count down.

He jumped astride the buggy and drove back towards the lift. A higher-pitched sound came from the rubber wheels; he was travelling faster. Everything was going to plan. He grinned. He passed the three men, who were still busy trying to reroute what looked like a telephone cable. They didn't look up as he sped past.

He parked feet from the lift, strode to the lift and closed the gates. Yerkin took one last look back through the lift gates as he swiped his card on the security reader. From the opposite direction, two men were walking towards the spot where he had left his orange toolbox; they might well be casualties. The lift shook into life, and he travelled back to the surface.

Yerkin removed his boiler suit and hard hat and threw them in the back of his white van. He fired up the engine and drove towards the exit, keeping well under the 15 kmph speed limit. He nodded to the guard and touched his security card against the sensor for the last time. The mechanism squealed. The gate opened, and he passed through. As the yellow and white gate closed behind him, a dull thud vibrated through the ground. Immediately afterwards, sirens and klaxons began to screech and wail, and red warning lights flashed over the lift shaft tower.

Vladislav Yerkin looked at the dashboard clock. It read exactly noon.

CHAPTER 1

Brad Willis was happy. He was very, very happy. The bundle of published scientific papers lying in front of him was proof. They had taken a lot of work to write – long hours searching for references had filled his days and nights. But he had succeeded. There they lay, all six of them. It was a record; he had never managed six papers in a month. There was a second pile containing two papers he had failed to publish this month. That was okay. Two out of eight was a good result. The other two would be a good start for next month. Still, he was very happy. He was an astronomer. What other profession would have paid him for doing what he would gladly have done for free? Brad ate, slept and lived for astronomy. Why weren't all scientists astronomers? It was the noblest of the sciences. He yawned and rubbed his red, swollen eyes. That's what staying up all night did to you.

One night was fine, but two in a row were wearisome. Still, he was happy.

Willis's desk was on one side of a spacious room. On the left-hand wall hung a twelve-foot whiteboard. Scrawled on it were the remains of the previous day's discussions. Above it hung nine clocks, each displaying the time at a major astronomical observatory. The leftmost one displayed the time on Mauna Kea in Hawaii; the rightmost one the time at Siding Spring in Eastern Australia. The centre clock – the only one with a black face – displayed the time here at the Institute of Astronomy, or IoA, in Cambridge. The black clock showed eight-thirty. The clock second from the left showed that at the Paranal Observatory in Chile, it was three-thirty. In summer, the time difference was five hours; in winter, it was only three. His allotted time on the telescope was almost over.

He missed the days when using a telescope abroad meant getting on a plane and flying out to an exotic destination. That used to be the only way to get hands-on with the instruments. The nights were made up of star-studded skies streaked with the Milky Way. On Paranal, it looks so white that it is often mistaken for a band of early morning cloud. Those were the days: he would spend the afternoons in the sunshine, recovering from the lack of sleep that was the reward for a long night's work. Today he did his observations from Cambridge using the internet and a plasma screen on his local computer. It wasn't the same, but he was happy.

Despite his contentment, Willis longed to go on trips that would take him from his cosy office and transport him halfway across the world to exotic places with palm trees, white sandy beaches and food that even the most critical aficionado would appreciate.

During a working night, things were sometimes hectic, and then there were periods of calm. He was experiencing one of these calm periods. He lifted his six-foot frame from the observing bench, opened a drawer in the adjoining desk and took out two cards with gun targets printed on them. He examined the better of the two as he brushed his mop of dark brown hair away from his face. Four holes lay within the target, one on the edge of the central circle and about two inches to the left. Yes, he should have done better. But this wasn't a bad attempt; after all, it had been his first practice in over five weeks.

Willis was solidly built but by no means heavy. He held up his large hands. They were strong enough to give him the edge at the practice range: a strong grip helped to hold the pistol rock-steady. He needed to keep up regular practice for the little sideline he sometimes got involved in.

On that subject, Reilly hadn't contacted him for months, many months. He had last spoken to him in February; it was now September. Things must be quiet at MI6. Willis wasn't a spy – not in his estimation, at any rate. He wasn't an agent. The Secret Intelligence Service merely considered him a useful asset. Mike Reilly wasn't his handler. Spies had those. No, he was merely a communication point when the SIS needed some freelance work done. Willis clasped and unclasped his fingers, then rubbed his palms together. Something had to happen soon. A break doing something different would be very welcome. He didn't want to think about Reilly now. Shaking his head, he placed the two cards back in the drawer.

An alert flashed on his computer screen. The Paranal telescope had acquired its final target, so Brad returned to his desk and concentrated on the task at hand. He downloaded his results for the night; analysing them could wait until tomorrow. Willis's eyes were stinging and watering, and his eyelids were heavy. His head beginning to droop, Willis put the final touches on his night's work and logged out of his terminal.

Twilight would arrive in Paranal soon, and some other astronomer would have booked the telescope for the rest of the night. Willis was ready for a rest. He went to the washroom before leaving. He had had a very productive night, and all he wanted now was a shower and some shut-eye. He splashed cold water on his face and marched out of the toilets.

Willis packed his haversack and shouldered it. When he opened his office door, a cool gust of air hit his face. Welcoming the coolness, he took a long breath and stepped outside. Papers on the notice board rippled in the draught. Above the rustle of the paper, another noise fought for attention. His desk phone was ringing, its buzzing a mere whisper fighting its way along the corridor. Damn. He turned and headed back to his office.

With his eyes almost closed, he lifted the black receiver from its cradle. The caller began to speak immediately. 'My name is Klaus Laufer. I am telephoning from Switzerland. I am based at the research facility at CERN.'

'CERN?' Willis was confused. 'What do you want at…' He squinted at the clock. 'Five to nine in the bloody morning? I haven't been to bed yet. I'm knackered. Why are you calling?' For a normal person, 8.55 a.m. would be reasonable. For an astronomer, it was early.

'The team fired up the Large Hadron Collider some weeks ago, Dr Willis. There are ramifications for the Supernova Cosmology Project at Berkeley – we fear that the building may be broken into, and questions are being asked about the findings of the project.'

'Why me? I've just finished a night shift. I need to go to bed. Is there no one else you can call? What—'

'Please, Dr Willis,' the voice interrupted. 'I don't have time to explain. Please get in contact with Berkeley Labs immediately. I don't know anyone I can contact at

Berkeley, and I have reason to believe that someone might attempt to force entry within the next hour. Please hurry. Trust me. CERN has already been compromised.' There was a pause. 'You must...'

The line went quiet, and the dialling tone returned. The connection had been terminated.

Bollocks. Who is Klaus Laufer? Brad thought. He searched for the directory to find the number for Berkeley. I know all the physicists at CERN from my particle physics days, but I've never heard of a Klaus Laufer. If someone is planning to break into the labs, why call me? Why not phone Berkeley? What is there to steal at Berkeley, anyway? Some desk computers might be lying out, but everything of any value would be locked away.

'I know,' he said. 'Greg Palmer – I'll phone him. He'll remember me. I seem to recall that his apartment isn't far from the lab.'

CHAPTER 2

The ringing phone woke Greg Palmer with a start. By the time he opened his eyes, he was already holding the phone to his ear. 'What? Who did you say? What the … do you know what time this is?' Palmer's left hand brushed his forehead as though trying to sweep the sleep away. The time, projected on the far bedroom wall from his LED alarm clock, was 12.55 a.m.

'Yes, this is Greg Palmer. Who did you say you were?'

'My name is Brad Willis. I'm ringing from the Institute of Astronomy in Cambridge.'

'The IoA?' barked Palmer. 'What do you want with me at this time?'

'I'm sorry, Greg, you're the only person I could think of. Do you remember me? We enjoyed a few sherbets in Birmingham last year at the National Astronomy Meeting.'

'Of course I remember. But it's still one o'clock in the goddamn morning.'

'This is urgent,' Willis said, 'or I wouldn't be calling you.' He repeated the message Klaus Laufer had conveyed a few minutes earlier. 'I know it's late where you are, but I haven't even been to bed yet. I don't have time to explain. Laufer wants you to get over to the Berkeley Labs immediately. If someone is about to break into the lab, you have to stop them. There must be something worth stealing there, or Laufer wouldn't have called me. I'm also fearful for his safety.' Willis described how Laufer had been cut off. 'This is extremely urgent. Please let me know as soon as you find out what's happening.'

'Okay. I'll check it out and let you know.' Palmer dropped the phone, staggered to the bathroom and splashed a handful of cold water on his face.

***

Palmer dialled the front desk. No one answered, so he hung up. Shit. He searched in the semi-darkness for the clothes he had scattered over the floor when he fell into bed. He realised he'd had a couple of large whiskies before crashing out. He dismissed the thought and pulled on his trousers. If someone was planning to break into the labs, how did Laufer find out about it in Switzerland? What was there to steal at Berkeley, anyway? Everything worth any value would be locked away. Willis has a fucking cheek. Who the hell does he think he is?

***

Two security guards sat behind a long desk in the foyer of the University of Berkeley's Astronomy Building. Six CCTV screens sat on the desk in front of them. Each screen scanned the entrances and corridors. A large fake palm tree adorned each side of the desk to soften its appearance. Health and safety would have disapproved of the unofficial microwave oven and kettle the guards had plugged into a spare wall socket. In the daytime, visitors to the Astronomy Building would be greeted with courteous smiles and directed to the correct departments, but there was not a lot to occupy guards there at 1.15 a.m. They had completed their routine checks and initialled their security checklist. A row of empty coffee cups sat along the desk; there had not been much else to do. They'd have to tidy up their lunchboxes and sandwich wrappers before the day shift got in at 6.30 a.m. Other than the odd bang and clatter and a pair of feral dogs sniffing around the main glass doors, it had been an uneventful shift.

The guard nearest the coffee machine stretched and picked up a novel from a shelf behind his head. Light flashed off the security badge pinned to his shirt. It read: 'H. Sherman, GSI Security'. He straightened the corner fold that was marking his page, sighed and started to read. Within seconds, the storyline had grabbed his attention.

The other guard sat with his legs crossed, his feet on the desk. The light from his iPhone illuminated his face, exaggerating its contours. He scrolled down the list of music displayed, selected a track, pressed Play and let the music meld with his thoughts.

Neither man was aware of a small plastic tube protruding an inch from the pebbles in the pots holding the palm trees. They didn't hear the faint hiss of gas that had been programmed to be released at exactly 1.20 a.m.

The gas was invisible, save for a few inches of white condensation that formed above the outlet of each tube. The condensation quickly cleared as it warmed in the heat of the foyer.

H. Sherman laid his book, face down, on the teak reception desk, yawned and slouched back in his seat. He wished he hadn't eaten that last turkey sandwich. Two screens away, music squeaked through the second guard's earphones, but their owner was oblivious to it. He was sound asleep. H. Sherman's arm fell to his side. The foyer was silent but for the faint hiss of escaping gas.

***

Dressed and still complaining to himself, Dr Greg Palmer drove to the research labs. His red hair was tousled and dishevelled. The cold night breeze wasn't helping to make him more alert. He had left the hood down on the BMW convertible the previous evening. His wavy hair was exposed to the wind above the windscreen. The car was cool. He pressed a radio button and heard the normal nondescript crap that DJs always played at one in the morning. Didn't night-shift-workers deserve decent music too? He had decided not to contact anyone else. What would he tell them? That some crackpot had called him in the middle of the night and asked him to check out the labs? No. It was better this way. At any rate, security would be in the building. He would tell them.

California wasn't cold at night, but he'd been warm from being in bed, and he was losing that heat fast. Goose bumps puckered his arms like Morse code on steroids. The pale blue of the street lights flashed past. They made him wish he could close his eyes and go back to sleep. He would have a cup of the weak bilge water that passed for coffee from the machine when he arrived.

The labs were quiet when Palmer drew up in front of the main building. The reception lights were off: no light showed from behind the large desk where the uniformed guards usually sat. A faint shimmer of pale blue light from the CCTV monitors illuminated the walls, reflecting off the two artificial palms that stood beside the desk.

He placed his ID card against the sensor on the door. A red LED flashed. Nothing else happened. He reversed the card. Still nothing. Resorting to brute force, he hammered against the glass door with his car keys. There was no movement inside, no sign of life.

Palmer's heart thumped. The car keys stuck to his hands. The sweat was sticky and uncomfortable. The outside of the building was dark apart from a dim glow coming from lights that illuminated the access path – the Department of Astronomy was very careful about light pollution. This was one of those rare times when a little more light would have been very welcome. Palmer cursed the low lighting. He followed the path, keeping close to the building wall.

The path continued around the corner to the astronomy administration offices. The distance between lamps was enough to allow him to see the outline of the path. A halo of light glowed below each lamp, but between them, there was nothing but darkness. Damn the lights. He passed some small high windows that gave a modicum of light. He cursed again. His eyes had adjusted to the dark, and he made out the vague outline of several doors. Wide panoramic windows indicated the location of the staff restaurant. Security lights illuminated the serving counters and the corridor leading to the ovens. He could smash the main glass door, perhaps? Then he dismissed that idea. But he might be able to force the internal latch on the supply delivery doors... He shook the doors. It might be possible to pry them open; he would need a tool.

Palmer looked out over the landscaped gardens. Trees were barely visible against an almost jet-black sky. He strained to make out a darker shape sitting several feet in front of the trees, behind a row of low bushes. He could make out a wooden storage shed against the tree-lined perimeter. He moved closer to investigate. It was old, and the wood was falling away, rotten. It was a gardener's shed – perhaps he would find some tools inside? The door was on the far side, hidden from the road and parking areas. Palmer had no idea how grateful he would soon be for this fact. He worked his way around, groping along the walls until he reached a door fastened with a padlock.

He pulled on the door. Pieces came away in his hands. First, a small strip came off, then a larger bit. Soon, enough wood had fallen off to allow him to pull the bolt free and force the door open.

Palmer stepped inside. His timing was perfect. As the frail walls engulfed him, the ground shook. A wall of wind blew the shed over, pinning him to the ground. Sparks flooded in from under the shed walls and, through the now empty window frame, a bright red flash lit up the sky.

Then came the blast. A wave of air raced past him, carrying glass fragments. The shards from the explosion embedded themselves, like shrapnel, in the soft, rotten timbers of what had been the shed. A second explosion followed. He found himself staring at a smoke-filled sky. The stars carried on twinkling above, oblivious. The shed had gone. He lay motionless on the earth. A pain in his chest forced him to breathe in short, sharp pants. Had something become lodged in his chest – a sliver of glass or a piece of the fragmented shed? Whatever it was, it hurt like hell. It felt like an invisible band was tightening around his chest. Was this what a heart attack felt like? There was no one near to help him. No one would hear.

Minutes passed. Palmer fought to stay conscious. He closed his eyes and tried to relax to ease the pain. He lay still, counting each breath. Each inhalation increased his chances of survival. Finally, the pain eased, and each count of ten breaths became freer and less painful than the previous ten. He rolled onto his side and pushed himself onto his knees.

The astronomy block was on fire. Flames poured from the first-floor windows, licking up the walls and over the window to what had been his office. Loud cracks accompanied the burning window frames and doors. He knelt for several minutes, unable to move further. The red glow of the fire merged with blue flashes as police and fire services arrived at the scene. A stream of service vehicles screamed to a halt in front of the lab. Their sirens relaxed their wails as the engines were cut, sounding like dying monsters. It took several minutes before two police officers saw Palmer. They rushed to his side and helped him to his feet.

'This is going to take some explaining.' The police officer was stating the obvious. Through the cracked crystal of Palmer's watch, he could see that the time was 1.34. He pressed his hand to his chest to lessen the pain. It was improving. He hoped he'd only been winded by the impact of the blast.

His self-pity abruptly stopped as paramedics carried two stretchers, on top of which were two body bags, past the smouldering stalks that had been the artificial palms. The security guards had not been as fortunate as he had.

'You say the call came from Switzerland, Dr Palmer?' The policeman had a strong Italian accent. He reassured Palmer that he didn't doubt his story for a minute. It was such a wild story that it had to be true.

'I got the message second-hand; the guy who called is in the UK but said he got a phone call from CERN in Switzerland. It's odds on that whoever rang is in deep crap – if he isn't dead already. The call was cut off.'

'We'll get the English police to trace the source of the call to your guy, Dr Palmer. It should confirm his story and alert the Swiss police to check out where the hell it came from.' The policeman shouted something into his chest microphone.

'You ought to contact the French cops, too. CERN is on the Swiss-French border.'

'It would have helped if your buddy had told you more about the original caller – like what accent he had.'

This omission troubled Palmer. He was normally very good at asking about such details – even in the middle of the night. Was he suffering from retrospective memory loss caused by the shock of the blast? No, that had happened before the blast. He would check with Brad Willis later. He sat for a few minutes in the police car until he could stand without falling. The crackling voices on the police radio irritated him. He was clearly in shock.

'I'd better arrange a lift to the hospital for you, then a ride home, Dr Palmer.'

Palmer shook his head. 'I'll be okay, thanks. I'm a little shaken, but it's nothing a bit of sleep won't cure.'

'Goddammit, man.' The officer pointed to Palmer's BMW. Glass covered every inch of its surface. The tan leather seats were ripped, and the two nearside wheel rims rested on the concrete; flying shards and metal fragments had punctured two tyres.

***

Small knots of spectators had formed on the footpaths around the campus. Even at this time of night, there were always enough passers-by to make a small crowd. No one noticed the tall man dressed in black trousers, a black shirt and a long black greatcoat that looked incongruous, even at night, in California. A claret birthmark above his left eye faded and darkened, illuminated by the red and blue flashing lights from the service trucks. Sergei's thin lips tightened into an expression that might have been interpreted as a smile. He had done well, he told himself. His employer would be pleased. His greatcoat billowed as he turned and melted into the darkness.

***

Greg Palmer dialled Willis's number as soon as the police car had dropped him off. 'Someone has only gone and blown up part of Berkeley.' He spat out the words, his voice shaking. 'You nearly got me killed.'

'Bloody 'ell, that's exactly what Laufer said would happen. I'm sorry you were put in danger,' Willis said, ignoring Palmer's tone.

'Two security guards have been killed. The whole block has been burnt down. Seems like the explosion was in the communications centre – that's where the flames were strongest.'

'We need to get to the bottom of this. Who the hell would want to blow up an astronomy department? I have a contact here in the UK in our Secret Intelligence Service. I'll ask him to liaise with the US to discover what the hell is going on.' Willis cleared his throat. 'How are you, Greg? Did you get hurt?'

'For real? You're asking that now? I have a few scratches, that's all. My car is in a much worse state – it's trashed. The police had to give me a ride home. I don't need fucking friends like you.'

'I'm really sorry, Greg. I had no idea that it would be as dangerous as it turned out, but I am glad that you aren't injured. We both need a good night's sleep. I'll speak to you tomorrow once I know what's happening.'

Willis hung up and immediately rang Reilly.

CHAPTER 3

It took a while for Willis to get in touch with Reilly. It was only after he became obstreperous with the person he was speaking to and insisted that she ask Reilly to call him back that he was put through.

'And that's the gist of it.' Willis finished giving Reilly a breakdown of what had happened at Berkeley.

'Why did this guy contact you?' asked Reilly. 'How did he get your name?'

'I have no idea. My astronomical connection is the only thing I can think of.'

'I will speak to my man in the States,' said Reilly. 'If he agrees, I suggest you fly over there and discover what you and Palmer, or whatever you said his name was, can find out.'

'I'm not certain that Palmer wants to get involved – he's pissed off with me already. We'll need to see how he reacts once he's recovered and had some sleep. Meanwhile, if you manage to make contact with your man, let me know.'

They hung up.

Willis threw himself on his bed. Maybe a couple of hours' shut-eye might be possible before he was due to leave. He felt the soft brush of fur against his leg. It was his cat, Ptolemy. Willis had named him after the astronomer Claudius Ptolemy, who had lived in Egypt because, like him, the cat thought that the universe revolved around him. It usually did. After Willis was in bed, the cat would come and lie over his feet. Tonight was no exception. After a few minutes, he could feel the warmth of the cat's body soak through the duvet onto his feet. A faint, regular, asthmatic wheeze filled the bedroom. Willis lay and listened to it, and slowly he relaxed.

***

Willis slept the sleep of the just. When his alarm went off, it took several seconds before he was able to open his eyes. His house in Madingley, near Cambridge, was small but big enough for a single man. Since Carole, his wife, had died two years ago, he had got used to living a simple life. He cooked for himself but survived with only one cup, plate and one set of utensils. He liked to keep life simple. Oh, and one bowl for Ptolemy.

He silenced the alarm. Resisting getting out of his warm, comfortable bed, Willis stared at the time on his alarm clock, letting his thoughts drift to more pleasant memories, such as eating with Carole in a Chinese restaurant on Marylebone Road in London.

Because she loved the dish so much, Carole selected crispy duck from the à la carte menu, but only after telling the waiter that she needed extra pancakes for all the duck on the plate. Although his thoughts had given him an urgent desire for crispy duck, he put it out of his mind. It was only breakfast time.

He bit the bullet and swung his legs out of bed. His eyes were still heavy but not as bad as they had been. A shower. He must have a shower. The pressure of the hot water stung his skin. The shower gel vibrated in the shower tray. He always missed his powerful shower whenever Reilly sent him on an assignment.

Now for some food before he had to leave. He managed a quick bite to eat and a cup of his favourite Brazilian coffee before the phone interrupted him. He answered it, his mouth full, still chewing on a piece of sausage. It was Reilly.

'Okay. I've made contact with Jamie Wilson – he's a naval type but assigned to the CIA at Langley. The Agency picks his brains on some special assignments, usually ones requiring technical approaches – kind of like your arrangement. I think you will like him. He wants you to visit him at the US Naval Observatory in Washington, DC. He will send a car to pick you up from Dulles Airport and take you to the observatory.'

'You didn't waste any time,' Willis said, smiling.

'There's no point in messing about. I've booked your flight – the details are in the email I've sent.'

Willis always kept a bag packed so he could quickly leave if he had to. This came from what he'd learned working for Reilly in the past. He lifted his house phone, dialled, waited until it had rung out twice and then hung up. It was his signal to Mrs Burns in the cottage next door. Within two minutes, the back door to his cottage opened. Mrs Burns had come through her back garden, as she always did.

'Good morning, Dr Willis, sir. Are you goin' travelling again?' Mrs Burns was an elderly Scots woman who sometimes 'did' for Willis – cleaning and shopping and feeding Ptolemy whenever Willis was away. She was a short, rotund lady with an enormous bosom and a generosity to match. She wore a wraparound pinny, of the kind his grandmother used to wear, in a dazzling floral pattern. Over her hair, she wore a hairnet. Yes – very much like his gran.

'I'm going away for a couple of days, no more. Will you look after Ptolemy and the cottage for me?'

'Don't I always?' came the reply. 'As long as you leave money for the cat food and litter.'

Willis always did, but she liked to make the point.

Willis pointed at an old, dented tea caddy on the top shelf of the Welsh dresser opposite the door. This was where he left money for Mrs Burns. She only used cash – no cheques. No credit cards. She deigned to have a savings account, but that's as far as she would go.

'I've put money in the caddy. If I'm away any longer, I'll transfer some money into your savings account as usual.' He told her he would be leaving later that evening. 'How is Rabbie doing?'

Rabbie was her husband. His real name was John. Willis called him Rabbie because he knew it made him smile. He took it in good spirits, and he had a great sense of humour. This was just as well as he was confined to a wheelchair and rarely got out. Willis always brought him something back from his travels. On his last trip to Paraguay, Willis bought John a T-shirt of the national football team, La Albirroja, the White and Red. He wore it proudly, its APF logo showing.

'I'll see you when I sees you, then.' She waved her hand. 'Ptolemy, come on. It's time for food.'

Ptolemy came in and stared up at Willis. He was sure the cat knew when he was leaving. Mind you, the oversized overnight bag at the front door could have been a clue. Ptolemy rubbed himself against Willis's legs and did a figure of eight around his ankles. Willis stroked his neck and brushed his hand over his back, then wrapped his fingers around his tail and pulled gently, letting it slip through his grasp.

'C'mon, Ptolemy,' Mrs Burns prompted.

Ptolemy followed her to the door. He stopped, looked over his shoulder, gave a mournful 'meow' and marched out in apparent disgust.

***

The plane was only partly full. Willis ordered three small bottles of Malbec. They would relax him and help him to sleep. After finishing off a tray of plastic food, he stretched out over several seats. The regular drone of the engines numbed his brain and helped him relax, so he succeeded in sleeping for the next few hours.

***

A car was waiting at Dulles Airport as promised. It bore US Navy plates, and the driver was in an officer's dress uniform. The journey took place in silence but for an occasional 'Yes, sir' or 'No, sir' from the driver in reply to Willis's efforts to be sociable.

The car turned left on the 495, crossed the Potomac River, turned onto the 190 and headed for the observatory. It entered Wisconsin Lane, then took the Observatory Lane entrance and drove towards the Circle.

A bold black and white sign announced their arrival. It read: 'The Department of the Navy, the United States Naval Observatory'. One Observatory Circle was an impressive building. Willis enjoyed the view. Its windows, framed by green shutters, contrasted against its white walls, and a canopy supported by double pillars covered its front door. The same canopy continued around to the right-hand side of the house, providing a covered walkway.

A large man in an admiral's uniform waited to greet Willis as he stepped out of the car.

'I am Admiral Jamie Wilson,' he shouted across the lawn. 'Welcome to the USNO. Please come this way.'

They walked towards the building. Willis's car had driven past the dome of the 26-inch-diameter telescope on the way in. It was in a central spot on the site, its majestic dome standing out against the skyline.

'It's a high-quality instrument,' Willis said admiringly to Wilson as they neared the entrance.

One Observatory Circle was built in the Queen Anne style. It was unsymmetrical; the hallway opened into the main room. They entered the building, turned right and went straight into a lavishly furnished suite. It oozed tradition yet had a luxurious atmosphere. The floor was covered in a thick tan-coloured carpet. Paler wallpaper framed a large oil painting that caught Willis's attention. A picture of a former Vice President of the US hung on another wall. But the most spectacular feature of the room was its window. It curved in a 270-degree arc and faced a curved walkway – the same walkway that bent around the right-hand corner of the house.

'This is a beautiful room, Admiral.'

'This is normally the residence of the Vice President of the United States, but it is being refurbished, and he has temporarily moved to the White House.'

'No wonder I'm overawed.' Willis gave a short laugh.

'Help yourself to a drink.'

The stout ex-pat Scot gestured in the direction of a drinks cabinet that could have featured in *The Guinness Book of Records* based on its size.

'That was one of my additions,' said the admiral. 'I wanted it to feel like home while I was supervising the refurbishment. We're upgrading all the security systems.'

Willis poured himself a large Scotch, not wanting to risk offending the huge man.

'I am very honoured to have received this VIP treatment, Admiral Wilson, but how do you think I can help Uncle Sam?'

'Forget the formalities. I'm Jamie. If we are to work together, we ought to relax more. May I call you Brad?'

'That's fine by me, Jamie, but the uniform is a bit imposing.'

'That's true. I left a formal engagement in the UK a little over ten hours ago. I won't have all this brass on for long. Let's check a few things out. You were a member of the Supernova Cosmology Project team – is that correct?'

'Yes,' Willis said. 'It was a large team. There were six researchers involved with the first paper we published back in 1998. I was one of the lead authors.'

'Lead authors?' Jamie Wilson's eyes narrowed. 'You had better explain.'

'In any scientific paper,' Willis said, 'the main authors are those who have led the research. Their names are always at the front of the full list and are rarely in alphabetical order. They are in the order of contribution: for example, the team leaders always come first.'

'And the others?' asked Wilson.

Willis sensed that Wilson thought this was important. 'The less major players are sometimes listed alphabetically, sometimes in order of the size of their contribution, if that can be ascertained. It might even include some young postgrads who are making their first contribution to a scientific paper.'

'Where did your name appear in the list, Brad?' Wilson took a swig from an oversized glass of Scotch.

'The joint team leader was Professor Michael Stone. I came after him on the list – only because his name precedes mine in the alphabet.'

'Where did Hemmel, Egas, Palmer and Gifford appear?'

'They were all lead authors like me.'

Willis frowned at Wilson, intimating he wanted an explanation.

'All these men, including Michael Stone but excepting Palmer, died in the past month – they have either been murdered or died in what looked like freak accidents.' Wilson threw back what remained of his whisky.

Willis took a deep breath and stood in silence for several seconds. 'Why haven't I heard of these deaths? It must be because they happened all over the world, making it difficult for anyone to connect them.'

What was the admiral suggesting? Why would anyone target the authors of a scientific paper – or, more accurately, a series of papers?

'Which authors haven't I mentioned?' Wilson asked.

Willis was struggling to remember, stunned by the implications of what Wilson had just told him. 'Er, Max Eller, Hugh Macklin and Matt Quimby.' He explained that they hadn't worked together as a group for some time, but they'd remained in touch and had shared any new ideas they had on the project.

'So the project isn't finished?' asked Wilson.

'Good grief, no,' Willis said. 'It's the sort of project that will never be finished. The result from one piece of research leads to more work for another team or another project. The chain will go on forever until we know everything about the subject. It's a never-ending process.'

Willis stared unseeingly at the carpet. He struggled with what he was being asked to believe. The idea that someone was killing scientists was irrational.

'So, the bottom line, Dr Willis…' Wilson sounded serious. '…is that I believe you're in great danger. And so are your remaining co-authors.'

'The evidence suggests that. I managed to work that out for myself, but that's crazy.'

'Crazy or not, we need to alert the other members of the team to this danger.'

Willis looked confused. 'Why don't you involve the relevant authorities? Why are you expecting me to help?'

'The police and special services are already involved. All we expect them to do is get evidence and solve the crimes that have already been committed. We need your help to work out what might still happen – and prevent it. There's another reason we will tell you about later. We need a lesson on what your research involved. Would you explain it using layman's terms?' He didn't wait for a reply. 'If you can, and I'm banking on it that you can, I want to invite Brigadier-General Joshua S. Baker over here tomorrow to put him in the picture.'

'That's fine with me if he fits into the story. I have invited Greg Palmer to join us – he was a member of the team too,' Willis said. 'I spoke to him last night, and he's due to arrive tomorrow. Palmer is uptight about the labs being destroyed and is happy to help in any way he can. But he is a civilian like me. I hope that's okay with you?'

'If you think he can be useful, then it's fine with me.'

'Admiral…' It was Willis's turn to be formal. 'Is there something you aren't telling me? Is there something else holding this mess together?'

'Well, there has been one more death that doesn't fit the pattern. I'm trying to get more information about it. I'm talking about Michael Fecher – he was the first person to be murdered. As soon as I know more, I will let you know. What can you tell me about the fire at Berkeley?'

'Very little. Palmer suspects that the fire was started by two explosions – one in reception and the other in the communications centre. He's checked with the police, and they concur. Trace amounts of military explosives were found, presumably C4. But other than that, not much evidence survived the fire.'

'I think we've gone as far as we can today. Brigadier-General Baker will arrive tomorrow – he will explain a possible link between the fire and the deaths. In the meantime, I recommend an early night. From what I have heard, you didn't sleep too well last night, and you have some catching up to do. So have I.'

Willis couldn't agree more. Although it was still early, he followed Wilson's lead. He served himself a large Scotch and followed the admiral and a naval orderly up the stairs that led to the bedrooms.

Michael Fecher had been the first leader of the project, even before Willis joined. What had happened to him?

CHAPTER 4

The previous day, Palmer had sat in the observing cage of the telescope, making fine adjustments to the secondary mirror as it tracked across the sky. Palmer's methods did not always fit well with his day-to-day masters at NASA, the funding body for most of the observatory's projects. The only thing saving his skin was that, time after time, he had extricated NASA from difficult situations. He was the Observatory Director. His task was to manage the administration, technical and support staff. He was also responsible for ensuring the smooth running of the facility. His job was not to sit in an observing cage – there were technicians to do that – but Palmer was a hands-on director.

His plan to arrive after lunch was not to be. Willis, via the US Navy, had contacted Palmer and asked him to travel to Washington, DC, as soon as possible. It irked Palmer to take instructions from Willis; he disliked being told what to do by a Brit. Some of them still treated the USA as a colony, Palmer thought. Willis had been his equal on the Supernova Cosmology Project, and Palmer found it difficult to accept this new status. He was his own man and needed to feel in control of his actions and destiny. He found it unacceptable to report to Brad Willis.

The US Navy had sent a chopper to take him on the final leg of his journey. Despite wearing ear protectors, Palmer's brain was throbbing as he approached his destination. The isolation in the cockpit made the journey seem more uncomfortable than it was. The city stretched out beneath him. Skyscrapers dominated the skyline. The Atlantic coastline was jagged, with waves crashing onto the beaches. The chopper veered inland. Dulles Airport lay on his western side. Shortly after he'd qualified as an astronomer, Palmer had spent some time at the USNO working on a navigation project to help the navy – but that was in the past. Best forgotten.

The descent was sudden and rapid, making Palmer glad he had missed breakfast. The roar of the engines increased, and a cloud of dust, dirt and blades of freshly cut grass enveloped the cockpit. They skimmed over Wisconsin Avenue before landing on a neatly trimmed lawn. When the debris cleared, the same prominent black and white sign that had welcomed Willis greeted Palmer. It told him he had arrived at the USNO.

***

Willis and Admiral Jamie Wilson were waiting in front of One Observatory Circle to welcome Palmer.

'I am Admiral Jamie Wilson.' He shouted so his voice would carry over the noise of the helicopter's engines. 'Welcome to the USNO. Please follow us.'

When they entered Wilson's office, he offered Palmer the same welcome as he had Willis.

'Help yourself to a drink.'

Wilson's secretary came in and asked Wilson into the outer reception area. Willis took the opportunity to update Palmer on the previous day's conversation on lead authors and the possible links to the supernova research project. Palmer listened to the information without comment, but his face revealed his disbelief. He said he thought it was illogical – though a remote possibility – that some malign force could be killing off astronomers merely because they had contributed to a goddamned paper. When Wilson returned, he refilled his glass. Willis and Palmer shook their heads, then glanced at each other. Willis nodded at the clock on the mantelpiece and raised his eyebrows.

Jamie Wilson pulled himself up to his full height. Willis estimated him to be at least six foot six in stature; he was as broad as he was tall. The surfeit of whisky – it was genuine Scotch he drank – seemed to be taking its toll. He gazed at Palmer. 'As I've told Brad, I have invited Brigadier-General Joshua S. Baker over here later today. I would like you both to outline your research to him, so he knows what it involves. The brigadier has a personal interest in the subject.'

Again, Willis and Palmer glanced at each other, searching for an explanation, wondering what would possibly entice a brigadier-general with no connection to the astronomical community to get involved in a project that had no apparent military significance.

***

Brigadier-General Joshua S. Baker arrived promptly at noon. Perhaps it was his droopy beige linen suit, which had seen better days, or his thin black acrylic polo-neck that endeared him to Willis. He decided that Baker was nothing like he had expected – there was no brass, no pomp and no military arrogance with this man. Willis took to Baker immediately. He wore his fair hair in a typical army style, only one stage away from a crew cut.

'Thank you for agreeing to meet me, Doctor – or is it Professor Willis? And you must be Dr Palmer.'

'Both apply,' Willis said, 'but I would prefer Brad.'

'And I'm Greg,' added Palmer.

'Excellent, then call me Josh. Let's get down to business. I need to understand what your research involved. Don't be confused about the army and navy working together. We always deal with the things that matter. Isn't that correct, Jamie?'

Wilson nodded and took another sip from his ever-present glass. Baker pulled up a chair, turned it around and sat astride it, leaning on its back. He rifled in the top pocket of his jacket and took out a tiny leather pouch, removed a pair of folded spectacles, unfolded them and put them on his nose.

Willis was grateful for the delay. He wasn't looking forward to trying to explain a decade of research to an army brigadier, even if he did like him. In his undergraduate classes, he was able to introduce things in stages to them, but he was not sure how best to structure this.

'We need to go back to the first half of the twentieth century to understand the basis of our research,' Willis finally said. 'An astronomer named Vesto Slipher discovered that galaxies were racing away from the Earth. Nothing much happened until Edwin Hubble discovered that the further away a galaxy was, the quicker it travelled.'

'Was this the same Hubble after whom NASA named the Space Telescope?'

'Exactly.' Willis nodded. 'NASA justified the funding of the Hubble Space Telescope – the HST – by promising that it would refine the speed the galaxies travelled at.'

'And did it?' interjected Baker.

'It helped, but the story is a lot more involved than that.'

'Keep going,' urged Baker. He was leaning forward over the chair back, absorbing every word.

After taking a deep breath, Willis realised that this might be easier than he had expected. It was clear that Baker was paying close attention and was capable of absorbing the basic concepts.

Willis took up the story. 'The Hubble Space Telescope narrowed the uncertainty of what is now known as the Hubble Constant, but it didn't reduce it far enough. This constant determines the age of the universe… The smaller it is, the older the universe and the further back in time the Big Bang occurred.'

'The birth of the universe?' Baker put in.

'Exactly,' Willis said.

The admiral sat fiddling with his ball pen, doodling on a piece of paper that lay on his desk. He wasn't as outwardly comfortable as the brigadier.

Willis continued. 'The holy grail of modern astronomy was proving the value of this speed. Many groups carried out research, and they published as many values for it as they did papers. Rarely did two teams agree. At the end of 1998, our group at Berkeley published a key paper. Another team from Harvard University published a similar paper with identical conclusions. This was heralded as the greatest twentieth-century discovery in astronomy: it is manna from heaven when two completely independent groups come up with the same results.'

'Don't keep us on tenterhooks.' Baker was getting impatient.

'What they discovered was a surprise. No one expected it. They discovered that the speed at which the galaxies were moving was accelerating.'

Baker wasn't looking too happy. Willis thought he had better move on. 'When Albert Einstein proposed his General Theory of Relativity, he found a problem. He had to stop the galaxies from collapsing in on themselves under gravity. So he invented a constant that created a method to hold them apart. Einstein was quoted later as saying that this was his greatest blunder.'

'Our discovery,' Palmer butted in proudly, 'suggested that Einstein was not wrong. We discovered a form of energy that filled the universe and was driving it apart. It suggested that the more the universe expanded, the more energy filled in the gaps. As a result, the new energy drove the universe apart even further and faster.'

'What is this energy?' asked Baker.

Willis took up the thread again. 'That's just it. We have no idea, Josh. The numbers have been refined over recent years, but the nature of the energy is unknown. This is where the research stands today. We call it dark energy for want of a better name. Now you're completely up to date, Admiral.'

Josh Baker took off his spectacles and folded them. He shook his head. 'I don't understand how this research has led to these murders. The research is completely theoretical – it has no practical application that I see.'

'I agree,' Willis said. 'Once we discover the rationale for the murders, I suspect everything else will fall into place – but I also believe that's going to be easier said than done.'

'I have another reason to suggest the murders are connected. After we finish this conversation, I will fill you in on the details.'

At this point, Wilson seemed to come awake. 'Let's go back a tad. How would this result affect Einstein's original equations?' He hadn't been asleep after all.

'It doesn't affect them in any way.' Willis shrugged. 'At worst, the new constant would need to go back in.'

'Another goddamned constant,' snapped Baker. 'Now we need another space telescope to find its value?'

'Not a space telescope, but something similar.' Palmer sat down on the chair next to Baker. 'That will be the next stage in this line of research.'

'How did you conduct the research? What tools did you use?'

'We used the world's best telescopes,' Willis explained. 'We needed to study stars as far away as possible, so we booked time on the two big Keck telescopes. The Keck I and Keck II telescopes are high on Mauna Kea mountain in Hawaii. Each of these telescopes has a light-collecting mirror ten metres in diameter. We also used the Hubble Space Telescope, thanks to the co-operation of the Space Telescope Science Institute in Baltimore. But the real tools we used were supernovae: exploding stars that are millions of times brighter than normal stars. They are visible halfway to the end of the observable universe.'

'And your project at Berkeley was the Supernova Cosmology Project.' Baker's face lit up as though a bolt of lightning had exploded in his brain.

'Yes, that's right.'

Brigadier Baker's jaw dropped. 'This is getting more and more complicated, but the pattern is clear.' He got up and walked to the window, frowning. This was the most serious Willis and Palmer had seen him since the meeting had begun. He turned around and threw his specs on the table.

'I know what the connection is to the first murder – of Professor Michael Fecher.' Baker stared straight at Willis.

'He was the team leader before Michael Stone took over: he was the inspiration for the whole project. Without his foresight, we would never have got off the ground… and he is dead?' Willis asked.

'He died in Prague,' added Palmer. 'He was murdered two months ago. His death shocked his family and associates, but they assumed it was a random, isolated incident. The

Prague police didn't make much of an effort to find his killer, although I can't blame them. Little evidence was found at the scene.'

Baker ran his fingers through his short hair. 'This problem has been around longer than we imagined.'

Illogical or not, the conclusion from the evidence was inescapable. They had to assume that everyone associated with the Supernova Cosmology Project was at risk. All members of the research team were being deliberately and methodically eliminated. Hemmel, Egas and Gifford were already dead in suspicious circumstances. Hemmel and Gifford had both been hit by a truck, and Egas had died of food poisoning. The necessary course of action was also obvious. Willis and Palmer had to discover who was doing this, why they were doing it and then stop them – before they too were eliminated.

'I need to know all you know about this affair, Brigadier. It will be risky, but if I sit and do nothing, the risk will be even greater – I fear the killings will continue until everyone who took part in the project is dead.' Willis focused on the brigadier. 'Enlist Palmer to help us, Josh. Increase our chances of survival – along with the chances of the remaining members of the team. I will return to the UK and request I get involved too. This needs to stop before more people are killed.'

'I was hoping you would come to that conclusion before I asked you to volunteer. I'm pleased to have you on board.'

***

Palmer had managed little sleep the night of the fire at Berkeley. He had even less tonight. Willis hadn't slept much either. They had retired upstairs in the hope they might relax; Jamie Wilson had even convinced them to sink a large glass of whisky, intimating that they would sleep like babies. He wasn't wrong. They tossed and turned like babies, and they were on course for staying awake all night. Willis's brain was in hyperdrive, thought after thought flooding through his mind. Finally, he sat up in bed and stared out of the window.

Josh Baker had agreed to give him a copy of the file he had created after he'd discovered the pattern to the deaths. As promised, Baker told them why he thought the deaths were linked. As soon as he revealed that co-author Susan Gifford was his niece, Willis realised how Baker had cottoned on to the pattern of deaths. Susan had died when she was hit by a truck. Baker had been investigating her death when the fire took place at Berkeley. That had been her workplace, so it didn't take Baker long to deduce that her close friend Hemmel's death was also unusual. After that, the other two deaths soon fell into place.

Susan Gifford had been one of the lead authors with Willis. The connection would not have been obvious without personal knowledge, gained either professionally or through a family connection, to one of the victims. In Baker's case, it was a family connection.

The 'accident' had only happened a few weeks ago. Otherwise, Willis would have known and cottoned on to the pattern of deaths immediately.

Willis recalled Susan Gifford well. She had been one of the more energetic members of the team. She loved analysing data, but the uncertainties in the data produced huge error bars in the results. She processed the numbers so they were useable. Some of the uncertainties were so large that the small changes they were searching for could easily go undetected. The team had been plagued with doubt: were their results valid or, due to some systematic or experimental errors, had they allowed errors to creep in? Other highly respected teams had had to withdraw papers in the past due to careless oversights. All quality papers are required to go through a peer-review process. Susan's work helped get positive peer reviews of their work, without which they might never have been published. Susan had spent more time with the data than anyone else in the team. Could that be why she had been killed?

***

They rose early the next day. Willis had booked his flight home. Palmer made plans to fly back to Berkeley to await Willis's instructions. Neither man was sure what to do next.

Willis's meeting with Reilly would change all that.

CHAPTER 5

The following morning, the twilight sky brightened, and a warm day once more blossomed on the Chilean peak. An orange glow on the horizon replaced the deep black of the night sky, signalling the end of the night on the mountain. For the past nine hours, the 8.2-metre-diameter astronomical telescope on Cerro Paranal had probed the depths of the visible universe. Its work completed, the cryogenically cooled imaging detector returned to the ambient temperature of its surroundings. All 5 tonnes of the 50-metre observatory dome rotated until its observing slit pointed away from the prevailing wind – essential to protect it from the daytime weather. Two precision motors sighed and drove the giant fork mounting back to its parking position. A distant quasar had been the last target of the night; it had been a last-minute target of opportunity. As a result, the huge reflecting telescope finished the night, pointing well to the west. This meant its last slew back to its parking position would be a long one. Under instruction from the control computer, the robotic monster obeyed the final command of the day and, with the grace of a practised ballerina, one of the world's largest optical telescopes swung eastwards.

Every morning after the telescope reached its rest position, at exactly 180 degrees azimuth, electronic encoders would send a signal to confirm that the slew had been completed successfully, then, the motors would stop, and the brake would be applied.

Today the signal never arrived. Instead, there was a gurgling scream. A sickening crunching sound echoed around the dome…

Safety circuits failed to trigger. All went silent.

The cavernous interior of the observatory dome amplified the sound of fresh blood dripping onto its concrete floor.

CHAPTER 6

Monika Fecher walked towards the apartments of the Royal Astronomical Society in London. She had already told the Society's secretary that she was not looking forward to relaying her news to the Council. Her father, Michael Fecher, had been robbed and killed in Prague, and the papers for his Edwin Hubble Memorial Lecture had been stolen. The Council would, no doubt, be sympathetic, but they would also want the Christmas lecture to take place. Although it was not her subject, she had promised to give a summary of his work. Without her father's notes, this would no longer be possible.

She walked through Burlington Arcade and turned left into Piccadilly. Across the road stood Fortnum & Mason, the food store to beat all food stores. Every time Monika and her father visited London, F&M had been one of their first stops. Monika's mum had always asked them to bring back English jams and jellies. Ever since she had been confined to a wheelchair after her accident, one of her simple pleasures had been freshly baked bread and English jam each morning.

The triple arches leading into Burlington Square drew nearer. Its square housed many British learned societies. The Royal Academy of Arts took pride of place at the back of the courtyard. It also housed the Royal Society of Chemistry, the Society of Antiquaries of London, the Geological Society of London and the Linnean Society. Monika would find the Royal Astronomical Society through the first door on the left.

She took a deep breath and took the few stairs to the front door. She was there to deliver bad news, and it wouldn't be pleasant. She reached out to press the visitors' button when a familiar voice whispered in her ear. 'Allow me.'

A hand came between her and the door and swiped a card in the security card reader. 'This will be a lot quicker than waiting for the office to open up for you.'

'Matt Quimby? I recognise that voice. I wasn't aware you had left Berkeley.'

Matt leaned forward and kissed her on the cheek. She was over five foot seven tall, but she only reached his shoulders. He grew his dark brown hair on the long side, but it swept back neatly and gracefully above his ears. Thin white streaks had begun to protrude into the brown.

Monika said, 'You look more like a captain of industry than a Berkeley professor.'

'Thank you, but I haven't left Berkeley. I'm just visiting Europe on a jolly.'

Monika smiled at him. 'You have never gone on a jolly in your life.'

'Okay, you have sussed me already, but you'll be happy when you find out why I'm here.'

The door was open, and Matt Quimby was already inside. He held the door to let her pass.

'Let me get you a coffee in the Fellows Room, and I will tell you all about it.'

Like many learned societies, the RAS didn't have members; it had Fellows. Such titles made their members feel a lot more important.

Matt swung open the heavy oak door. He turned a china cup over in its saucer and placed it under a coffee machine that sat incongruously on a nineteenth-century mahogany desk. The Fellows Room, reminiscent of a gentlemen's club, had all the opulence of such. Its large armchairs added to its ambience. Paintings of past Fellows adorned its walls. Matt sat down on one of a pair of worn leather Chesterfields that sat behind a low coffee table. He placed the coffee cups on the table beside them.

'Sugar? Milk?'

'You know your way around these rooms,' said Monika. 'How do you know Burlington House so well? One sugar, thanks.'

'I visit here quite often. I have been working on cosmology at Cambridge. Cosmology – that's the real science of the universe,' he teased, 'not piddling little planets like you choose to study.'

'They're hardly piddling,' retorted Monika, not taking him seriously. 'Not if I detect them light years away, around distant stars.'

They always teased each other when they met.

'I'm trying to finish off the work your father started, but I'm not making such a good job of it. I was sorry to read about what happened to him.'

'I'm working hard to get myself through it,' said Monika, 'but what is this news you say I will be happy to hear?'

'Well, I'd like to volunteer to do the Christmas lecture for you, if you like. If you agree, you can relax a bit.'

'That's marvellous, Matt – that would be great. It will get Council off my back. I was dreading today's meeting.'

'I know that Christmas is a long way off, but it will be a weight off your mind. You'll be able to enjoy Thanksgiving without worrying about writing a lecture. But there are conditions attached,' he said, winking.

'And what might they be?'

'I get to take you to dinner.'

'Will you go up to the Council Room now, please?' The Executive Secretary leaned through the half open door into the Fellows Room. 'Take your coffee with you, if you wish – we would like to get going early. The President seems impatient to get started.'

Monika and Matt didn't answer but picked up their coffees and followed him. The Council Room had been moved to the top floor, the direct result of the Society's recent refurbishment of the building. The glass-walled lift would not have been out of place as an art nouveau creation in an Agatha Christie film. One could imagine Hercule Poirot stepping into the lift. Two other Fellows joined them, and they continued to the top floor in silence.

The Council chairs had invisible names on them – or so it seemed. Some Fellows liked to sit left or right of the President, and others claimed what were clearly their regular seats. Whether this was because of some perceived status the positions inferred, Monika was unclear. She and Matt took the two remaining places at the furthest end of the room and sat with their backs to a window. Bookcases lined the sides of the room and reached the far window directly behind the President.

'Fellow officers, members of Council and guests.' The President stood up. 'Thank you for attending this extraordinary meeting at such short notice. The original agenda today was to address the government's cuts in research spending for the coming fiscal year. But with your permission, I would like to postpone that until the next meeting. Other events have taken precedence.'

Murmurs echoed around the room. 'What else could be more important to the astronomical community than the current cuts in research grants?'

The President raised his voice and continued. 'I fear that we might be facing a challenge we have never experienced in the history of the Society. At 08.25 hrs Universal Time today, the Astronomy Building at Berkeley was destroyed by an incendiary device.'

There was silence, only interrupted by the sound of papers being rustled. Members shifted in their chairs, but the Fellows' attention was focused on the President. Members exchanged confused glances. Had they misheard the President's statement?

'Within two hours, the ATLAS particle detector and supporting facilities at CERN had been damaged by a similar device. More details are coming through as we speak. Professor Davies, please would you continue?'

Everyone in the room turned to the left of the President as a tall, lanky man sporting a goatee beard rose. He took a long, deliberate breath as though to compose himself.

'Fortunately, the timing of the explosions meant that loss of life was at a minimum, but it was not zero. Two night watchmen at Berkeley and one maintenance engineer at CERN lost their lives.'

'Are terrorists involved?' an elderly man interjected from the foot of the table.

'They were almost simultaneous attacks, so terrorism hasn't been ruled out. But it is too early to say. We can say, however, that whoever is doing this is targeting scientific establishments. It might be anti-science activists or even rebel Creationists, but we know of none who are capable of this. Any organisation with international connections, as this one must have, would be well known to the authorities.'

He took out a bundle of photocopied papers and distributed them around the table. 'This is a list of astronomical facilities funded or partially funded by the UK. What we – what you – now have to do is to get in touch with everyone we know and alert them to the possible danger. They will need to tighten up their security processes for the foreseeable future. Dr Quimby, we asked you to attend today as we believe that the Institute of Astronomy at Cambridge is a high-risk target.'

'I agree,' said Matt. 'Because of our supernova research co-operation with Berkeley, we must be a target. We also need to alert observatories in Hawaii, Chile, Tenerife, and of course, ESO, the European Southern Observatory. And let's not forget the microwave and radio telescopes.'

'Agreed.' The President was on his feet again. 'Let's bring this meeting to a close. Return to your respective institutions and alert the management teams to the possible threat. We might be overreacting, but better safe than sorry. I declare the meeting closed. Thank you, ladies and gentlemen.'

Fellows milled around, waiting for the tea to arrive, discussing what they had heard.

'Looks like I won't be taking you to dinner after all,' joked Matt.

'Not dinner, but how about we go to Pall Mall, and I buy you afternoon tea at the Athenaeum? Our trains don't leave for at least three hours.' Monika smiled.

'Deal, but that will only be a temporary replacement. Agreed?'

CHAPTER 7

Brad Willis awoke to a relentless drumming on the door.

'Dr Willis … Dr Willis, open up.'

Willis rolled out of bed, half asleep, and walked towards the sound. He hadn't yet recovered from the long flight home. He staggered downstairs, groping for the banister, his eyes still closed. He shuffled towards the door and undid the latch. In the doorway stood a man who looked military but wore an open-necked shirt, dark jeans and a tan raincoat. He pushed past Willis and walked into the middle of the lounge.

'My name is John Summer. I have been asked to meet you and take you to London, to the Albert Embankment.'

Willis had been there before. The Albert Embankment was the London address of MI6.

The light from the morning sun assaulted Willis's eyes. He switched on the room light and turned his back on the patio window. He stood in a dark corner of the room and stared at his uninvited guest. He had a ruddy complexion and stood a little under six feet. His raincoat looked almost new, but he came across as being untidy. The combination of tan coat and reddish hair didn't work for him. Willis opened his mouth to speak, but his guest spoke first.

'Dr Willis, you might be a common link between what happened this morning in California and Switzerland.'

'In Switzerland?'

'It's almost noon, Dr Willis. Haven't you seen the late morning news?'

The visitor picked up Willis's TV remote and switched on the BBC news. The television screen showed a split image: on the left of the screen was the smoking shell of the Berkeley Astronomy Building and the office window where Willis had sat barely eighteen weeks earlier; on the right was a fire-damaged tunnel. As he looked at the carnage, Willis recalled an earlier life where he had spent long hours working on particle physics in that very tunnel at CERN, hoping that he might discover a revolutionary new particle that would make his name as a young research scientist.

'CERN?' Willis said, but Summer's earlier statement had given it away. The parallel with the London Tube bombings was obvious.

Summer nodded.

'Who needs to speak to me in MI6? Is it Mike Reilly?' Willis asked, although he knew it could be no one else.

'You will find out when you get there, and that's all I am permitted to tell you.'

Willis wasn't sure whether to be intrigued, complimented or afraid. He opted for all three. What bastards could be wilfully destroying these scientific establishments – and why?

By the time Willis had dressed, John Summer had consumed three cups of his best Brazilian coffee. Willis was thankful he had not taken any longer to get ready.

***

A black SUV with dark-tinted windows waited on Willis's driveway. The plates on the car stood out: the number belonged to the military – Royal Navy if his memory served him correctly. They drove for only ten minutes before the limo turned off into a side lane. Willis recognised the road: it led to a small private airport six miles from the IoA campus. Carole, his late wife, had given him a series of flying lessons for his birthday, and he had learned to fly at this very airport. The plane he had first flown was at the side of the runway, sitting outside the controller's office. The ID on its fuselage, by coincidence, included Carole's initials. But those had been happier times. He pushed the thoughts to the back of his mind and locked them away.

Willis smiled. He had already guessed the plates on the SUV were Royal Navy. He had also guessed that their flight would be short. What he saw next removed doubt on both counts. Standing fifty yards clear of the control building stood a Hawk T2 training jet. It bore the RN insignia. This was too much of a coincidence. First, he had seen the small plane with Carole's initials, and now a Hawk T2 – the plane he had progressed to afterwards. He itched to fly it again, but today he would have to be satisfied to be a passenger.

'This is where I leave you, Dr Willis.' Summer gave him a firm handshake. 'Good luck. We will no doubt meet again.'

Willis thanked him for his help and strode towards the jet.

Willis was familiar with the Hawk. Its single Rolls-Royce Ardour turbofan engine made it capable of short take-offs and landings. This eliminated the need for a long runway – but with such power comes bone-shattering noise. He climbed on board, strapped himself in and waited. The Hawk revved its engine, rose into the sky and sped off westwards.

***

It took minutes to reach London. The Hawk circled while the pilot confirmed his landing permissions. Every bone in Willis's body seemed to vibrate as they flew over Greenwich Observatory and the Naval College. The towering structure of the Shard stood out against the skyline. Finally, they landed at City Airport.

The jet dropped a deafened Willis off close to the control tower, his ears numb and his feet still vibrating on the solid tarmac. The wonder of modern technology took off minutes after it had landed – and, of course, once the pilot had made sure that Willis was well clear of its jet exhausts. In the distance, a man waved at Willis, signalling towards another identical black SUV. He climbed into the back seat as two motorcycle outriders came alongside to escort him to 85 Albert Embankment, SE1. Once he was comfortable in the rear seat of the SUV, Willis stared out of the partly open window, letting the gentle breeze blow onto his face as he watched the London streets flash past.

The car dropped him off at Vauxhall Cross. This was the plainer side of the Secret Intelligence Service building. The side facing the Thames was unnecessarily elaborate: it resembled a cross between a Mayan and Aztec temple. A bright young man, who looked no older than twenty-five, approached, guided Willis through the thick metal security gates, and then they walked under the building's huge arch. Willis followed the man up the stairs, past a series of pseudo marble statues, to the first floor and continued along a short corridor. He opened a door at the far end for Willis to enter. Inside, the familiar face of Mike Reilly greeted Willis. Willis's memory of his last visit was still fresh.

Reilly sat facing the door. He had surely lost some hair in the past few months, Willis thought. His balding head, sparsely covered with white hair, made him look older than his age, forty-five.

Willis had come to know Reilly while working in South America. He had saved Jim Armstrong, one of Reilly's men, from being assassinated. Willis had uncovered a plan to trap Armstrong in a city-centre bar. When he found him, Armstrong had been shot and was losing blood. Willis's prowess with a hand gun had saved the day – and Armstrong's life. He had disarmed both Armstrong's assailants and handed them over to the local police. Willis was arrested for carrying an offensive weapon, but Reilly had pulled strings to have him and Armstrong released. So had begun an exciting relationship and one that Willis enjoyed.

Reilly stood up and shook Willis's hand, grasping it in both of his.

'Let's retire to the main conference room.' Reilly led the way, and Willis followed. They entered a large oval room. It hadn't looked like this the last time he had visited: white irregular panelling like that found in sound recording studios now lined the walls and ceiling. Reilly took a seat at one end of the table and signalled to Willis to sit on his right.

'It's been a while, Brad. How have you been since Paraguay? I hope those ribs have mended well by now.'

'You didn't ask me here to reminisce, Mike,' said Willis. 'What excrement has hit the fan this time?'

Reilly didn't need any further encouragement. 'You said your mate Greg Palmer was almost killed earlier – that he'd got much too close for comfort to a blast at the Berkeley Astronomy Building. But as you will have heard on the news, there has also been an attack at CERN. Somebody planted a bomb on the main magnet of one of the detectors. The magnet sustained considerable damage. Some other science buildings have also been threatened. We need you in Europe ASAP. This job fits your talents. This problem will need a technical solution. Your particle physics background will come in handy. You understand the anatomy of the Large Hadron Collider, and that should help you investigate its sabotage.'

'I saw the news about CERN, and I feel bad about putting Greg in danger,' Willis said. 'I rang him and asked him to investigate after I got that cry for help from CERN.' He had already told Reilly how he had received a call from Klaus Laufer in CERN and how Laufer had warned him of an attack he believed would happen, at short notice, at Berkeley.

'We also expect trouble at the Institute of Astronomy,' continued Reilly. 'Other than the fact they are attacking scientific institutions, they seem to be completely random and without motive. There is no single activist group we can identify that has such diverse interests.'

Reilly handed Willis an envelope. Inside was an airline reservation, typed on a piece of plain copier paper. This was typical whenever Reilly used military aircraft. Willis read: 'To Cointrin-GVA.' It was signed by Reilly.

'Hand that over when you get to the airport.'

'Geneva?' Willis's mouth twisted. 'Why do you think a visit to Geneva will prevent an assault on the IoA in Cambridge?'

'I will fill in the details on the way to the airport. You're already packed, I assume?'

Willis nodded. 'I brought my suitcase when John Summer mentioned the Albert Embankment address.'

'That piece of paper will get you aboard a BAe 146 cargo carrier. There is one leaving RAF Northolt in about ninety minutes. It is already scheduled to fly a ministerial team, so it will drop you off on the way.'

Whenever Reilly arranged a get-together, a trip was inevitable. Willis's job as an astronomer gave him an excuse to visit almost any city in the world without raising suspicion. Observatories, universities and conventions always welcomed a man of Willis's reputation. It was Reilly who had recruited Willis; he had been the perfect candidate. Tactics had changed since the old days of the cold war with the Soviet Union. Problems today needed technical solutions, and Willis's background suited this well. He had earned his first PhD in Cambridge. He then went to Berkeley, where he did the ground-breaking research that would earn him a reputation that would allow him access to educational and scientific establishments throughout the world.

He had been a mature student. He hadn't submitted his PhD dissertation until he was twenty-three – and then that had been after several false starts. False starts that had let him stray into the world of particle physics. False starts that MI6 knew would be useful in this new technological world. Reilly knew that Willis's knowledge would be invaluable when they arrived at the world's largest particle physics laboratory in Switzerland.

***

Reilly sat on Willis's left as they sped towards RAF Northolt in yet another SUV, shuffling through a pile of papers as he spoke. 'We ought to get someone in from the States to give you a hand, Brad – for diplomatic reasons if nothing else. They've had a site targeted, so it'll be in their interest to co-operate.'

His case contained different-coloured files; Willis could only imagine what the colours signified.

'Should I get your mate, Palmer, to fly over and join you?'

'That a good choice,' Willis said. 'I recommend Palmer. Josh Baker has already asked him to volunteer. He's a good guy.'

Reilly continued to shuffle through his papers. 'I have here a full list of all personnel at CERN. I asked them for it this morning when I suggested that you might fly out to help. There's no mention of a Klaus Laufer holding any post –

from the directors down to the cleaners.' He glared at Willis as if challenging him to find out why that should be. 'Take this copy with you. I have another in the office.' He handed Willis the list of several thousand names.

'The explosives in Geneva were placed where they would do maximum damage, so we need to assume—'

'That either it was an inside job or that inside expertise was available,' interrupted Willis.

'I suspect the latter. Whoever set the explosion was familiar with the security systems and the layout of the site. Not many people have access to the tunnel and know the components of the system. The whole installation is technical, and it would have taken a specialist to know where to site the bomb.'

'I'll need to investigate who has regular access – and the knowledge.'

'Update me when you get there, and let me know if you find out who this Laufer fellow is.'

When they arrived at RAF Northolt, the BAe 146 was ready and waiting.

'It's a CMk3,' said Reilly. 'A great workhorse.'

The four engines of the 146 were idling, ready for take-off. Plumes of hot air raced from the engines' exhausts, making the tree line behind them shimmer as the searing gas rose into the air and dispersed.

Reilly shook Willis's hand once more. 'Good luck and stay safe.'

He turned around and strode back to the SUV that had brought them.

As he boarded the plane, Willis thought about the team of colleagues he had worked with and the relationships he'd built up with them over the years. Friends who were now dead; killed for no reason other than that they were astronomers. He ground his teeth. The muscles in his cheeks bulged as he fought the rage that was beginning to take over his body. He had to catch whoever was doing this – and stop them.

CHAPTER 8

Willis braced himself for landing. He didn't have a phobia of flying, but, like most engineers and scientists, he had a respect for everything mechanical or electronic. He appreciated the technologies involved – and knew how fragile they were. Unlike most passengers, he always hoped that his plane hadn't been recently serviced. He preferred it to have several flights in its logbook after the last maintenance. This ensured that the maintenance men had found and eliminated any subsequent maintenance-induced 'bugs'. Even the most careful technician causes some disturbance, no matter how slight. The BAe 146 had an excellent reputation for safety, and Willis was confident that the navy's engineers would have meticulously serviced and maintained the jet to high military standards.

The last time he had been in Geneva had been with Sophie – Sophie Fenwick. How he wished they had chosen the same science. He hadn't spoken to her since they had gone to study their separate subjects: she had selected particle physics; he, astronomy. They had parted in the reception of the Crowne Plaza Hotel. They had promised to keep in touch, as friends often do, but they never did. After all, he had soon met, fallen in love with and married Carole. That had put Sophie out of his mind, although he had fond thoughts of her from time to time.

He wondered what she would think about his present activities. What she would think about Reilly. He wished he'd confided in her about his role with British intelligence, but he never had.

As he had expected, the landing was smooth and uneventful. Geneva Airport only has one real runway, not counting the small grass runway running parallel to it. The latter is only for small private aircraft. A row of Cessna 152s sat diagonally facing a small administration building, while barely twenty feet away, a Piper Cherokee was trying to effect a safe landing in a strengthening crosswind.

One aircraft sat further out, proud of the others. A group of four men stood huddled in earnest conversation around its tail. Now and again, the one nearest the building would look in the general direction of the main runway and say something into a mobile phone.

Willis looked at the man. Something about him made Willis uneasy. He had a dark red birthmark above his left eye, which drooped slightly. The man was staring at Willis – why was he paying him so much attention? – then, he turned and walked inside a small office. Willis put it to the back of his mind. He proceeded to passport control and his waiting car.

CHAPTER 9

Organisation Européenne pour la Recherche Nucléaire, commonly known as CERN, was a huge establishment. It was the largest particle physics research facility in the world and the most complex. It was so large that part of it was in France and part in Switzerland, with the larger part in France. The huge accelerator ring was 27 km in diameter and housed about 9,300 electromagnets. It was capable of colliding particles together with enough force to generate a temperature equal to that found in the Big Bang, the temperature that had existed at the birth of the universe.

Willis stood in front of the glass doors that opened onto the reception area at the Meyrin site, the main entrance on the Swiss side of the border. He let his mind return to the heady days of particle research. Although he remembered the glass doors, some things had changed since his last visit – such as the security lock, which had been upgraded to require iris recognition.

A stocky woman with dark hair tied in a bun was attempting to walk quickly towards him. A pair of heavy Cuban-heeled shoes slowed her progress.

'Herr Willis, Herr Doktor Willis,' she shouted from the doorway. 'I am Frau Holtz. I am the personal assistant to Herr Yeung. Please come with me.' She led him through the glass doors and up to a security desk. 'I must apologise, Herr Doktor, but I must process you through safety.'

A uniformed guard handed him a clip-on lapel badge. 'Please wear this at all times on the outside of your clothing, Dr Willis.'

The dosimeter was no stranger to Willis; it hadn't changed since his last visit. The trademark RADOS was used across the base. The dosimeter was in two parts: the upper part had a transparent window for recording neutron radiation; the lower black part did the same thing for gamma and beta radiation. Willis clipped it to the lapel of his jacket.

'Herr Yeung had it brought over from Building 55/1 for you,' said Frau Holtz. 'He used your old registration details.'

Willis signed the declaration, where he promised to pay CHF 350 should he lose the dosimeter. Then he followed Frau Holtz up the entrance stairs and into the lift. Within minutes he was at the Director-General's office, but its appearance surprised him. This was larger and more open than the office he remembered, without the whiteboards and bookcases that once had covered the back wall.

'Dr Willis, it is good to meet with you.' Ernst Yeung indicated towards a luxurious cream leather chair. It tried to devour Willis when he sat in it. Yeung was a rotund man in his middle fifties. His fair hair was casually brushed back across his head – so casually that it was continually in need of attention. He kept brushing it back with monotonous regularity. His light, checked suit was clearly intended to disguise the scattering of dandruff on his shoulders.

'How come you managed to land this comfortable role?' asked Willis.

Yeung spoke with a strong Bavarian accent. 'Director-General is not such an easy role,' he protested. 'I have so many bosses and people interested in how CERN is progressing. There are now twenty member states contributing funds, another eight – including the US, EU and UNESCO – are observing, and about another twenty-three participants, plus associates, take part in different aspects of the programmes. All have personal interests to pursue. Anyway, what can I do for you? I thought you had switched over to astronomy?'

'It doesn't look as though there's much difference between the two – we are both chasing the Big Bang. It looks like your lot might be closer to it than we astronomers are.'

'It is all bullshit,' said Yeung. He had a slight American twang. Like most mainland Europeans, his English had been heavily influenced by American idioms and phrases from movies and TV programmes. 'It's all marketing and PR. You will have read that the LHC – the Large Hadron Collider – has been nicknamed the Big Bang machine?' Again, he swept his hair from his face.

'Well, they have to justify the billions of euros in funding they have allocated to the project.' Willis grinned. 'I'm sorry – I didn't answer your question. I'm involved with a project to tighten up safety in some of the large projects in and outside Europe. My brief covers your equivalent, Fermilab in North America, and the large internationally funded astronomical observatories.'

Willis had put this cover story together with Reilly. It eliminated the need to involve governments and politics to get access to CERN. The French wouldn't welcome an outsider meddling, especially a Brit. Willis had great respect for the value the French put on science, unlike his government; however, he hated their enthusiasm for red tape and paperwork.

'I am not under any illusion, Willis.' Yeung had changed his attitude. 'I know why you are here, and I object to you nosing into my area. We can sort out any problems that occur here on our own.'

'Be that as it may, Dr Yeung…' Willis had become equally formal. 'I am here officially, and I trust I will have your full co-operation.'

Yeung grunted.

It's going to be like that, then, thought Willis, but didn't voice the words.

'I would like to pick your brains, if I may. They've told me about the explosion you had here earlier this week and about a few other incidents that have happened. All this is for my report only, you understand?' Willis waited for confirmation from Yeung. 'I assure you that I will publish nothing until you have had sight of it.'

Yeung didn't confirm he'd heard. 'About two thousand, six hundred people work at CERN at any one time. That number includes contractors. We are very lucky that the explosion happened on a holiday Thursday in Geneva; it was the holiday of Jeûne genevois. Casualties would have been much greater if it had been a normal working day.'

'Would it be possible to go and look at the place where it happened?'

'It happened almost a week ago, Willis. Jeûne genevois is on the Thursday after the first Sunday in September. Today is 11 September, and we haven't been sitting at our desks and doing nothing. You are welcome to inspect it, but you won't find anything we haven't. Our people investigated before they tidied up, but they found nothing.'

Yeung leaned over and tapped out four digits on a telephone. 'Is Jacques there? Good. Ask him to come to my office.' He turned back towards Willis. 'Jacques Villiers is in charge of Technical Support. He will answer any questions you might have and will let you know the extent of the original damage.'

When the thin, scrawny man came in, Yeung briefed him on what Willis needed. He and Willis walked towards the entrance shaft leading from the surface to the tunnel's entrance. The lift was already at ground level when they arrived. They got in. It dropped steeply and reached the tunnel in not much more than a minute.

Jacques Villiers forced another pen into the already full pocket of his white lab coat. He looked like a typical lab technician. 'Please follow me, but be careful – the grille on the ramp will be slippery if you are wearing composite soles.' Villiers's English was passable, but, as is common with engineers, language was not his forte. Willis could see him concentrate on forming each sentence in his mind before he spoke. On the outside rim of the tunnel, a narrow track acted as a Lilliputian road. There was a three-wheeled electric vehicle to Willis's left, with a man Willis assumed was a technician in a pristine red boiler suit astride it. He had to squeeze past it to keep up with Villiers.

'We won't need to ride,' said Villiers. 'It is only about fifty metres or so on the right.' The tunnel stretched far into the distance. It curved only slightly as it vanished towards the French border. Villiers stopped. 'This is where the explosion took place. It damaged the accelerator magnet, but the most serious damage occurred to the detector of the LHC. The chamber that detects the subatomic muon particles is full of liquid argon. Its purpose is not for cooling; it is an integral part of the detector, and it reacts to the particles as they pass through it. It is not dangerous. There is no chance of secondary explosions, but we have delayed the project for a year. We cryogenically cool most of the elements here to make them into superconductors.'

'I understand – this is to increase the strength of their magnetic fields and help them produce the acceleration required.'

'Exactly. It is the escaping coolant that causes the damage and the danger to anyone nearby.'

'Where were the explosives placed?' asked Willis.

'It was a simple plastic explosive, the forensic guys said. It was wrapped around the main direct-current connectors on the ATLAS magnet. It was well hidden. The outer section of the detector will have to be changed, of course.'

'What other damage occurred?'

'The ATLAS detector is as large as a five-storey building. We must replace the magnets around part of the track. Any other damage is almost trivial. At the site of the explosion, the track around the tunnel was a write-off, so we will have to rebuild it. The coolant for the cryogenics leaked out, but that is trivial compared to the damage to the muon chamber. Our biggest challenge is trying to rebuild the ATLAS without bringing it to the surface.'

'So, there has only been one full-power experimental run since the last upgrade? Is that correct?' Willis bent and pulled at a loose panel on the trackway, then stood up and followed Villiers.

'Yes,' said Villiers. 'But that's the odd thing about the attack – it didn't happen until after the last experiment.'

'Why is that odd?'

'Well, in the days and weeks beforehand, contractors were all over the place. Security increased as soon as we cleared the accelerator for the trial. It would have been much easier to stage the attack sooner – at the weekend, even. Why wait till three days after the system had come online?'

'I'm not sure. I have seen all there is to see here. What is Dr Yeung like to work for?' Willis saw Villiers's eye twitch.

'He's okay.'

That was not the reply Willis expected from one of Yeung's right-hand men. He decided to let the matter drop; he would have another opportunity to broach the subject.

'To whom should I speak next?'

'The most obvious person would be the project leader,' said Villiers. 'The project office is at the far end of reception. I will take you.'

'No need, Jacques. You have been most helpful, thank you very much.'

'Once you come out of the lift, enter through the swing doors. You will find the project leader's office at the very end of the corridor on the left-hand side. It is in a temporary building while the main one is being renovated. You had better take a security card for the lift. I have a spare.' He handed it to Willis. Villiers walked off, waving and not looking back. Willis could tell he was absorbed by the repair tasks that were his main challenge for the next few weeks.

Willis soon found the door, following Villiers's directions. A plastic nameplate described the room's occupant:

PROJECT LEADER

S.F.

Willis knocked and entered.

A long conference table, two whiteboards and a digital projector filled the small room. At the far end, a slim woman with auburn hair to her shoulders sat with her back to Willis. He walked to the desk.

'Excuse me, may I introduce myself? I am Brad Willis.'

'I know who you are, Star Man.'

The chair swivelled around before Willis had time to recover from the surprise. He was staring incredulously into the eyes of S.F.

'Doctor Sophie Fenwick?' His voice was a whisper.

CHAPTER 10

Monika Fecher and Matt Quimby turned right out of Burlington House and walked through Burlington Arcade. It was the second time that day Monika had passed the archway. She peered across at Matt. Although he was American, he walked on her left: presumably, he did this to shield her from the traffic. Someone must have told him that most cultured Englishmen did this, and it was a sign of chivalry. No one else in Piccadilly seemed to know this fact – or, if they did, they chose not to heed it. Men and women were walking in groups and pairs with no obvious sides favoured. He kept his position anyway.

Monika smiled at the uniformed usher standing at the entrance to the arcade. He was a relic from a bygone era, but his braided top hat didn't look out of place in these surroundings. The arcade was lined with shops, mainly jewellers, some selling watches, both second-hand and new. The most common brands were Patek Phillippe and Rolex. A few clothes shops displayed their goods. None was priced.

This was always a sign that they were well beyond the average person's budget.

A shoeshine boy sat astride his wooden trestle, legs apart, busily buffing the left shoe of a tall, overweight man reading a newspaper. Monika turned to Matt. 'I'd like to return before the gates finally close. Some of this jewellery intrigues me. Shall we walk back via the arcade? I prefer that walk back to Oxford Street.'

Neither Monika nor Matt paid any attention to the man in the open gabardine raincoat walking on the inside of the pavement. He kept close to the shop fronts and stayed two steps behind Monika.

Time was getting short, so they decided to walk back along Piccadilly. As they turned, the man hid in a shop doorway and then continued to follow them when they turned onto Regent Street.

The Athenaeum is located on the north corner of Waterloo Place at 107 Pall Mall. It is an important address for the RAS. Monika liked its atmosphere. She had been introduced to it by the RAS, which held a Dining Club meeting there once a month. Attendance at the dinner was by invitation only; to be chosen as a permanent member was an even higher honour.

Robert, the senior waiter, greeted Monika. 'Good afternoon, madam. Would you like tea for two as usual?'

She smiled in response. She and Matt eased themselves into two of the four settees positioned around the central coffee table. They sat on adjacent corners to make conversation easier. Dark oak panelling encased the room. Long red velvet curtains adorned the ground-floor windows and matched the thick maroon carpet.

'Cambridge is one of the hubs for the CERN data network. I expect there won't be any demand for volume data passing through there from CERN in the foreseeable future.'

Monika looked puzzled. ‘Are you making a statement or thinking out loud?’

He continued, ‘The IoA wasn’t designed to be a secure establishment. It does the usual checks on visitors, but there isn’t enough security to prevent entry if someone is intent on gaining access.’

‘I agree. The telescopes are mostly antique, more of historical interest or for teaching undergrads. All the real work is done in La Palma in the Canaries or one of the Southern European Observatories. But they did hit the administration building at Berkeley. That doesn’t make much sense either.’

‘My first task will be to spend time at the computer centre. We need to assume that whatever was the target at Berkeley will also be a target there.’ He gave a long sigh. ‘This job is tough enough without all this crap.’

Robert returned and placed a silver teapot with two cups and four perfectly shaped scones between them. ‘Earl Grey, as usual, madam. Will there be anything else?’

Monika thanked him, and he glided away. Matt stared at the assortment of scones, jam, butter and cream supplied by Robert and frowned. Monika smiled. ‘First, you cut the scones and butter them. Then add the jam and cream.’ She gave a demonstration with the first scone. Matt followed her lead.

‘This is delicious,’ he said after devouring the scone in two bites.

‘That’s something else you have learned about England, and it’s a lot more useful than knowing on which side of a lady one should walk.’

Matt frowned as though he didn’t understand.

‘The next thing I will teach you is not to eat so quickly. Anyone would think you had attended boarding school.’

The comment seemed to go completely over his head.

'You never did tell me why you came to Cambridge.'

'Partly business, partly pleasure,' said Matt. 'I have a younger brother over here who is doing a gap year. I wanted to see him and touch base with old colleagues at Cambridge at the same time.'

'And the business part?'

'I'm combining data from a research trip I took with one of the members of the IoA last year. I'm hoping to get better results by doubling the amount of data. It's all very boring, but I am sure it will be worth it in the end.'

Then their peaceful afternoon tea was interrupted by a man who came flying through the air over Monika's shoulder, clutching Matt's briefcase under his right arm. Following him was Robert, his arms outstretched, pushing the man onto the table. A zillion pieces of glass sprayed into the air from the glass table. Silver, china, Earl Grey tea, scones, jam, cream and Robert all spread themselves over the Athenaeum's deep-pile carpet.

The man managed to scramble to his feet and turned to run. He was still holding Matt's briefcase – but Robert had hold of the other end. He tugged, but Robert's grip was stronger. The man's coat tore, and he lurched forward. Monika and Matt reeled backwards, their mouths open, as the man careered out through the swing door and onto Pall Mall.

'I am most sorry for the inconvenience,' said Robert, brushing the cream and jam from his jacket. 'May I ask you to take another table?' He placed Matt's briefcase on an adjacent settee. 'Now,' he said, 'it was Earl Grey and scones, wasn't it?'

Monika and Matt rose silently, glanced at each other and then obediently moved to the fresh table as instructed.

'What the crap was that?' said Monika. Her hands shook, and her voice trembled.

'We are being attacked in England too – I think we need to assume that he was one of the bad guys,' said Matt.

'But why did he want my briefcase? All I have in it are the notes I made for your father's Christmas lecture.'

CHAPTER 11

'You didn't keep in touch,' said Sophie.

'Neither did you.'

Their words were playful, but there was a sting in Sophie's voice. She stood up slowly from her desk. Her russet hair bounced off her shoulders as she walked around and kissed Willis on the cheek. She stood teasingly close and stared into his brilliant blue eyes. 'Those blue eyes bring back some pleasant memories.'

'Is that all I get?' he asked, smiling.

'I work here. We ought to stay professional. Anyway, that's all you deserve for not phoning – or even texting. Was it so difficult to contact me?'

Willis took her arm so that he could look into her eyes for a few seconds longer. They were as he had remembered them: hazel around the outside with flecks of green around the iris. She wore a dark blue two-piece suit and an open-necked white blouse. She was about three inches shorter than he was. He wished he could tell her why he hadn't been in touch – how Reilly had rushed him off to South America for three months. But that was no reason to have ignored her. His gaze fell as guilt took over.

'It's a long story. You know that I got married?'

'Of course I did – I don't walk around with my head in the clouds. But that was a long time after we parted – almost four years after. You had ample time to call me before then. How is Carole?'

He caught his breath. 'Carole … she's dead. She was killed by a hit-and-run driver. He's never been caught.'

'I'm so sorry, Brad. That was insensitive.'

'You weren't to know. But tell me, how did you manage to become LHC project leader?' Willis was desperate to change the subject.

'Someone has to be around to take the flak when things go wrong. And there's a lot of it flying about here.'

'I can imagine,' Willis said.

'The truth is, Ernst Yeung remembered me from when we were here as students. He had read my research papers on the Higgs boson and thought I would be ideal to lead the project for him. As I have neither German nor French connections, I suspect it suited the politics too.'

'Ah, the Higgs boson,' teased Willis. 'The God Particle?'

'Not you too,' said Sophie. 'That's usually the slant the press puts on it.'

The God Particle was a joke among scientists. It was the title of a very informative book by Leon Lederman, who had been director of the Fermi National Accelerator Laboratory, or Fermilab as it was popularly known, but Lederman had intended *The God Particle* to be a popular book. Before its publication, he had shared the Nobel Prize for physics in 1988. The book became a bestseller.

'The whole point of building the LHC, and especially the ATLAS detector, was to find the Higgs boson,' said

Sophie. At that time, the Higgs boson existed only in the minds of particle physicists, but it fitted the theory so well. The Nobel Prize was awarded to Peter Higgs when it was finally discovered. Peter had been the first person to propose it.

'I am only the project leader, but some of the physicists working here might manage a Nobel Prize from their follow-up research. Anyway, I would rather have a proper office than this temporary hut,' said Sophie.

'More work on the Higgs boson will have to wait until the ATLAS is repaired,' Willis said.

'Villiers is a good man. It will take over a year to get it working again if we need to lift all 7,000 tonnes of it to the surface. He's working on a plan to repair it in situ, but it's not without its problems. At least it is all happening at the right time. We don't run experiments in the winter; it uses too much of the electrical energy that is needed by people who live in the surrounding towns.'

'Could your competition have sabotaged the accelerator for you?'

'There is no competition,' said Sophie. 'It needs all the power CERN produces to observe the Higgs boson – even Fermilab can't get close.'

'How successful was the last experiment?'

'The experiments are analysed over a long period, so it's never down to only the last experiment. It takes two to three years of combining data before we can come to any firm conclusions. Only then do we make an announcement.'

'And was the last run important?'

'Not for the discovery of the Higgs. That was achieved years ago, but it was important for the latest research.'

'Where are the data stored? Is it secure?'

'It's all held on computer tapes in a secure data vault. We have greater computer processing power available to us than any other research establishment. We use a system named GRID, which is a distributed processing system. It's very like the screensavers SETI – you know, the Search for Extraterrestrial Intelligence – sends out for folk to run on their home PCs to try to find extra-terrestrial life, but millions of times more powerful.'

Willis's brain was working overtime. 'And then what? You break the data down into modules and distribute them around the network for processing?'

'That's about it,' said Sophie.

'May I inspect them?'

'Now?'

'Why not?'

Sophie checked the card around her neck, spun around, and stepped towards the door. 'We hold the computer tapes in a robotic retrieval system.'

Willis had been in similar storage facilities before, but he'd never been in one this big.

Sophie approached the keypad. A proximity sensor registered her ID badge, and she entered a code. Lights flashed. She presented her right eye to a biometric laser reader set on the wall. It scanned her eye to check her identity. Fifteen seconds later, a steel door slid open to reveal a basket containing a tape canister.

Willis lifted the canister, weighed it in his hand, and quickly broke its seal. He snapped the lid off and threw it on the desk.

It was empty. The tape had gone.

CHAPTER 12

'Buying me dinner is the least you could do after ruining my day,' said Sophie. The restaurant wasn't crowded; it was still early in the evening. The gingham tablecloths added to the French atmosphere the restaurant was trying to create, and the watercolours of the Eiffel Tower and the Seine embankment completed the effect.

'We might have ruined Ernst Yeung's day as well.' Willis reached out for the ice bucket and refilled Sophie's glass, then his own. 'Whoever is doing this must be competition.'

'No way,' said Sophie, shaking her head.

'How about someone on the team, then?'

'If it were someone in the team, they would have known we closed for the winter and left it until after the break – or at least until near the end of the break. The way they did it means we have extra time to make the repairs.'

The wine waiter glanced at the ice bucket and checked the level of the champagne. He made eye contact with Willis.

Willis nodded, and he hurried to find another bottle. Willis waited for him to vanish behind two large swinging doors before he spoke. 'It doesn't make any sense.'

'I wouldn't worry about it, Brad. It's only one set of data, and it's not of any use to anyone until we get enough readings to get a statistical analysis. The security breach is more serious than the loss of data. But you're supposed to be treating me to dinner. Even if it is years too late, it's better late than never. Let's stop talking shop.'

'Yes, let's.' Willis stretched out his hand and rested it on Sophie's. She smiled, then drew her hand slowly away. Neither said anything.

Willis recollected how the restaurant had been decorated the last time they'd been here. White linen tablecloths had been replaced with the red and white gingham ones; one of the pictures might be new, he wasn't sure, but the pale blue wall covering was as it had always been. The waiters were even the same. They hadn't remembered him – why should they? – but Willis rarely forgot a face.

Last time, they had sat in the corner. The pillar there had shielded them from most of the other tables and had offered a modicum of privacy. Willis had considered suggesting to Sophie that they sit there, but two men in German greatcoats had swiftly arrived and claimed it.

'How long do you expect to be in Geneva this time?' asked Sophie.

'I need to make recommendations for security improvements when I get home, so a week or so at most.'

Sophie looked satisfied. 'At least it will be longer than twenty-four hours *this* time.'

She was wearing her hair longer than the last time they had met. It dropped softly over her temples and framed her face in curls. Willis's gaze was drawn to her lips.

'You never told me you liked whitebait.' It was half a statement and half a question.

'I like all kinds of fish,' Willis said. 'They are healthy and good for you.'

'Well, they have certainly kept you in good shape.'

'You're in pretty good shape yourself, princess.'

Sophie smiled at the compliment and took another bite of her melba toast.

But Willis's attention was on the two men who had taken the corner table. They seemed vaguely familiar. He frowned.

By the time dessert was over, Sophie and Willis had caught up on their social lives since they'd last met at university. They had covered every possible aspect except for work, which was still a taboo subject. Willis's social life was the poorer of the two, partly due to his working nights at the observatory and partly due to a huge part of his life that he hadn't yet disclosed to Sophie. After looking into her eyes for a full five minutes, Willis felt guilty for not telling her about his association with Reilly, so he decided to tell her now, even if it meant she blamed it for ruining their relationship.

Willis took a slug from his wine glass and swallowed. 'There's something else you ought to know. I work unofficially for British intelligence.' He leaned over and refilled her glass.

'You what?'

'I was recruited shortly before I went to South America. I report to a guy called Reilly who is based in London.'

'Bloody hell. I wasn't expecting that.'

'I'm here on business. My role is to investigate the sabotage of the detector – and a few other incidents that have taken place.'

He and Sophie sat in silence for several minutes. She rubbed her temples with the palms of her hands, clearly shocked. 'Are you in danger?'

'I don't think so – not yet at least, but I've only just started my investigation.'

'Was that why you never called me?'

'No, it wasn't. I'm so sorry. I should have got in touch long before I met Carole or Reilly.'

'I need some time to digest this bombshell. Let's change the subject.'

Willis leaned forward and topped up her glass. She hadn't taken a drink since he had last filled it; it was automatic on Willis's part. As he poured the wine, a movement from the other side of the room caught his eye. He looked over Sophie's shoulder at the men in the corner of the restaurant.

'Are you trying to get me drunk so you can take advantage of me, Dr Willis?'

'As far as I recall, I don't need to get you drunk, Dr Fenwick.'

'Shhh … someone might be listening.'

The conversation had become more relaxed.

But they ought to leave. He had been studying the two men across the room for over an hour. Willis suspected that they weren't here to welcome him to Switzerland. Willis signalled the waiter and paid for the meal, then helped Sophie with her coat. 'Why don't you escort me home for a change?'

'And where might that be?'

'Two floors up,' Willis said, speaking loudly so his voice would carry.

'Well, that's very handy, but I think we need to keep things platonic. It's been quite a long time, Star Man, and I need to be in the office early tomorrow.'

'We promised not to mention work tonight.'

Willis rearranged Sophie's collar as they moved away from the table. The two men at the corner table had also stood and put their coats on. It wasn't until the taller of the two put his phone to his ear that Willis remembered where he had seen him before. He had a red birthmark over one of his eyes. He had been tailing Willis since the airport.

'Excuse me.' Willis signalled to the waiter. When the waiter arrived, Willis put one arm around Sophie's waist and the other around the waiter's shoulders. He spoke to the waiter as he manhandled him and Sophie towards the kitchen.

'I must thank your chef. That was the best filet mignon I have tasted in Switzerland.' He spoke loudly to allow his voice to carry.

Sophie opened her mouth to say something, but Willis cast her a look and shook his head. She took his cue and kept quiet. He hadn't ordered filet mignon. Although it was a clumsy move, it succeeded: Willis wanted to get away from the two men. Gaining access to the kitchen might mean he could find a rear exit there.

The two men stopped and glowered at each other.

The three barged through the double swing doors.

'Sorry to mess you about, but those two men are following us,' Willis said quickly. 'Do you have a back door we can use?'

'Yes, to the left of the freezer.' The waiter pointed to a tall stainless cabinet behind the central row of grills. 'You will never get away in high heels.' He shouted to one of his junior chefs. 'It's after eleven, Andre. Go home early and give these nice people a lift on the way.'

Until the waiter called to him, Willis hadn't even noticed the short, thin man. He rushed out from behind the largest grill waving his car keys, pointing in the direction of the back door and shouting, 'I'm Andre, please follow me.'

'Thank you,' whispered Willis. He, Sophie and Andre raced for the back door. In a car, they would be gone before the pair inside came to investigate.

'Your mignon was magnificent!' Willis shouted for the benefit of the two men before he and Sophie vanished through the exit.

His jaw dropped when he saw Andre's car: it was a Mercedes Smart car. It was so tiny that Willis would have a hard time getting into it.

'I will get on the small ledge at the back,' whispered Sophie.

Although it seemed like an eternity, it was no more than fifteen seconds before they were all inside the Smart car, and it was racing out of the alley, its horn blaring. Andre bullied his way across the lines of traffic driving towards the A1.

Willis had time to look back. The two men in greatcoats were standing in the lane, gesticulating, before they raced back into the hotel.

'Looks like I'm taking you home after all,' said Sophie, forcing a smile. Her hands were shaking.

Christ, thought Willis, they might find my room.

CHAPTER 13

Back at her house, Sophie threw herself on her couch. 'What's going on, Brad? What were those two men after?'

'I wish I knew. They knew I was coming to Geneva – I saw one of them standing near a private plane at the airport.'

'Why on earth would they be after you?'

'I have no idea. No one except my boss knew I was coming to Geneva. It must have something to do with my investigation. I hope we managed to lose them.' Willis took Sophie's hand, pulled her to her feet and cradled her in his arms. Their lips came together softly. The soft smell of her hair brought back memories from years earlier.

She backed away. 'No, Brad, it's been too long. I'm not ready for this.' Her perfume seemed to cling to him even as she moved away.

'I understand – I left you without saying goodbye. I was just hoping…'

They sat for a while staring at the ceiling and the patterns of light the passing traffic cast onto the cream walls. Sophie's head rested on his shoulder. She was humming under her breath and twirling a lock of her hair around her finger. Willis remembered how she used to hum when they were together. After they made love, she would always have a grin on her face from ear to ear, like a cat that had stolen not only the cream but the master's prize salmon too. He inhaled the familiar smell of her perfume, feeling melancholy, then he took a step away from her and dropped heavily onto the other chair, giving her a look that wouldn't have been out of place on a puppy.

'I'm stuck with you for tonight,' she said sternly. 'You had better sleep on the couch.'

It felt strange to be lying so close to Sophie, but she seemed miles away.

Willis regretted they hadn't met up more often; they had been so close as students. Most evenings, they had studied together, just to be in each other's company. Saturdays and Sundays, they spent in the park, provided the weather allowed. He had often asked himself if he loved her, but the answer always eluded him. He blamed the inexperience of youth. But that was an excuse, and Willis knew it. He was ten years older than Sophie. He had returned to university after dropping out in his first year. On his return, it had been largely thanks to Sophie that he had found enough focus to study – and study he did. He'd found the first-class honours easy to get, partly because he loved the subject but mainly due to Sophie's encouragement.

He and Sophie had gone to different universities to do their PhDs. He had thrown himself into it; he had to. He missed her, and he used his studies to help him forget about her. The problem was that it had worked too well. Even now, he had no idea what he wanted.

It was down to pure chance that they had met today. What would happen this time, he asked himself. Would he let her go again? Did he know what he wanted now?

Just then, Sophie's phone rang and dragged him back to reality. She picked it up and listened for a few seconds.

'Yes, okay.' She was no longer smiling. The glow had vanished from her eyes. She looked at Willis and opened her mouth to speak.

He waited.

'Jacques Villiers has been m-m-murdered.'

CHAPTER 14

Just after 10 a.m. the following morning, Willis returned to his hotel with Sophie. He pushed open the door to his room and then froze.

'Oh shit. We've had visitors.'

The room was a mess. Clothes and papers were scattered across the floor, and the desk drawers had been pulled out and emptied.

Frantically, he looked around. 'The damned laptop's gone.'

He called Reilly. 'Mike, two men followed me and broke into my room last night. The bastards have stolen my laptop. Are you sure the hard drive will erase itself if the code isn't entered?'

Nothing else, other than his laptop, seemed to be missing.

'Yeah, I'm sure. What else is missing?' said Reilly.

'Nothing, I don't think...' He told Reilly about the previous evening's events, including the news that Villiers was dead. 'Listen, if I describe these two men we met in the restaurant last night, can you ID them?'

'Go ahead.'

'One had a dark red birthmark over his left eye – his eye looked as if it might have been damaged at one time. The eyelid drooped, covering part of the iris. He had thin, straight lips. Looked menacing. I can't describe the second man – there was a pillar between us that obscured his face from his view. They wore identical black coats, but one coat had a beige trim, the other a maroon one. Bit odd.'

He then told Reilly about the conversation he'd had with Jacques Villiers. He added Villiers's comment that it was not a logical time to have sabotaged the accelerator.

'I'll speak to forensics when I get back to CERN and find out how he was killed,' Willis said.

'Good,' said Reilly. 'The Yanks are sending your mate to help. I told them you wanted to work with Greg Palmer. He has other information that might be related to what is happening in Switzerland. He'll give you the details – but another astronomer has died.'

'Not another one! How many more will there be? I worked with Palmer on the Supernova Project – he had already volunteered to come. I told you I had asked him.' While Reilly was talking, Willis was wondering what to make of him. He had definitely told Reilly about Palmer and their previous experiences, but now Reilly was informing him of facts as though they were news that had just come to light. After thinking some more about it, Willis decided it was just Reilly's way of sorting things out in his mind: after all, Willis wasn't his only contact, so he would need some kind of system to remember all the information he was told.

'Of course,' said Reilly. 'I expected you might, as he is an astrophysicist, a civilian like you, but he has been temporarily seconded to US Naval intelligence. I will let him fill you in on all the details. He will be arriving on the first flight this afternoon via Munich. Meanwhile, I will try to get a fix on your friend with the birthmark. Your description should be enough for us to pin down who he is.'

They hung up.

Willis turned to Sophie, who had been standing silently by the settee. 'I should move out of the hotel. They know where I am now, and I don't want them to come back. I am sorry to put you in danger.'

'Why don't you move in with me at Bellevue? There will be safety in numbers.'

Willis was about to kiss her when she added, 'You can take the spare bedroom.'

CHAPTER 15

Matt Quimby arrived at the Hoyle Building at the Institute of Astronomy in Cambridge after a rushed bowl of muesli. He left his car in the car park nearest the building after managing to get the last place. He walked the short distance across the grass to the main entrance. On his way, he passed the statue of Sir Fred Hoyle, the founder of the Institute.

Every time he arrived at Madingley Road, he was overcome by a feeling of awe. So many of the astronomical giants of the twentieth century had been based in this building. Many of them had battled with and uncovered the secrets of the universe. Hoyle had been a great man; he and his colleagues had worked out how the Sun managed to shine. They had devised the nuclear equations that explained how stars burn their fuel. His work was elegant, as most good scientific ideas are. This work and the Big Bang theory predicted the quantities of all the elements in the universe. Indeed, it was Hoyle who had coined the term 'Big Bang'.

Hoyle was not awarded the Nobel Prize along with the other members of his team. Everyone in the profession knew that had been a political decision. He had often spoken out against the Establishment. The decision will always be to the shame of the Nobel Selection Committee: history will record it as such.

Matt reached the main reception and signed in, then turned left towards the majestic staircase leading to the first floor. The interior of the building had the atmosphere of a church; it demanded respect. It was like an alchemist's workshop where the great secrets of the universe would unfold. He passed the office of the present Astronomer Royal, Sir Martin Rees, a great man who was at one time also the President of the Royal Society. Matt turned right down a corridor, past the men's toilets, and stopped in front of the door to a box room. This was to be his office for the duration of his stay at Cambridge. He was resentful that the office was so small – the broom cupboard next door was the same size. In the States, he would have walked out if such a tiny allocation had been offered to him, but, at Cambridge, any office allocation at all was a compliment and recognition of the contribution he was making.

He eased the key into the lock, turned it and opened the door. At first sight, all appeared to be in order. If anything, it was tidier than when he had left it. His right knee rubbed against the desk drawer closest to the window, and it partially opened. Matt knew he had locked the drawer before going to London the previous day. He checked the left drawer. It was also open, and splinters of wood and varnish revealed that someone had forced it.

It took only minutes to check the contents of both drawers. He had brought the minimum of belongings to England, so it was easy. The piles of paper on the desk had also moved: there were fewer piles than before, but he was confident that nothing was missing. His box files of papers and the books on the shelves lay untouched, the thick layer of dust covering them attesting to this fact.

He lifted the phone on his desk and informed security. Within minutes the room was full of guards in grey uniforms with silver badges embossed with 'GB Security'. There were only three of them, but they more than filled his tiny office.

'Is anything missing?' the nearest guard asked.

'No, nothing has been taken,' said Matt. 'How did whoever it was, get in? The door wasn't forced, and I had my key with me in London yesterday.'

'I can't rightly say, Mr Quimby, sir. It looks like another office was gone over in the same way,' said the tallest of the guards. He must have been the most senior: there was one extra star on his front pocket. Matt asked himself if he would get a job with Ronald McDonald once he'd earned another three stars. 'Nothing is missing from that office either, sir.'

'Whose office was it?' asked Quimby.

'It was Jim Smart's office.'

Matt's heart sank. Jim was the network support engineer for telecoms. His role was to configure and program the data communication servers: in other words, the computers that controlled the flow of information in and out of the Institute.

Matt lifted the desk phone a second time and dialled 131, the number of the secretary for the Hoyle Building.

'I need to hold an urgent meeting with the management team.'

'But…' Dick Evans, the secretary, was about to protest.

'I want it in the next thirty minutes.' Matt hung up.

Twenty minutes later, fourteen of the key players had assembled around the oval teak table in the meeting room. Some held coffee in plastic cups they had hurriedly collected from machines on the way. There were only eight seats around the table, so some people had to stand. Matt remained standing, freeing up an extra chair.

After the last straggler had arrived, Matt addressed the management team. ‘Gentlemen, there has been a series of security incidents around the globe in the last few days.’ He turned to the whiteboard behind him, took a marker from the tray on the wall and proceeded to list the events the RAS President had told him about the previous day in London.

‘The IoA is believed to be a high-profile target. My office and that of Jim Smart were broken into sometime between eight yesterday and ten-thirty today. We need to put in place a series of emergency measures immediately.’ He paused for effect, then added, ‘But I fear we may already be too late.’

CHAPTER 16

Even pristine Switzerland has grubby rooms. This was one of them.

It was sparsely furnished. It held two single beds, an ageing chest of drawers that had seen better times, a small round table and two chairs. The scratch marks on the chair legs were evidence that their previous owner had at least one cat.

A solitary wire hung from the middle of the cracked ceiling. Attached to it was a fringed lampshade that played host to half a dozen houseflies, while hundreds of small black dots on the shade and the yellowed bulb showed that several generations had preceded them.

Thanks to the brown wallpaper and the dark grey blankets, which absorbed most of the remaining light from the sixty-watt bulb, the two black greatcoats lying on the bed were almost invisible. The man nearest the table lifted a brown paper bag that was wrapped around a clear glass bottle. He proceeded to fill two plastic beakers. 'This one eez a lot harder than the others,' he said, pushing one of the beakers across the table.

The other man nodded and threw back its contents. With a swing of his arm, the man with the claret birthmark waved a persistent fly from his other eye, which he then rubbed as if trying to remove the drooping eyelid that partly covered his bloodshot eye.

'Villiers is dead, but the timing eez crap. There is still a lot to do to get rid of the other evidence.'

'This Englishman is already a problem. *Da.* We must get rid of heem too. We should have killed heem at the airport before he had a chance to get in touch with Meyrin site. He was very clever at avoiding us today.' He filled the beakers for the second time.

'Our employer pays well – we must succeed. We have come too far to fail now.' The second man took the proffered plastic cup and emptied it.

'*Da.* I am pleased that we visited his hotel room tonight.'

He dropped Willis's laptop on the bed, lifted the lid and hit the power button. From the inside pocket of his greatcoat, he removed a stainless steel meat skewer, lifted a cloth and began to polish it.

'We veel try again tomorrow.'

CHAPTER 17

Willis was waiting for Palmer in Arrivals. He assessed Greg Palmer as he walked towards him. Willis was taller than his new partner and about ten years younger. Even so, he conceded that Palmer might have beaten him in a hundred-yard dash. He was sinewy and fitter than Willis. Palmer's ruddy hair made him look ten years younger: Willis knew that Palmer was approaching fifty-five, but he didn't look a day over forty-five.

Each man had been told to co-operate fully with the other.

'I hope Baker and your guy are wrong about what's going on,' said Palmer. He spat the words in Willis's direction.

'Baker has told me I have to report to you.'

'Good.' Willis ignored the snide remark. 'But if they are, the sooner we find out what's going on, the better. Anyway, co-operation includes suitcases.' Willis took one of Palmer's cases and walked towards the car.

Yeung had arranged for a limousine to pick up the two men to give them a chance to chat on the way to his office. It had been a long flight, but Palmer was used to making long trips; he told Willis that he had slept most of the way. He had brought his usual supply of melatonin tablets, which he took for four days before any long flight. Melatonin was reputed to reset the body's biological clock more quickly, thus curing jet lag. Palmer complained, this time, that he hadn't had the benefit of four days' notice before the flight. Willis sensed a sharpness in this comment too. Having listened to Palmer's comments and the tone in which he'd delivered them, Willis was having doubts about Palmer's suitability for the task at hand. He decided to pay special attention to Palmer's actions and attitude for the next few days.

'The two men who followed Sophie and me at the Plaza Hotel will no doubt try again,' Willis said. 'We need to check that they're not still following us. They seem to have an uncanny way of knowing where we're going before we do.' Willis took a furtive look around the limo as the driver put Palmer's bags in the boot.

While they were being driven, Palmer and Willis reviewed everything that had happened in more detail. Palmer described the events on the night of the fire at the Astronomy Building. He went on to review what the brigadier had told them about members of the Supernova Project and why he, Palmer, disagreed with the reasons they were targets. Willis still wasn't sure the brigadier was right, but it was all they had to go on for the time being. He challenged Palmer to provide an alternative reason, but none was forthcoming.

It was Willis's turn. Willis told Palmer that the brigadier was also a senior member of the CIA, in case recent events hadn't made that clear. Palmer had missed that discussion, as he had arrived a day after Willis. Willis filled

Palmer in on the events surrounding CERN. He told him about Villiers's murder and the two men in the black greatcoats who had trashed his hotel room. As well-trained scientists, each man kept to the bare facts. There would be plenty of time later to work on theories. More of the facts needed to be known first; otherwise, it would only be guesswork.

It was clear why Baker and Reilly had wanted to bring the two men together. Their stories intertwined; even so, the facts didn't follow any logical pattern.

Things didn't get any clearer when Palmer told Willis the latest news: that Willis's favourite telescope had killed a technician in a freak accident. The drive mechanism had crushed him against one of the telescope's pillars. It had been the morning after Willis had left for CERN. The Chilean police were investigating, but they had turned up nothing yet.

'But that can't be related, surely?' said Palmer. 'A junior guy like him can't possibly have played a role in a series of events that spanned two continents. He was only a young lad. His death must be unrelated.'

Neither man had yet found any common thread, or motive, to explain any of the killings.

'We need to check out the brigadier's idea that members of the Supernova Project have been targeted,' Willis said. 'If you give me your list of those who have died, I will add the others to it. I'll find out if Lucy, my PA, can uncover anything for us by going through the journals. She can check which subjects the victims published papers on and see if they have anything in common. You will also meet Sophie Fenwick – she'll help us with anything we need at CERN.'

'I believe I met her at the Particle Physics and Astronomy Research Council in England before it was emasculated in … was it 2007?'

'Sometime around then. You won't need any introduction, then?'

'Oh, I will. I doubt if she'll even recognise me; we exchanged fewer than half a dozen words.'

'The plan is to go directly to meet Ernst Yeung, the Director-General of CERN. We can sort your hotel out later,' Willis said. 'Ernst will fix it so we have access to any areas we might need. So far, five people have been murdered for no clear reason – six if we can't find Klaus Laufer, who told me about the threat to Berkeley.' Willis shook his head. 'I don't recall reading any of Laufer's work in particle physics or astronomy. No one here recognises his name or has any idea who he is. That's odd. We should have been able to find some reference to him in the literature…'

There was a sudden squeal of rubber as the car braked hard. Willis and Palmer were thrown forward in their seats. A dark brown car sped off in front of them.

'Phew, that was a near thing,' said Palmer.

'Sorry, sir. He came out of nowhere.' The driver was apologetic.

Willis released his grip on the door handle. 'Another coincidence? If we don't get to the bottom of this soon, who knows how many more will die?'

'I agree,' said Palmer. 'I never considered physics to be a dangerous profession before.'

CHAPTER 18

'Good afternoon, Frau Holtz.' Willis smiled. 'May I introduce Greg Palmer from Berkeley? Dr Yeung is expecting us.' He gestured towards Yeung's office. Frau Holtz smiled at Willis and nodded. He indicated to Palmer to follow him.

Yeung was on the phone when they arrived. They entered his office, which had three glass walls, providing Yeung with a panoramic view of the open-plan office that surrounded him.

Yeung ended his call. 'My sincere apologies, gentlemen. I am making the final arrangements for our two murdered engineers.' He waved and indicated to the two leather seats. Willis let Palmer select the large cream chair that had nearly suffocated him on his earlier visit. He smiled at Palmer's look of surprise as it started to devour him.

'Yes, yes, that's fine, set that up … and make sure we tell everyone.' The phone was back at Yeung's ear. 'Okay, good.' He replaced the handset on its charging station.

'Good afternoon, Dr Palmer. It is not entirely a pleasure to meet you.'

'Thank you,' Palmer said slowly, his mouth open, looking aghast at Yeung's sharp comment. Palmer continued, 'Brad brought me up to date on the way over – thank you for the use of the car. The murder of your men is disturbing.'

Yeung walked around to the front of the desk and leaned against it. 'Disturbing isn't the right word. I put my office and the facilities here at your disposal.' He smirked at Willis. 'I also know you are not here to learn about health and safety, Dr Willis. For the time being, I will continue to pretend not to know why you are here – that will prevent international complications and unnecessary questions. But I expect you to keep out of my way as much as possible.' He lifted his eyebrows as he shifted his gaze to Palmer. 'You will, of course, both have my fullest co-operation. You may use my office if you so wish. I have told your office that they may contact you through myself or Frau Holtz at any time.' He was looking at Willis as he spoke.

His help will be as useful as a wooden barbecue, thought Willis. Even from Willis's short acquaintance with Yeung, he was already wondering how much he should confide in the man. Willis hadn't expected such a hostile attitude – and it wouldn't help him achieve what he needed to achieve.

'Thank you, Ernst,' he said. 'I am aware that you have almost three thousand people working here at CERN, but could you provide me with a computerised list of names so we can check whether they have any connection to the men who have been killed? I already have a list from my boss in the UK, but I want to ensure that I have the latest version.'

'Of course. In what format would you like it?'

'I would like it in a straight comma-separated file. My people in London will start work on it as soon as possible.'

'Consider it done, but I expect to be kept up to date on all progress you make.'

'I have already promised you a copy of my full report when it is completed.'

Yeung snorted.

'My American boss believes that the deaths of the men involved in the Supernova Project at Berkeley are all linked,' said Palmer. 'Brad and I have agreed, for the time being, to follow that route first. It is the only lead we have.'

'I see. Now, is there anything else I might assist you with?' said Yeung, seeming uninterested.

'I would like Greg to meet Sophie Fenwick,' Willis said. 'Maybe she can help by looking at the problem from CERN's point of view.'

After bidding Yeung farewell, Willis and Palmer walked along the corridor to Sophie's office.

'What did you make of that man? Did he strike you as someone who would co-operate fully with us, or do you think he could hold us back?' Willis asked.

'Definitely the latter. I don't think we should use his office. I don't trust him.'

When they arrived, the door was ajar, and a dozen or so men huddled in front of Sophie's whiteboard.

'I'm over here,' she said, raising her voice over the heated discussion that was taking place at the board.

'It's a hive of activity here today,' Willis said, 'for a change.' He was trying to tease Sophie; it wasn't working. 'What's going on?'

'We have ensured that the tunnel area around the explosion site is safe. We were able to get close enough to the detector case to check the damage. It wasn't quite what we expected.'

'Is it a lot worse?' asked Palmer.

'The main damage is exactly as we originally thought,' said Sophie. 'But a charge had been set inside the magnet loop as well as outside.'

'So?' Willis shrugged. 'That proves it was a thorough job.'

'Excuse us, Dr Fenwick, we're going to the lab,' one of the men said to Sophie.

'Thanks, Claude. I'll ring you later … and thanks for your help.' Sophie turned back to Willis. 'Oh, it was a thorough job, alright, but that's not the only odd thing.' Sophie swung her PC screen to face Willis and Greg. 'Have a look at this. It's an electron microscope image of the central focus chamber in the detector.' She pointed to a pattern of tiny holes in what looked like a polished metallic block. 'This is the bit that does all the work. We needed a close-up view of it to discover if the blast had strained the metal or if it was showing any fatigue. We were about to order some photos when I found this on Villiers's computer. I had been checking it to see if he had left any unfinished tasks.'

'What scale is this on?' asked Willis.

'The largest holes there are around three microns across, but the smaller ones are a factor of ten smaller.'

'That makes the largest about three-millionths of a metre in diameter – that's small but not exceptionally small. CERN is comfortable with sizes a lot smaller than that. Now, if you'd said a femtometre—'

'The size isn't what's important,' interrupted Sophie. 'It's their direction that's the problem. Some are tracking at right angles to the blast – that doesn't make sense.'

'Could they have ricocheted off the sides of the magnet?' said Palmer.

'No. That doesn't explain it,' said Sophie. 'I haven't told you about another oddity: every track passes through the central focus of the detector.'

'Surely that means that the explosion was in the centre of the circular magnet?' Willis said.

Sophie hit the enter key. The image on the screen changed. 'This is a view of the inside of the detector. Look – there's no damage, no blast debris, no residue of any kind, only these damned holes.'

'And Villiers knew this? Is this why he was killed?' asked Palmer.

'I doubt Jacques knew about this. Hold on, let's look at the times on these files.' She closed the images and opened the file manager. 'Here we are,' she said, pointing to a date and time. 'These files were emailed to Jacques's computer late on the morning of the fourteenth of September. He never read the email. He was dead by the time it arrived.'

'He must have asked for the photographs to be taken,' said Palmer. 'That's why the lab emailed them to him.'

Willis lifted the phone and dialled the lab. 'Is that Brunner? Can you tell me who ordered the photographs that you sent to Jacques Villiers on the fourteenth? Yes. Okay. Yes, thanks.' He placed the phone back on its base. 'Villiers asked for them to be taken, so he must have suspected something.'

'And if somebody knew what he was about to discover, that would have been reason enough to kill him,' said Palmer.

'But what did he discover?' asked Sophie. 'Only subatomic particles could make that pattern – particles that were created at the centre of the detector. They must have radiated out from there – but that's impossible. I'm the project leader of this experiment and, trust me, that there is no energy strong enough or technology good enough to make particle holes like this … in fact, any holes at all.'

'What haven't we seen? Whatever it is, is it connected to the murder of Jacques Villiers?' Willis asked. 'We need to find something else the victims have in common other than supernova research if we are to make any progress.'

'There is one thing we have discovered,' said Greg. 'Whoever killed Jacques Villiers must be a member of CERN and may be based at the Meyrin site.'

Willis placed a hand on Greg's shoulder. 'A valid point. If Greg is right, we had better keep our suspicions to ourselves for the time being.'

CHAPTER 19

Double oak doors swung open. The twelve men rose from the dining table simultaneously. They placed their cigars and wine glasses back on the table and moved towards the adjoining room. No bell had rung; no usher had made an announcement. They knew it was time. The pleasantries were over. Now it was time for business.

Their footsteps were silent on the thick carpet; their voices echoed off the vaulted ceiling of the dining room. Their dinner jackets hung heavy with military decorations.

The second room was much larger. It was lavishly furnished: a long oak boardroom table took up most of the space, its dark wood contrasting against the plush red carpet. Oil paintings covered the walls. The crystals in the chandelier overhead competed for brilliance with diamond cufflinks, gold chains and bracelets. The men all wore one thing in common: a small triangular badge encrusted with black diamonds pinned to one lapel.

'What do you have to report on the status in Geneva and Cambridge?' The man at the top of the table turned to the man on his right.

He rose. 'I am pleased to report that your instructions have been carried out.'

'Thank you.'

'And in Berkeley?'

The last man on the left stood and nodded. 'All completed.'

'Thank you. And what is the position with the Englishman and the American?'

'Both are in Geneva, Pythagoras,' the man on his immediate left said. 'We're following their activities with interest. We have the Englishman's laptop, and we have removed the hard drive. It had the British intelligence self-erase subroutine installed, but we disabled it. The information it contains shows that at present they are no threat to our plans. We will not eliminate them unless we have to – we should call back Sergei and Yerkin.'

The first man rose and spoke again. 'The more interventions we make, the closer to us the investigations will lead. Villiers was unfortunate; we had no alternative. We should call off Sergei and Yerkin, but I recommend that we make sure they don't go too far for the time being. We will kill those meddling fools, Willis and Palmer, if they interfere again.'

'I agree. We might need Sergei and Yerkin at short notice. We will meet again in one week.' The man at the top of the table, who had answered to Pythagoras, rose and turned towards the double oak doors. Eleven sets of fists thumped the table, drumming him out.

CHAPTER 20

Sophie sat at her desk, spinning a pencil between her middle and index fingers. Palmer stood at the water cooler, filling a plastic cup for the umpteenth time in the last ninety minutes.

'You'll wear the leather away in that chair arm if you keep rubbing at it.' Palmer walked over to Willis and smacked his hand with a wooden ruler.

'And you will damage your bladder if you drink any more water.' Willis moved his attention from the arm of his chair and started to play with a button on his shirtsleeve. 'I had an old tutor at university who had a favourite saying when things weren't going as planned. He would say, "Let's go back to basics. We're missing something." That's what we need to do here.'

'Well, it sure as hell isn't obvious,' said Palmer. 'I can't see it.'

'Let's list all we know on the whiteboard,' Willis said.

Sophie opened a desk drawer and threw a box of markers in Willis's direction. He caught the packet, spun around on the chair and was on his feet in one fluid movement. On the left of the board, Willis added a column showing the locations of all the murders. Next to that, he added the names of the victims. In the third column, he wrote 'Areas of research' and then filled in the column for each victim.

Palmer pointed at the board. 'You haven't listed Michael Fecher – he was the first victim.'

Willis stopped writing and looked at Palmer. 'He was my professor at uni.'

'He was at the International Astronomical Union General Assembly in Prague when someone put a meat skewer or something damn similar through his heart. The local police assumed it was a robbery gone wrong. His briefcase was broken open, and its contents scattered around.'

'He was the first project leader of the Supernova Project, wasn't he? But he hadn't done any real research for years.'

'But he would still have been up to date with the latest findings.' Sophie moved closer to the board.

'I don't think he would have been.' Willis added Michael Fecher's name and details to the column. He left 'Area of research' blank. 'He would have read or even refereed the latest papers, but that's about all. He wasn't privy to anything worth him getting killed for. It would all have been in the public domain.'

'All these people were researching different things.' Sophie gestured at the names and the columns on the whiteboard. 'I keep telling myself that supernovae research and particle accelerators have little in common except at the most basic level. Even then, there's nothing worth killing for.'

Willis wrote a question mark in the blank space next to Michael Fecher's name. 'What if he was doing some private research? He might have brought some results to the IAU in Prague to discuss them with colleagues, but I doubt it. He was in his seventies, after all.' Although Willis had great respect for Michael Fecher, who had been Willis's mentor at university, he doubted he was up to date on current astronomical research.

'Don't be bloody ageist.' Sophie slapped him on the back of his neck.

'Okay then, I know his daughter. Let's ask her – she might know.' He smoothed his hair down, erased the question mark and wrote 'Monika Fecher' in its place. Then he moved over to Sophie's desk and sat down. 'She's in England. I'll email her and ask if she can help us.'

'Even if she gives us a connection to her father, there are still other gaps in the connections that need explaining.' Palmer's gaze moved down the names on the list. 'There's no connection here at all that I can see.'

'You might have hit on the answer there, Greg. Maybe there is no connection – not with research anyway, not using this approach.' After logging on to his personal email account, Willis pressed Send on Sophie's PC and stood upright. 'We need to find something these people have in common other than research. So far, I think we've been barking up the wrong tree.'

'The young research assistant killed in Chile can't have anything in common with all these others. There can't be a connection there.' Sophie drew a red circle around his name. She drew a blue one around Villiers's name and a green circle around Fecher's name. 'These three, I would say, are outliers. They're less complicated than the rest, but they're not like the others. If we can focus on these, it might give us a lead on the remaining group.'

She put the pens back in the holder at the side of the board. The three stood in silence for some time, trying to think of any other possible links between the victims. Their concentration was interrupted by a ping from Sophie's PC. Sophie went over to her desk and moved the mouse. The screensaver vanished, and her email screen blinked on.

'It's my flaming office, but you're getting emails.' She clicked the mouse again. 'It's from Monika Fecher. She says: "As far as I am aware, Dad was not involved in any current research. I am almost sure he wasn't doing any private work either. Matt Quimby might know better; he was very close to Dad. Don't forget, I'm a planetary scientist, and Dad might have shared more with Matt. I will be in Cambridge tomorrow and will ask him. He is busy investigating a break-in at the communications centre at the IoA. If I can be of any more help, here's my number in London. I will be here for the next half hour."' Sophie looked up. 'And she's given a number for central London.'

'That was a prompt response,' said Greg. 'I forgot about the time difference. London is behind Geneva, so she would still be at her desk.'

'Let me see that number.' Willis reached the desk in two impatient strides. He had lifted the receiver and was dialling before Sophie could make another comment about him taking over her office.

'Hello?'

'Is that Monika Fecher?'

'Brad, it's good to hear from you again. It's like a blast from the past.'

'It sure is, Monika, but I need a favour. Thanks for getting back to me so quickly. Could you find out what, if anything, was taken in the break-in at Cambridge? Perhaps you could ask Matt for me?'

'I don't need to do that. The only thing that was taken was a COMLOG tape.'

'A COMLOG tape?'

'Yes. It has no value whatsoever; it records the flow of data through the Cambridge node of the network. The source and destination of every piece of information that is sent on the entire network, including the internet, is logged on the tape. It's only important if there's a communications fault and they need to troubleshoot the network.'

'I see. Thanks.' There was a pause. 'What did your dad do besides teach? Did he have an administrative role?'

Willis listened to Monika's reply in silence. 'I will give you a buzz tomorrow after you speak to Matt.' He thanked her and replaced the receiver, then turned to Sophie and Palmer. 'At last – I have found a connection between two of the killings.'

CHAPTER 21

'Well? Don't just stand there. Tell us what the connection is,' said Sophie. 'What did Monika tell you?'

'Monika told me that a computer tape was stolen in the break-in at Cambridge.' Brad's gaze darted from left to right. He did this whenever the neurons in his brain strained to make sense of information. 'This means that the entire data network plays a role in the mystery. But what kind of role? She said her father had requested some data bundles from CERN because Berkeley wanted to work on them.' He walked over to the whiteboard again and cleaned off the lists they had made earlier.

'He's making another list,' said Sophie. 'He has some kind of list-making compulsive disorder.'

Willis wasn't listening. He was busy writing. As he wrote, he read aloud, 'One: Michael Fecher had a data security role as well as his teaching job. Two: it was the collision results from the last trial run of the collider that were missing from the canister Sophie showed me yesterday. Three: a communications log tape was stolen from

Cambridge. Four: all the incidents have had a computer facility connected to them. The explosion in the Berkeley facility was in the telecom section.'

Willis put down the pen. 'Sophie, didn't you tell me a distributed network of computers processed the CERN data?'

'Yes – it's named GRID,' Sophie said. 'It's the only way we could get enough processing power to do all the calculations in a reasonable timeframe.'

Willis leaned over and offered Sophie a marker. 'Can you draw a map of the network on the whiteboard and show us where all the nodes and servers are? The pattern might be clearer if we can visualise the locations.'

'No way,' said Sophie. 'There are thousands of computers connected to the network. It goes worldwide. Every research establishment or university is capable of receiving modules of data. They process it and return it to CERN.'

'When you distribute the data, how do you know who receives it? How do you get the results back?'

'There's a program that manages all the tasks, both in and out. It records who gets what and when we should expect it back. This is all stored on…'

'The COMLOG tapes?' Willis finished her sentence.

'Yes. They will have different names in different places, of course.'

'What about making a list of all the research locations that might get data at any given time? That must be on the mainframe somewhere,' said Palmer.

Sophie picked up the phone and asked the data centre to send her a paper copy of the list.

Five minutes later, the door to Sophie's office opened. A lanky man with his hair tied back in a ponytail handed Sophie several sheets of perforated printer paper. The three gathered around the list. Palmer took a yellow marker pen and highlighted the locations. Berkeley was the first he marked, then Cambridge, then CERN itself. 'Does anyone have any other location I should add?'

They read down the list. Palmer highlighted the observatory in Chile. 'The data facility in Chile is not as large as the others – we use the rooms for different purposes at different times, and they're not dedicated like the rest. You can get from the main telescope dome down into the computer room.' Palmer paused again. 'Shit! That's the fucking connection: the door, the telescope and the crushed research assistant. They had to get access to the telescope to destroy the COMLOG tape in the computer centre.'

Willis puffed out his cheeks and then expelled air through his teeth. 'The pattern is undeniable; the CERN data is what is valuable. Someone is trying, successfully by the look of it, to erase the audit trail from every server that received data from the last experiment at CERN. Something must have been recorded that wasn't expected – and that must have caused the holes in the ATLAS detector that the electron microscope imaged.' Although he had thought about it ever since hearing the suggestion that the holes existed, Willis had been unable to focus on the real connection between the killings and why they had been necessary, but now things were beginning to fall into place.

'How are the data allocated?' said Palmer. 'It looks like it's in alphabetical order, from what we have so far: Berkeley, Cambridge, CERN and Chile.'

'It would have been in this case, as this was the first allocation,' said Sophie. 'In future allocations, the server would send the data to whoever had completed processing the previous data set the soonest. They would also have had a software flag set that meant they were ready to accept new data.'

Palmer read out some names and locations from further down the list: 'Fermilab, Georgia, Harvard, Kazakhstan … and, at the very bottom, Uzbekistan. This list is very inconsistent – some names are of organisations, others are locations, states or countries.'

'The name used is the name given by the member of GRID when they register to make their computing power available,' said Sophie. 'The name doesn't matter. As long as it never changes, the data will arrive at its destination. The name is mapped to an address on the network.'

'So, the next set of data would have gone to Fermilab, assuming there was any more to send?' Willis said.

'Yes, if there was enough data to send and Fermilab had their flag up to accept data. Otherwise, it would have gone to the next location on the list that had its flag up. It works like a miniature version of the World Wide Web, but it's a closed user group – that is, everything goes out from CERN to its collaborators and must come back here.'

Willis was thinking out loud. 'Whatever happened in the detector is important. It was spotted by whoever processed that section of the data. So…'

'So, they stole the original data tape from here to conceal the results,' said Palmer.

It was Willis's turn. 'And then they attacked computers around the world to destroy the COMLOG tapes and the backup tapes to hide their tracks. Without the log, we will never work out who got what data or who has the only copy of the results.' He was irritated that it had taken so long to come to this conclusion, and he reckoned if they hadn't made false starts in the first place, they would have made better progress.

Willis banged his fist on the table in triumph. The data centres were a crucial link in the chain of events. He'd solved the first part of the puzzle.

CHAPTER 22

Willis fidgeted with his pen. He was uncomfortable. This was going to be a challenge. He was about to meet a group of particle physicists, and as a result, he might be out of his depth, but there was no alternative. What could have caused the holes in the supercooled magnet inside the ATLAS detector? Willis had studied the physics of the very small and the physics of the very large, but that had been years ago. In physics today, a year can bring a century of change. He could only imagine what these guys were doing at CERN now. He knew how far astronomy had progressed since he was an undergrad. When he tried to compare that with the world of particle physics, it was frightening.

Sophie and Willis were at the lectern in the main conference room at CERN. Sophie spoke first. 'Thank you very much, ladies and gentlemen, for abandoning your respective departments and coming along at such short notice, especially since we were unable to give you a reason for holding this meeting. Let me try to explain now. For those of you who don't know me, I'm Dr Sophie Fenwick. I am the project manager for the particle accelerator. This is Dr Willis, who is leading the investigation into the deaths of the two engineers.'

The screen behind her showed an image of part of the ATLAS magnet. Sophie had drawn red circles around holes recorded on the image. The diameter of the circles had been scaled to match the diameters of the holes: larger circles were drawn around the larger holes. In the bottom left-hand corner of the PowerPoint slide was a horizontal red line; above it was the scale, two microns. Hoping his nervousness wouldn't show either in his manner or his voice, Willis braced himself for the moment of truth as he prepared to follow Sophie. Taking a deep breath, he stepped forward. 'I have asked you here today because you are among the top theoretical physicists in the world. What you can see on the screen is a scanning electron microscope picture of part of the magnet from ATLAS. As you are aware, ATLAS is one of the particle detectors within the LHC and is essential for its continued operation. We discovered these holes after the last live test of the collider. Unfortunately, after the experiment, we lost all our computer data. The detector will be out of action for some time. I know this is an unusual request, but we need to discover what could have caused this effect. We want you to work together to find out what could have caused these holes.'

A short, grey-haired Japanese gentleman stood. 'I am Itagaki, from Sumoto, Japan. Please, why is this so important to know so immediately?'

'Thank you, Professor Itagaki. I am so pleased you were able to come today – I have read most of your papers. One reason why we need to know is that we want to repair the detector as soon as possible. This attack put us at least a year behind schedule, and we fear it might happen again.'

When Professor Itagaki sat down, Willis was happy that the first answer had gone unchallenged. His elation was to be short-lived.

'Harold Ellington, from Oxford, England. What are the other reasons for all the urgency … the real reasons?'

'Thank you for being so forthright, Dr Ellington.'

Willis had expected this. These were intelligent people, after all. They would want to add value to any discussion, and they would not let anyone hoodwink them. Willis and Sophie had a reply prepared.

'There have been a few incidents recently at research establishments around the world, as you are no doubt aware. There was an explosive device planted inside the ATLAS detector. We are helping the authorities with their enquiries. We have explained most of the damage, but not these holes.'

Ellington rose to ask a supplementary question.

A voice from the back of the room shouted, 'We've discovered the Higgs boson already.'

Laughter filled the room.

Another voice added, 'We can all go home. Our work here at CERN is complete.'

Another roar of laughter.

'Maybe it's anti-gravity particles or dark matter?' shouted a third voice.

Ellington had dropped back into his seat, but his glare made it clear that he didn't appreciate the frivolity. Willis was thankful for the distraction, but it was time to bring things back on track.

'Okay, okay, settle down, please. We need to solve this. Jacques Villiers was killed – and his death might well be associated with what is on the screen here.'

All in the room went respectfully quiet.

After all his concern, Willis was pleased that things were going so well and that the dread he'd anticipated had evaporated as soon as he had taken the lectern.

'Rudi Braun, Max Planck Institute.'

Sophie turned to look at the young man who had spoken. He might still have been in his teens. His blond hair hung to his shoulders. His voice was like that of a choirboy, ready to break. A bright red open-necked shirt contrasted against his pale skin, and his bright blue eyes danced with an enthusiasm that came only with youth. 'Whatever produced these holes has to have high energy or mass. It would make sense if it had both high energy and high mass. There is nothing in our recipe book of subatomic particles that could cause that effect. Someone joked about the Higgs boson. That is the closest we have to a particle that might have enough power to penetrate this thickness of metal, but it's not powerful enough.'

'Paul Renault, Paris, France.' Another man rose to his feet. He looked as young as Rudi Braun. Like Rudi, he dressed casually: his distressed jeans wouldn't have looked out of place on a station busker. 'It could be a completely new particle we haven't even theorised about yet.'

Willis shouldn't have been surprised by the age of these research scientists. He reminded himself that very few scientists had won Nobel prizes for work that they had done after the age of twenty-four. Perhaps prejudices and mental baggage stifle original thought after that age, he thought – not for the first time. As he looked out at his attentive audience, he saw a sea of eager faces staring back, each showing their eagerness to solve the puzzle at hand.

'What if it was a combination of two particles?' This came from a young woman. 'There are some theoretical particles we could never hope to isolate. What if they came on piggyback? One with high mass, perhaps the Higgs particle. The other would need to carry a great deal of energy.' She sat down without identifying herself.

The room went quiet. The older members of the research teams shifted uneasily in their chairs. There was a shaking of heads. This suggestion did not sit well with them, although none spoke up against it. Even before he was a serious student, Willis had experienced this closed-mindedness and reluctance to accept new ideas, especially from researchers of a certain age – and this room was full of researchers nearing that watershed.

'There is the inflaton.' Harold Ellington was back on his feet. 'This is only a theoretical particle; we aren't even actively trying to find it. The inflaton was proposed years ago as the force behind the expansion of the universe, after its creation, after the Big Bang. Astronomers have observed the ongoing expansion of the space between the galaxies for years. I suspect this would be overkill because the inflaton might have too much power. You will be aware of the problem, no doubt, Dr Willis. The speed with which the universe grew during its first few seconds is a testament to that. Janet's idea isn't that wild. Two particles might theoretically interact and give us this effect. The Higgs particle would have to be one of them. What the other one might be is anyone's guess.'

'Thank you, Professor Ellington,' Willis said. 'Perhaps we can discuss this further after the meeting?'

Sophie clapped her hands. 'Ladies and gentlemen, now you are aware of the size of the problem we're trying to solve. I would like you to give this some consideration and come back to Dr Willis or me if you have any further ideas.'

The audience shuffled in their seats. Some quickly left the room; others huddled together in groups to discuss the challenge they had been set. In the small informal groups that formed, the atmosphere was electric: researchers gathered in deep, sometimes argumentative, discussion, batting ideas around and having them batted back by their colleagues.

Willis grabbed the opportunity to buttonhole Harold Ellington before he left. He introduced himself and got straight to the point. 'Many thanks for your input today. It was most useful. This inflaton particle you mentioned – what if it were a lot stronger? Much, much stronger?'

'That would make it an ideal candidate to partner with the Higgs particle. Such a combination would be very powerful. It would be powerful enough to make the holes Dr Fenwick found.' Ellington looked at Willis. 'I must apologise. I don't recognise your name – which area of science did you say you were working in?'

'I'm an astronomer, Professor Ellington. I was part of the Supernova Cosmology Project. In 1998 we discovered not only that the universe was expanding, as you described but also that the rate of expansion was speeding up.'

'I read about that work; it was of the highest quality.'

'Thank you,' Willis said. 'Following on from our work, the COBE and the WMAP space satellites revealed that baryonic matter – that is, everyday matter – makes up only four per cent of the universe. The other ninety-six per cent is made up of dark energy and dark matter. You might recall that the speed of the expansion predicted by astronomers is many times that predicted by particle physicists.' He emphasised 'many times.'

'I am way ahead of you, Dr Willis. My God, that's perfect. You are suggesting that not only have we detected Higgs particles but that we have also detected dark energy at the same time. Jesus. That would solve the world's energy problem in one fell swoop.'

'How might we be able to detect it? I was under the impression that the LHC doesn't have enough power to detect such a combined particle.'

'You are correct, Dr Willis, but we do have enough power to detect the Higgs boson – we have done that already. If the Higgs combined with another particle that added to its energy, we might detect it as it broke apart again. We would need less energy in the collider to detect the combined pair after they had split.'

'Would the inflaton be a suitable candidate to fill the role?'

'That is a distinct possibility.'

CHAPTER 23

'What is so urgent that it requires action between meetings?' The question came from the man who was the senior of the two. He stood at one end of the black oak table. The glow from the chandelier above exaggerated the shadows on his face. He looked angry and impatient. The second man hurried towards him.

'There has been a development.' His breathlessness made him rush his words. 'The American and the Brit are making progress. We need to eliminate them before they get any closer.'

'Where are they now?'

'They're still in Geneva, but they have spoken with the researchers at Cambridge, and they are beginning to recognise a pattern.'

'Are Sergei and Yerkin still in Geneva?'

'No, Pythagoras. Yerkin is, but we sent Sergei to England.'

'This is getting a lot messier than I would have liked.' Pythagoras sat down and paused to consider his reply. 'Get Yerkin and tell him to sort it. Tell him to do whatever it takes – but to do it as soon as possible. We were too complacent before. Let's not hold back. Let's eliminate everyone who is in our way.'

'I had already set it up with Yerkin, subject to your approval, Pythagoras.' The man took a mobile from his inside pocket and pressed a few buttons. The Samsung vibrated twice. 'It is done.'

CHAPTER 24

Willis, Palmer and Sophie met back in Sophie's office at her request. 'The connection with astronomy and dark energy has come as much as a surprise to me as it has to you. The difference is that I'm no astronomer.' Sophie spoke so fast that some of her words merged together. 'Brad's conversation with Ellington didn't mean much to me. I need an explanation of what it was all about and what, if anything, we have discovered.'

'Okay,' Willis said. 'Here's a quick astronomy lesson, but you don't need to know any of this, so don't worry if you get lost. Greg, help me out if I get something wrong or miss anything out.'

'I will grade you at the end – marks out of ten,' said Palmer. 'We had to describe this to Baker a few days ago, so it should be fresh in our minds.'

'Sophie, how much do you know about the expansion of the universe?' asked Willis.

'What I do know comes from my university foundation course. Not much. Edwin Hubble was the first astronomer to notice that all the galaxies were moving away from each other at different speeds. It has something to do with the Doppler Effect.' As he thought back to his earlier explanation to Baker, Willis gave a sigh of relief. This explanation would be much easier and quicker since Sophie had some background in the subject.

'Full marks,' Willis said. 'The Doppler Effect is simply the changing pitch of the sound you hear when an ambulance or a police car rushes past you with its siren on. It has one pitch when it is approaching and a different one when it is moving away. What's more, the faster a vehicle is moving, the greater the change in pitch. It is fortunate for astronomers that the same thing happens to light. If an astronomer records the incoming light as redder than it should be, he knows that the object is moving away, and the opposite is true. If the object is approaching, the light will get bluer. The more the colour is shifted, the faster the object is moving.'

'The big contribution Edwin Hubble made was to relate the amount an object's light reddened to how far away the object was,' said Palmer.

'So Hubble discovered that the fainter groups of stars – the fainter galaxies – were redder than the brighter ones?'

'More or less,' Willis said. 'He managed to calibrate the reddening. Astronomers used it to measure the huge distances to galaxies, and, over the years, we have been improving the accuracy of his calibration. Initially, that was what the Supernova Cosmology Project was all about.'

'Improving on Edwin Hubble's results?' said Sophie.

'Yes. They used the brightness of the supernovae to do this. Supernovae are stars that explode at the end of their lives – they are very bright and are still visible even when they are at immense distances from Earth. There are different types of supernovae, but one type, in particular, is very useful for this kind of work. These supernovae always emit the same amount of light, so by measuring how bright they appear to be from the Earth, we can measure their distance. It's the same as measuring how bright a forty-watt lamp is: the further away it is, the fainter it gets, but you need to know that it's a forty-watt lamp in the first place. These special supernovae make that possible. The surprise came when the supernovae measurements and Hubble's redshift, as the reddening of light is known, gave different values for the distances of the furthest galaxies.'

'Back to the drawing board, then?' asked Sophie.

'It certainly stirred the pot a bit,' Palmer said wryly.

Up to this point, Willis had made everything seem so simple, but things were about to become more complicated, thanks to the introduction of the unexpected result found by two different groups of observers. Willis continued, 'This meant that the speed of the universe's expansion was increasing.' He was enjoying himself. This was his subject, and the expression on Sophie's and Palmer's faces reflected his passion for astronomy. This was why he loved teaching it: there was nothing more rewarding than watching students as the facts clicked into place and they realised the significance of what they were being told.

'What's making it speed up?' Sophie asked, looking interested.

'This was where imaginations ran wild. Astronomers suggested a new form of energy to explain the increase in speed. They called it dark energy. They had no idea what dark energy was – that's why they called it "dark" – but it successfully explained their observations. The energy could be carried by the inflaton particles Harold Ellington suggested. As it happens, it helped to solve another problem they were having, but that isn't relevant here.'

'Go on,' said Sophie. 'Don't stop at an interesting bit.'

'Well, there wasn't enough "stuff" in the universe to make the theories work. There needed to be exactly the right amount of matter in the universe. The problem was that they only found about four per cent of what they needed. The idea of dark energy helped to fill a lot of the deficit – it gave another seventy-four per cent, to be exact. Astronomers still have twenty-two per cent to find. They're still looking for something else, likely another type of matter, to fill the gap.'

'Now tell me why the Higgs particle is so exciting if it's combined with this energy,' said Palmer. 'You understand it.'

Because it had been years since Willis had studied particle physics, he knew he would struggle to make the explanation easy, but he was determined to give it his best shot.

'I only understand some of it,' Willis said. 'The special thing about the Higgs is that it sticks to the space around it. It is in a sort of field, very like a magnetic field. It is this particle that gives things mass. Without mass, there is no momentum, no inertia and no gravity.'

'And how does dark energy fit in?' said Sophie.

'Dark energy is almost the opposite. It has no mass, but it drives massive objects apart. It could push Higgs particles apart if it interacted with them. Once we have them moving, there is mass and energy, real kinetic energy. It could cause the damage to the magnet that you photographed.'

'That makes sense of Ellington's comment that it could solve the planet's energy crisis,' said Palmer. 'Isn't this all too easy – finding it on the last test run, I mean?'

'That was a surprise. But why not? That's what the particle accelerator was designed to do, and it creates enough energy to do it. Sometimes that's how great discoveries are made.' Willis threw his pencil on the desk.

'That means if our killers, or their bosses, have become aware of this, it's dangerous.' Fear was written over Palmer's face. 'This has potential as a new energy source – it is immense. It's certainly enough motivation to drive them to murder people to control it.'

'It's not that simple,' said Sophie. 'Finding a particle like this is only the beginning. It would take years of research to discover a way to harness it so that it will eventually become a useful source of energy.'

'We had better keep at it. I need a drink,' Willis said, 'but I think we're making progress.'

Willis's mobile rang. It was Reilly. 'What have you been up to? You're upsetting the Director-General of CERN.'

'I knew he was upset. He tried to pull rank on me to release parts of my report early. He insisted on getting copies of everything I discovered as I discovered it.'

'Well, he's made an official complaint. He wants you off the enquiry.'

'Look, Mike, I have no idea yet who's involved in this mess. We suspect that at least one member of CERN is involved. I need to make sure all this remains under wraps until I'm sure about what's going on. If I tell one person, I'll lose control of who knows and who doesn't.'

'Still, you had better keep him sweet.'

'If you want me to resign, I will, but I've got to have a free hand to run the investigation as I see fit.'

Shit. That was all Willis needed – to have an irritated Director-General breathing down his neck, expecting him to jump at his every command and threatening to report him if he didn't. 'There's no need for that. Try to keep him onside for as long as possible. He could be a powerful enemy if you irritate him. Consider yourself bollocked but carry on as usual unless I tell you otherwise. I have confidence in you.'

'Thanks, boss. That's much appreciated. I'll try not to ruffle his feathers.'

Willis slammed his mobile down on the table. 'Shit,' he said. 'Yeung's made a formal complaint. That's not going to help us get things done any easier. I certainly need a drink after that.'

'Well, you have been throwing your weight about a bit.' Palmer's words were toxic. 'It's about time someone put you back in your box.'

'Oh, grow up, Palmer, and accept things as they are. Join the bloody team for a change.'

'Let's go for dinner,' said Sophie, breaking the tension. 'I know a good restaurant.'

'I'll be with you once I've called Mike Reilly back. There's something I need him to do for me.' Willis lifted his mobile and walked out of the room.

CHAPTER 25

Vladislav Yerkin had planned the project in great detail. It was his attention to detail that made him successful. He considered himself a perfectionist. This was what he lived for: while other men excelled at mundane careers, he took pride in designing and implementing his tasks. He would do the same on this project. His bosses had told him that it was not necessary to put anything too elaborate together. But an artist always gives his best performance, and this was no exception. He repeated this to himself as he moved towards the wire fence, which was about five metres high.

This stage would not be difficult. There was no tight security in the truck compound, no fancy card readers or biometric iris recognition scanners to worry about, only passively activated halogen lights. Stray movements triggered them several times an hour – so much so that the security guard had stopped taking notice of them. Nevertheless, Yerkin wore a thermal suit that he had stored at –30°C for the last eighteen hours. The heat detectors could still be set off by those parts of his body that weren't covered, but his idea should be effective enough not to alert the guard.

Yerkin laid a canvas bag on the damp grass and removed a set of tungsten bolt cutters. The chain on the gate gave way without putting up a fight. Immediately to the right of the gate was a sign that read 'EKHART ERDÖLHÄNDLER'. Oil distributors. He stood behind it. It was yet another precaution, but it would prevent him from being spotted from the guard's office window. Never had Yerkin considered himself to be over-cautious, but he did like to make sure that nothing unexpected happened to upset his well-laid plans, over which he had taken so much care.

He swung the gate open enough to slide his body between it and the fence pole. The gate creaked. It needed oil. The security lights flashed on – not from Yerkin's movement from some other stimulus. Like most criminals, he welcomed lights. They helped him to see the layout of the yard more easily, and they cast strong shadows. Yerkin took the opportunity. He moved into the blackness created by the lights and made his way along the garage wall towards the guard's open window.

From inside the office, a crowd roared. The sounds of a football match flooded the yard. Someone had scored. The guard punched the air with his fists, turned, and reached out for another bottle of Stella Artois. By the time he had slumped back in his chair, Yerkin was past the window and at the doorway. He opened his canvas bag and removed a towelling bundle. As he unwrapped it, a slither of blue light from the television escaped from a crack in the door.

It sparkled off the polished steel of Yerkin's knife.

Yerkin peered into the guard's office. The guard was sitting with his back to the door. His shoulder-length hair trailed over the back of his armchair. It spread out in a fan shape, framing a shiny bald patch in the centre of his head.

He was a dumpy man: his neck merged with his shoulders. Yerkin pushed the tip of the knife against the door and waited for the next roar from the crowd.

When it came, he pushed the door open and grabbed the guard under the chin with his left hand. In one swift movement, he drew the knife across the front of the guard's throat. The guard flailed about in his chair. A thin line of red oozed out from where the blade had passed as the guard continued to struggle. The line thickened until a flood of red poured down the front of his shirt. Where it soaked into his blue jacket, it turned black.

Yerkin had watched so many of his victims die. He imagined what his prey was experiencing. The guard would have seen – too late – Yerkin's reflection on the television screen. His arms would have become heavy. His legs would have tingled. He would have shivered. He would have been paralysed. Yerkin slackened his grip and walked in front of him. He could almost taste the experience of death. The last thing the guard would witness was the smile of satisfaction on Yerkin's face, and then the room would go dim. He would then fall forward into a sea of eternal darkness.

On the wall opposite the window, a plywood board held six rows of keys, each belonging to a heavy-duty *Lastwagen*. Yerkin scanned the board until he found the keys for the fuel tankers. His fingers moved along the line and stopped at the *Tankenwagen* that had the most fuel. He memorised its number plate and lifted its keys from their hook.

From the guard's desk, he removed the set of keys that opened the second security gate. He picked up his canvas bag and set off for the storage yard.

The fourth key he tried opened the gate to the secure yard. Once inside, he found the tanker he had chosen. It was a good choice. Its mudguards covered its wheels down to their rims: this meant that the tanker was full and weighed down by its load of petroleum.

He turned the key in the ignition. Nothing happened. Then he spotted a green light flashing on an instrument panel above the gearshift: it was the device required by European law to record the driver's speed and time at the wheel. He had to enable it before the engine would start. He kicked at its black plastic housing, smashing it into pieces. He turned the key again. This time the engine burst into life.

He moved the tanker forward in first gear and let it roll to a stop in front of the wire gates. Yerkin jumped out and opened the gates. This time there was no one around to hear the creaking of the gate. Once the tanker was outside the entrance, he stopped again and closed the gate, leaving the cut chain dangling from the lock. He waited until he was two hundred yards away before switching on the tanker's lights.

Yerkin was very pleased with himself. He had taken no chances. It would be at least fifteen hours before the guard's body was discovered. He changed gear and drove towards Meyrin.

He loved his work. True, he was a mercenary, but he would be happy to work for nothing. If only he signed his work, he would be a household name. To the people who mattered, he was famous. They knew who he was – and how to hire him. When he'd begun his new career, very few people had heard of him. Now, his reputation had grown. Clients competed for his services in the knowledge that their contract would be executed cleanly.

When he arrived at Gate A of the LHC complex, all the lights were out except for the window at the entrance barrier. This was how he had planned it. Gate A closed at seven in the evening. Had he gone to Gate B, it would have been busy and fully illuminated. It was open twenty-four hours a day, seven days a week. Gate A suited his plans better, as the target area was closer to Gate A. No one would take notice of a tanker parked on the road.

He let the tanker roll to a halt, killed the engine and switched off the lights. He removed a CD from his canvas bag, slid it into the player and turned the volume down until it was just a soothing background sound.

All he had to do now was wait.

CHAPTER 26

Mike Reilly flashed his MI6 badge to the policeman at the gate, just as he had done many times before. As he moved into the hall, he shuffled among groups of professional lobbyists. He tried not to be seen, keeping his gaze low as if inspecting the floor tiles.

It was a Wednesday, and he was in the Houses of Parliament in London. It was Prime Minister's Question Time. For many MPs, this was the highlight of their week. As was traditional, MPs had the opportunity to question the PM on any subject they wished. There was one condition: anyone submitting a question must forward it, in advance, to the Speaker of the House. This allowed the PM to prepare a detailed answer before the session. Since most questions presented are to score political points, this rarely happened. To overcome this, MPs usually asked a trivial question about the PM's plans: for example, about his engagements for the forthcoming week. The MP, once on their feet, was then allowed to ask a supplementary question – and this was the real question. The idea was to catch the PM off guard, but it rarely did. Every PM has a team of staff that anticipate any subject and prepares answers for him. This practice of concealing the real question was an abuse of the system, but it was never challenged, and each party believed it gave them an advantage. Listening to the PM's clever answers impressed Joe Public on the rare occasion he might select the wrong television channel on a Wednesday afternoon. These televised proceedings weren't a thing that would grab the interest of the average member of the public.

Question Time was well under way when Reilly arrived early for his appointment. As was usual, and since he was early, he made his way up to the public gallery. He enjoyed the afternoon's entertainment with other members of the public and a few representatives from the media.

This was one of the few times he admired politicians. He often amused himself by mentally attempting to answer a question before the PM. He compared their answers, but Reilly was never close. No matter how clever an answer he gave, the PM's answer outshone it. Their performance at Question Time could make or break the career of a PM.

There would be no problem in that area today. The current PM was confident and knowledgeable. He fielded many issues not anticipated by his team and did so skilfully. This was despite an equally skilful and devious leader of the opposition.

The House of Commons stretched out below Reilly. Rows of green benches faced each other like soldiers on a battlefield. Reilly had arrived in time to see an MP be introduced. The customary question was asked: 'Will the Prime Minister please tell me what his plans are for the coming week?'

The Prime Minister gave his usual response. 'May I refer the Honourable Member to the answer I gave the Honourable Member for Cardiff earlier?'

'Thank you, Prime Minister. I would like to ask the Prime Minister what plans the government has to stop the injustice in Myanmar? Why has he not introduced sanctions before?'

There were puerile shouts and cries of, 'Hear, hear!' as opposition members thumped the benches.

Reilly preferred questions on local issues or the National Health Service to international or political ones. He stood a better chance of putting a half-decent answer together on those. There was still half an hour to go before they were likely to stop for a break. He leaned back in his seat and relaxed. Although Reilly found most questions interesting, for the last ten minutes, there had been a barrage of banal point-scoring questions, annoying him – and the Prime Minister – so there was little chance that he would miss anything of consequence.

Loud laughter echoed throughout the chamber. Reilly stirred and opened his eyes. A short, rotund gent stood at the front of the opposition benches. The buttons of his waistcoat strained to hold the Harris tweed together.

'I am glad the House finds the answer to the last question amusing.' He waited for the murmurs to subside. 'Would the Prime Minister comment on the latest swings in stock market values? The press is suggesting that the stock market is being engineered by a group of foreign businessmen. Many of my constituents rely on fair markets to ensure their pensions.'

'I can assure the Right Honourable Member for Govan West that there is no evidence that markets are being engineered. We are currently going through a period of unusual global economic growth – India and China are demanding more commodities than there is supply. This is simply an example of a temporary misbalance between supply and demand. Fluctuations do occur – that is all we are experiencing at present. The Bank of England and the

Chancellery will be monitoring the situation, and this House will be the first to know if there is a problem.'

'I must inform the House that was the last question of the session.' The Speaker of the House nodded to the PM. He and several others rose and left the chamber.

So did Reilly.

***

'I trust my answer to the last question was accurate, Mike?'

The antechamber was dark and oak-panelled. Reilly had never been in this room before, but the PM was clearly anxious to hear his report.

'It was entirely factual, according to the evidence you have, Prime Minister.'

'The evidence I have? What the hell does that mean?'

Now Reilly was searching for that elusive answer. He didn't intend to deceive, but he was struggling to find the best words to use.

'Spit it out, man. Don't try to dress it up; that's my job. Now, what the hell is going on?'

Reilly took a deep breath. 'There have been attacks in the US, UK and Switzerland. We believe they are all linked – and it looks as though they're energy-related. It's not the energy supply itself that's being targeted, although we are protecting the pipelines in case. The attacks are aimed at technologies that might be energy-related.'

'You mean hybrid automotive systems, electrical drives?'

'No, it is more related to a form of atomic power. The scientists involved are researching pure science – there are no technological applications yet. It might just be an attempt to influence the markets.'

'Do we know who might be involved?'

'Not at the moment, Prime Minister, but we do have people in the position to find out. We are co-operating with the Americans.'

'Good. I want a report to arrive at Downing Street with my cornflakes every day. Is that clear?'

'Yes, Prime Minister. I also intend to contact the Metropolitan Police for help. We have a good relationship with the Met, but if I go through my usual sources, I will attract attention. Any political help you can give to make that run smoothly would be appreciated. It needs to be handled with discretion. I would prefer it if I met them on neutral ground, not at Police HQ. Perhaps the Home Secretary would make a request?' While Reilly was confident that the Home Secretary would be able to help, he was reticent about approaching the PM with such an unusual request. He hoped that the PM wouldn't ask the nature of his enquiry.

'Of course – she's in the next room.' The PM lifted the phone and dialled a number. 'Mike Reilly, MI6, is coming through.' He gave brief details of Reilly's request, then he added, 'Make sure he gets access to Miriam.'

'Thank you, Prime Minister.' Reilly shook his hand and made for the door.

'Reilly?'

'Yes, Prime Minister?'

'Keep me informed.'

Reilly gave a short nod and left.

***

'Mr Reilly, I believe you want me to set up a discreet meeting between you and the Metropolitan Police?' The Home Secretary was making notes in a notebook.

'Yes, ma'am.'

'Thank you, Reilly, but I am not the Queen – not yet, anyway. My name's Miriam.'

'Thank you, Miriam.'

'And which department would you like to meet with, Mr Reilly?'

'The Child Porn Department, Home Secretary.'

'I suspect you mean the Sexual Offences Exploitation and Child Abuse Command.'

CHAPTER 27

'*Une table pour trois*, Marcel?'

'*Bien sûr*, Madame Fenwick.' The waiter led Sophie over to a corner. 'Your favourite table,' he said in English. Gracefully he swept a chair away from the position he had chosen for Sophie and waited for her to reach the table. He had tucked it skilfully under her before he made ineffective gestures at the two men's chairs. As if by magic, he produced three jumbo-sized menu cards from behind a curtain and handed them out ceremoniously to Sophie, Willis and Palmer. The fourth card was the wine list. He stood, looking from Sophie to the men. Willis reached out and took the card. Marcel smiled and gave a bow. 'We have some excellent wine tonight. If I may, I would like to recommend the Sancerre or, if sir prefers red, the Crozes-Hermitage is excellent.'

'Thank you, Marcel. We will have one of each, please.' Willis handed the list back without opening it. Another short bow and Marcel vanished.

Sophie leaned forward. 'What are we celebrating, Brad? Our discovery?'

'We haven't made a discovery yet. All this is conjecture.'

'It would be nice, though, if it was true.'

'I'm not so sure. It will depend on who has been willing to kill all these people to get it, and what they intend to do with it now they have it.'

The waiter returned and took their orders, then replaced Willis's and Palmer's knives with steak knives.

'How well do you know Ernst Yeung?' Willis was looking at Sophie. Since he had been introduced to Yeung, Willis had sensed an animosity between them as well as something deeper, something that didn't fit with what Willis expected from a man in Yeung's position.

'The Director-General? You're not thinking that… No. You don't get to be that senior and then mess things up with this sort of thing.'

'I have met him before, once, but it was at a symposium. I don't know much about him.'

'I only knew him from my student days and now, here at CERN. He was responsible for hiring me, so I'm biased.' Sophie smiled. 'He has always been very helpful.'

Willis glanced in Palmer's direction. Palmer shook his head, intimating that he didn't know Yeung either. There remained a lot to be said between Palmer and Willis. Palmer cleared his throat. 'Someone is passing on information to the enemy. If I find out who it is, I will kill them myself.'

'I will ask Reilly what he can find out for us regarding Yeung. Will you ask Baker?' Willis said.

Palmer nodded reluctantly.

'What is it with you, Palmer? Why are you so negative? Spit it out, man.'

'I don't enjoy being told what to do. I am the same status as you, so why should you be bossing me around?'

'I wasn't aware that I've been bossing anyone around – how could you possibly have formed that opinion?'

'It's always "Do this, do that, Palmer." I'm fed up with it.'

'If you're that unhappy, maybe I should suggest to Baker that you return to the States.'

'See? There you go again. Now you're talking about reporting me.'

Willis shook his head. He couldn't get inside this man's brain. What was he on about?

'Settle down, boys,' said Sophie. 'Let's enjoy our meal. You can talk about this another time when I'm not here to listen to your disagreement.'

The next hour passed swiftly. Sophie's choice of restaurant had been a good one: the food was excellent, and Willis doubted that he had needed a steak knife. His meat was cooked to perfection. If he had wished for anything different, it would have been for a smaller portion, but he couldn't bring himself to leave any on the plate. The wine was of a similar note. Only a quarter bottle of white remained after the main course. After a few glasses of wine, Willis mellowed, making him enjoy the evening. If Palmer wasn't there, it would be much better, he mused. He would have Sophie all to himself.

Willis lifted the empty red wine bottle and spun it around in his fingers. 'Will I order another bottle?'

'What is that noise?' Willis was fumbling in his pocket. 'It's not my mobile.'

'It's mine, sorry.' Sophie took her mobile from her handbag and pressed a few buttons. 'His ears must have been burning. It's a text from Ernst Yeung. It says he is in my office with Harold Ellington and will we come straight away – it's urgent. What has Ellington discovered that won't wait until morning?'

'Well, I won't drive over there. I have had too much wine. The Swiss police would lock me up for a week,' said Palmer.

'Me neither,' Willis said. 'Let's get a taxi.'

No sooner had Willis stood up than Marcel was at his side. 'A problem, *monsieur*?'

'No thanks, Marcel, but we need to go. Please will you find us a taxi?'

'Marcel, make that two taxis,' said Sophie. 'Brad, you and Greg take the first one. I will stay and pay the bill – that will save some time. I will follow on immediately. I promised it was my treat anyway.'

Marcel vanished and returned with the bill.

'If I had known, I would have ordered a more expensive wine.' Willis kissed her on the cheek, and he and Palmer walked to the exit.

Marcel was as efficient at getting taxis as he was at waiting at tables. A grey Mercedes cab met them at the end of the restaurant's blue and white canopy, its diesel engine throbbing. While they drove, Willis racked his brain. What could possibly be urgent enough for Yeung to call Sophie in the evening? Especially given his track record of being unco-operative.

It took less than ten minutes to reach the complex. Willis paid the fare, and they pushed through the swing doors into the building. They went past Frau Holtz's empty desk and tried the door of Yeung's office. It was locked, which was not unexpected for this time of night. They continued along the corridor, aiming for the last door on the left. Sophie's office. The main corridor lights were out, but small red safety LEDs along the wall gave enough light for them to navigate their way.

Sophie's office door was open. Light spilled out, illuminating the wooden tiles in the corridor. The reading light on her desk was on, and Brad could see the unmistakable outline of Ernst Yeung sitting in the chair, his back to the door.

'Evening, Ernst. I hope this was worth leaving a good bottle of wine for? Why isn't Ellington here?' Willis stepped forward and walked round in front of Yeung.

He froze.

Yeung stared sightlessly ahead. His mouth was open, and there was a neat round hole in the centre of his forehead surrounded by congealed blood. A thin river of blood guided Willis down to Yeung's hands. He was still holding his mobile. Willis looked at the mobile. A call was still connected.

'Hello, hello?' he said.

No one answered. He ended the call and put the mobile on the desk. 'Better phone Sophie,' he said. 'Tell her to turn the cab around, go home, and stay away from here.'

Palmer had a brief conversation with Sophie, but he gave her none of the gory detail. He said just enough to keep her away. 'I need a drink,' Palmer said afterwards.

Then it dawned on Willis. The mobile. The open line. The call he had terminated.

'Run!' he shouted. 'We need to get out of here!'

Palmer needed no prompting. Both men ran for the door – ran for their lives.

A tornado of sound assaulted Willis's ears. The crunch of steel. Panels flew from the walls. A blast of wind blew Willis into a doorway, where he landed, on his back, on top of Palmer. My God, it's another bomb, he thought. This is the end. He prepared himself for the inevitable. A blinding light flooded the room. Twice. No sooner had the lights flashed on than they vanished. Intense darkness took their place.

The room? What room? Willis was looking at the sky. He could see stars. The darkness of the night invaded his world. Speeding out of the front gate was a tanker, its lights extinguished. On its side, Willis could make out the words 'EKHART ERDÖLHÄNDLER'.

A thick veil rolled over him. He slumped back to the floor, no longer conscious of his surroundings.

***

Vladislav Yerkin was pleased with himself. It had all gone like clockwork. He turned the tanker's lights back on and drove towards the border and to France.

CHAPTER 28

Reilly got out of his taxi in front of the archway leading into Guy's Hospital. He was ahead of schedule, so he decided to enjoy a walk. He crossed the road and walked towards Borough Market, despite the slight drizzle that formed droplets on the front of his spectacles. The drizzle gave the air freshness, and a mild breeze forced the smells of the market's produce into the streets and the surrounding lanes. The market teemed with shoppers and tourists, as was normal at this time of day. The pavements were already strewn with empty fruit and vegetable boxes. Squashed tomatoes and melons littered the walkways. The market had been only open for a few hours. Shouts of stallholders echoed off the bare brickwork and the glazed roof, trying to attract buyers to their produce.

It was hardly necessary. The stalls held treasures to tempt even the most resolute of shoppers. The aroma of exotic fruits, vegetables, cheeses, shellfish and gastronomic delights overcame the senses from all directions. The scents of oranges and lemons invaded his nostrils. This was Reilly's favourite market. On his way home, he would stop and buy his wife Madeline a selection of fish and cheese.

The rain had stopped by the time he reached the end of Stoney Street. The bustle of the market faded into the background when he turned left into Clink Street. When he passed the entrance to the Clink Prison Museum, he smiled. Would this have been a better place to meet the leader of the Sexual Offences Exploitation and Child Abuse Command of the Metropolitan Police? Clink Prison was surely appropriate; it was one of the oldest prisons in London. It had held men and women from Tudor times until 1780. It was said that William Shakespeare once visited a friend here.

But Reilly had agreed to meet Bill Chalmers in a much more salubrious place: Connoisseur's Paradise, an establishment dedicated to the promotion and enjoyment of good wine and good food. As the name implied, wine was its primary interest. The main door into Connoisseur's was on the corner of Clink Street and Stoney Street. Reilly skipped up the steps and introduced himself at the reception desk inside the glass doors.

While he walked to the restaurant, thoughts whizzed through Reilly's mind. How best should he approach his Scotland Yard contact? He decided to take a direct approach, keeping things simple and telling him the facts as they were.

'Your colleague has already arrived, Mr Reilly. Please come this way.' The receptionist lifted two menus and led the way inside.

Reilly found Bill Chalmers sitting alone at a table in a corner. He had his back to the wall and was seated well away from the windows that faced Stoney Street. Dark wooden furniture decorated the interior, and a glass gondola containing desserts jutted out into the middle of the room.

'Good afternoon, Bill. Thank you for taking the time to meet me this afternoon.' Reilly had chosen the time with care; they were the only two seated in the restaurant. It was noon. Connoisseur's had only just opened; they would have thirty minutes or so before the tables filled and customers flocked in. They would have finished most of their business by then.

'Don't thank me, Mike. I had damn close to a royal command to attend. You have friends in high places.' Chalmers was short and thin. What remained of his hair was a dirty grey; it surrounded a shiny pate. His suit was well worn. Reilly was unsure which would win the 'shiner of the year' contest – his suit or his bald head. His shirt was crumpled, and what looked like a soup stain decorated his tie. Reilly imagined picking Chalmers out of a line-up of suspects rather than Chalmers being in charge of catching them.

'I apologise for all this palaver,' said Reilly. 'It is important that only you and the commissioner know about this. I would normally have come in and asked for your help, but this is too sensitive for me to be caught talking to the Met.'

'Someone in a high place has been acting inappropriately, and you need my help? I warn you, in advance, I won't do a cover-up if that's what you're after.'

The waiter arrived to take their drinks order. He wasn't at all pleased with Chalmers' choice of drink. He walked away, shaking his head and whispering, 'Why would anyone come to a place like this and ask for a fucking beer?'

'No, it's nothing like that, I assure you. My interest lies in business crime. Something is going on that is worrying the Prime Minister. He would like your help to resolve it.'

'He has it, that goes without saying, but how does he expect me to help?'

Although Reilly had put considerable thought into how he would approach Chalmers, now he was sitting in front of him, he dismissed his earlier decision and started talking, rolling out most of the facts at once. 'Contacting you was my idea. I'm interested in your internet skills. I want you to track some data transmitted out of Switzerland and find out where it went. You guys track data all the time. I could ask GCHQ, but I'd rather keep it under wraps.'

'I can't help you there. I'm sorry. There are privacy issues and political issues with tracking another nation's networks.'

'You won't have any issues. The data has already travelled through Cambridge University's servers. We can even give you some of the file headers that accompanied the data to help you track them.'

'What you're describing isn't the internet – it's a corporate network, a private network.'

'Yes, it is. Some of the data go over dedicated lines, while some go over the internet. It depends on the content and the time of the transmission. But communications servers are the common link, and you guys are shit-hot at getting into those.'

Chalmers didn't look convinced. 'You have your own systems. They're a lot better equipped than our network.'

'I have no doubt they are,' admitted Reilly, 'but the data is long gone now, and there's no way to track it in real time. Our monitoring tapes don't tell us anything; we were looking in the wrong places to find this sort of thing out. We … I was hoping that your archive tapes might give us a clue.'

'That is one hell of a long shot. Unless we were monitoring the Institute of Astronomy, there would be nothing on record.'

'I realise that, but it's our only idea at the moment. Will you help?'

'File headers are useful, but they don't easily fit with what we designed our system algorithms to do. We work on keywords. The more keywords you get me, the better chance I'll have of getting a lead.'

As Chalmers spoke, Reilly became increasingly concerned. The restrictions with the Met's system might prevent them from getting any information from the Cambridge network. 'Okay, I will ask. Will numeric sequences work instead of keywords?'

Chalmers nodded. 'By the way, we encrypt everything stored on the hard drive at headquarters. So anything you send me will be safe.' He handed Reilly a small electronic device resembling a calculator. 'Here is a private data box. It will give you a code to get access to the data. Later, when you log on, it will give you another four-digit code. Type in the code, and you will get another code to respond with. You will have thirty seconds to enter it.'

Reilly was having serious doubts whether Chalmers could help or not. If this was the level of technology that they were still using, they would have little chance of achieving anything worthwhile.

'I understand, Bill. These things went out of fashion about a decade ago. Sort this for me, and maybe I'll try to pull some strings to get you some modern equipment.'

'Are you trying to bribe an officer of the law?'

Reilly smiled. 'If that's what it will take to stop these bastards, then yes.'

'I'm going to enjoy working with you, Commander Reilly.'

Reilly inclined his head. 'Will we have some lunch now? Courtesy of the Prime Minister?'

'Great idea. In that case, may I swap my beer for a bottle of Clos du Mesnil?'

'Get me a result on this, and I'll ask the PM to get you a case of the bloody stuff.'

CHAPTER 29

The world was not only still dark; it was also damp. Willis's brain hurt as if he had spent three nights out on Irish stout. His back ached, he dared not move his right leg, and there was an incessant buzzing in his ears. It took fifteen seconds for Willis to realise that the buzzing was coming from his mobile. He tried to reach up into his shirt pocket, but his hands refused to move. He tugged. There was a tearing sound, and his arm swung violently upwards, free of whatever had been constraining it. His wrist crashed against the corner of a drinks machine, and pain shot up his arm and into his brain. The buzzing stopped. Whoever was calling had given up. He dropped his hand back to his side and waited for the pain to pass. The drinks machine was leaking; a puddle of water had formed around his legs.

His brain worked slowly, like a sprinter trying to run through treacle. Flashes of memory came to him every few seconds, but when he tried to hold on to them, they faded into the darkness. The same flash of memory returned time after time: each time, Willis welcomed it afresh. He dipped in and out of consciousness, the same mental tape playing over and over again in his mind.

Parts of images materialised. He recalled hearing a cacophony of scratching and crunching. Bright headlights. A wall vanishing. A huge wheel bulldozing past his ankle. All this, then darkness forced itself upon him again.

Willis regained consciousness yet again. His leg was hurting like hell. There was a metal cabinet lying on it. Damn, he thought. It could be broken. He pushed the cabinet. It didn't move. It was only then that Willis remembered Palmer. Poor Palmer. Willis must have landed on top of him. He could feel Palmer's leg under his back. He tried to shuffle to his left to remove his weight from Palmer. One almighty push and the cabinet slithered along the corridor. The men lay at one end. Willis could have sworn that his leg straightened out.

'Shit, it's broken,' he said, but no more pain came. Either his leg was fine, or something had crushed it to mash. As he struggled into a sitting position, the smell of burning plastic attacked his nostrils. 'Shit, the fucking place is on fire.'

Willis's body reacted automatically. Sweat cascaded down his cheeks. Adrenalin pumped through his body. It was a sensation that he had experienced many times before. His body was preparing itself for action. An overwhelming surge of power pervaded him. He had experienced this before when he was under great stress, and he was becoming used to it, almost welcoming the adrenalin that it brought. His doctors had given it a name: PTSD. He had rejected it. They weren't normal symptoms of PTSD. Willis had his own theory. It was grief. Willis would use his newly found power to get out. He dragged himself upright, favouring his stronger leg. A little weight on his leg reassured him it wasn't broken. Palmer … he needed to get Palmer out, away from the smoke. He was lying with his leg at an odd angle. Willis grabbed him by the arms and dragged him past the fallen cabinet and along the corridor. The smoke was thickening, its obnoxious stench grabbing at his throat. He heaved Palmer into the reception area. With a final tug, he pulled Palmer's limp body one more yard and propped him against a wall. It was an uncomfortable position, but at least he would be safe. He staggered over to Palmer and fell to the ground like a sack of potatoes as darkness reclaimed him.

He had no idea how long he lay there. Blue flashing lights and the noise of sirens filled the hall. Thank God – the emergency services had finally arrived.

Footsteps echoed in the distance from what had been Sophie's office. There was a crash as the front door was smashed open. Two men in dark uniforms approached, one carrying a torch. He shone his torch into Willis's face. The light was agony. It was like a laser, focused on each eye, burning a hole through to the back of his skull and exploding like a miniature bomb in his head.

The man spoke into a radio. 'There are two men here. One is conscious, but he has damaged his leg. The other guy is out for the count, and his leg is twisted.'

Willis tried to move again but feared it might be worsening Palmer's condition. He had changed position while he was unconscious and was dangerously close to Palmer.

'Don't move.' The man wore a police uniform. 'Stay still until we are sure you've broken nothing. First, we need to check your leg. Can you move your toes? Good. Now try to bend your knee.' The officer was taking the weight of Willis's leg, his other hand gripping his ankle. 'Excellent. It is very badly bruised, but you will be able to play football again – if you ever could, that is.' The policeman waved over to a paramedic who had joined him. 'Let's slide him out and attend to the other guy.'

Every part of Willis's body ached as the men dragged him away from Palmer and left him lying under a table. A table leg blocked his view of Palmer.

Even supposing that Palmer's leg wasn't broken, Willis still felt responsible for getting him into this mess. He had asked for him to come to Switzerland in the first place, and Palmer didn't deserve this.

'How does he look?' Willis's words were croaky and faint.

'What you say, fella?' asked the policeman. 'Take it easy until the paramedic gets a chance to check you out. Your friend looks okay. He's unconscious, but it looks like he hasn't done any real damage.' The policeman shook his head. Palmer's leg was twisted awkwardly behind his back.

Willis was relieved. He relaxed, and, once more, the darkness enveloped him. He sank back into comfortable, welcome oblivion.

When he finally woke again, he was lying in bed. Tubes and wires trailed up from his torso and connected to machines at each side of the bed.

'Hello, Star Man.' Sophie's voice was soft and welcoming. 'You're lucky to be alive.' She smiled and squeezed his hand.

'How long have I been here?'

'A day and a bit. You're not too bad. The doctor sedated you until he'd done all his tests. He thinks you will be out in a couple of days at the most.'

'And Greg?' Willis mumbled.

'Greg wasn't as lucky. His left leg is broken. The surgeon has operated and fitted a pin, but he will be out of action for several weeks.'

'What happened?'

'Well, I managed to get a new office, but I would have preferred another method…' Her smile made Willis feel better. 'There is nothing left of it. Someone drove a fuel tanker through the wall. It's just as well it was a prefabricated hut.'

'What did they find out about Ernst Yeung? Someone shot him...'

'Yes. It looks like a .38 bullet, but we will know for sure when forensics have finished with it.'

'If someone wanted Palmer and me dead, why didn't they just shoot us too? They were clearly able to get into the room if they killed Yeung. That would have been much cleaner and much more reliable.'

Sophie pursed her lips and shrugged her shoulders. 'I don't know. It's crazy – it was an overkill situation. There must have been an easier way of trying to kill you than driving a tanker through the bloody building.'

'We might have a fanatical killer on our hands – someone who enjoys killing and has turned it into an art form. The method and skill are as important to him as the outcome.'

'Well, the outcome was a failure. Whoever hired him won't be pleased.'

'Bring the doc. I want to get out of here.'

'You'll be lucky. There's no way they'll let you out till you are mended.' Under protest, Sophie finally went to summon the doctor.

Willis was stiff and sore but not sore enough to want to stay in hospital. After a long verbal battle with his consultant, he eventually got his discharge papers. He persuaded Sophie to give him a lift to the police headquarters. She agreed – again, under protest.

Slowly he eased his aching right leg out of Sophie's car, lifting it with both hands, said his farewells, and waddled, like a duck, into police headquarters.

La Plas's office was dark and miserable. Every item was brown. Rust marks surrounded the handles of the filing cabinet. Used cardboard coffee cups littered the desk. Stains on the worn leather surface of the desk were evidence that more coffee had been drunk – and spilled – there in the recent past. This was nothing like the neat image of Switzerland Willis had imagined.

'Good morning, Mr Willis. I am told you that are helping CERN security with their problems?' Pierre la Plas was tall, middle-aged, and not unlike Willis's mental image of Inspector Maigret. There was even an unlit pipe on his desk. La Plas caught Willis looking at it. 'It's this health and safety crap. I'm not allowed to smoke here any more in case I affect my colleagues.' His English was excellent. 'Sorry, Mr Willis. I had forgotten that was how you earned your living.'

'It's not the same branch of health and safety. I am very pleased to say. What have you found out? The gun that was used on Yeung…'

'Nothing there. It's clean. And there's nothing on Interpol records either. The tanker was stolen from a fuel delivery company, and the security guard was killed – he had his throat cut. It was a fucking mess to clean up, I can tell you.'

'And the mobile?'

'The mobile belonged to Yeung. There's nothing suspicious there either.'

Although Willis was confident in Maigret's ability, he wondered how thoroughly he had investigated Yeung's mobile, as he hadn't mentioned the last number that he had dialled.

Willis told la Plas about the open line. The burly man pushed his chair back, pulled a sealed plastic bag from his desk drawer and took out a mobile. Its case was smashed, and bits of it were missing. He took two rubber bands and used them to hold the fragments together. He switched it on using a paper tissue to protect any prints that might remain. To his obvious delight, the display still worked.

Willis thought it odd that a seasoned assassin hadn't protected his phone with a password. Maybe that was because he had so little confidence in security systems that he decided it wasn't worth the effort.

'Thank you, Apple.' Willis sighed. 'What was the number he was connected to?'

La Plas pressed Recent Call List.

'I don't have my spectacles, Mr Willis, so what does it say?' He held out the phone to Willis. Willis took a ballpoint from a pot on the desk and wrote the number down twice. He tore off one copy for himself and passed the other to la Plas. 'It's a foreign number, and it starts with +73.'

La Plas typed in the number on his PC. 'There is no such country listed.'

'Try +7,' Willis suggested.

After another few seconds of two-fingered typing, la Plas exclaimed, '*Merde*, it's Kazakhstan.'

'Where in Kazakhstan?' asked Willis. 'What are the next three numbers?'

There was a pause. 'They're 7122 … it's Atyraū, Atyraū Province, Kazakhstan.'

Kazakhstan was one of the locations on the data trail from CERN. It was another piece of the puzzle. Willis was making progress – albeit slow. Also, disconnecting the open phone line hadn't been the trigger for the truck to crash into the building; he assumed whoever had been driving the truck must have been watching them. Willis shuddered. Things were getting more dangerous.

CHAPTER 30

'I'll need to take you around the back way, mate. Nothing will be moving from here to the bridge. Know what I mean?'

'Which way will you take me, then?'

'The quickest way will be up Savoy Place and Adam Street onto the Strand. Know what I mean? Will that be okay, mate?'

'That will be fine.' Reilly sighed. He was used to London traffic, but he had expected it to be a bit quieter at this time of day.

'There's some demo going on at Westminster – lorry drivers are having a slow drive past. Something to do with the tax on diesel. It hits my job too, but we cabbies can't afford to come off the road for a demo.'

The black cab swung around at the traffic lights and then turned left onto Savoy Place. London black cab drivers were well known for their conversation, which suited tourists fine. They would learn a bit more about the city, and the cabbie would end up with a bigger tip. But Reilly found the cabbie's chatter a pain in the ass. During his ride to meet

Chalmers, he had hoped for some quiet so he could concentrate on what he might tell him.

'Nearly never made it to work this morning. Got stuck coming in from the East End – the traffic was heavy even then.'

'I don't know that side of town well,' Reilly lied. He wanted to stop the conversation by pretending to be uninterested. It didn't take much effort.

Chalmers had asked to meet him as he had some results that he thought might be of interest to Reilly. They had opted to meet at Covent Garden, where there were enough small coffee shops and snack bars to meet relatively anonymously. The crowds would be increasing as lunchtime approached, and, with luck, live music might be playing on the lower level to drown out their conversation.

'I've lived in Essex all my life, and my dad and his dad before him, but things are changing so fast now. Know what I mean?'

Reilly ignored him. He wasn't being anti-social; he was mulling over what Chalmers might have for him. Had he found something, or was he being extra-cautious asking for another face-to-face meeting?

The taxi turned into the Strand and drove west before going north into Bedford Street.

'If you drop me off at Henrietta Street, that would be perfect.'

At last, Reilly's goal was almost in sight. With luck, he would get away from this futile chit-chat and still have time to think about how his conversation might go with Chalmers before they met.

The cabbie leaned back through his sliding window. 'Twelve quid, mate.'

Reilly handed him a ten and a five pound note. 'Keep the change.'

'Thank you, mate. Thank you very much.'

The locks on the cab released, and the red lights on the doors went out. Reilly opened the door and stepped out.

'I trust you will be as generous to me too?' Chalmers stood two taxis away, in the process of paying off his cab. 'I feared I might have kept you waiting – the lorry demonstration held me up.'

'Me too,' said Reilly. 'Let's get inside, away from the street.'

They went into the old flower market. It had been tastefully redeveloped, and rows of small craft and gift shops lined the area with, of course, a few restaurants and pubs.

They walked around the railing that surrounded the lower level containing the coffee shops. Chalmers peered over the rail at the floor below. He nodded towards a table sitting by itself in a corner. Reilly signalled back in agreement, and they aimed for the stairs. They settled at the table. Chalmers put his briefcase to one side. Reilly chased some flies away with a swipe of his hand and wiped up some spilled coffee from the red and white checked tablecloth.

Chalmers was wearing the suit he had worn at their last meeting. Reilly could have sworn he was also wearing the same shirt. The soup stain removed any doubt about the tie.

'Coffee?' asked Reilly. Chalmers nodded and put his raincoat on the seat opposite.

Reilly brought two cups of coffee and two Danish pastries back to the table. He emptied the tray and discarded it on the nearest empty table.

'Had a good couple of days?'

Chalmers shook his head and took a sip of coffee. 'There are some real weird bastards in this world. If I had my way, they would be all taken out and fucking shot. Instead, some fucking do-gooder or social worker or judge sets them loose again. The bastard we took to court this morning is out on probation for the third fucking time. Do you believe that? The third fucking time?'

'A simple "no" would have sufficed.'

'I'm sorry, but this job gets me down every so often.'

'Why do you keep doing it?'

'For the same reason, you keep doing what you do. I win more than I lose.'

'Are you going to help me win this one?'

'You set us a good one. We got no fixes on any of the number patterns or the file headers – in fact, we found zilch in any of the archives. Whether, like you, we were looking in the wrong places or whether they have done a damn good job of covering their tracks, we have no idea.'

'I suspect the latter. This lot has been very thorough.'

Reilly took a sip of his coffee and slumped back in his seat, despondent. 'Well, thank you anyway. It was worth a try, but I've run out of ideas now.'

'I am really, really sorry that the Metropolitan Police have been unable to help you.' Chalmers stared intently into Reilly's eyes. He winked as he pushed a computer printout across the table. 'If we had been able to hack into a foreign private network, it might have been possible to check current activity on the network. Unfortunately, that is not within my brief.'

Reilly studied his colleague inquisitively, prompting him to go on.

'Any information gained that way would be useless in a court of law anyway, even in the country where the data had been nicked from.'

The penny finally dropped. Chalmers was being cryptic.

'If it had been within your brief, what sort of thing might you have been able to do?' Reilly asked.

'The chances of us getting anything would still have been very small, and it would have needed a stroke of luck. It might have been possible to put a tracker on each of the servers to log any new data that might come along that route.'

'How would that do any good? The experiment is closed for the winter and for essential repairs that are needed. No data will be transmitted this side of Christmas.'

'Now, that is one thing that *is* within the remit of the Met. We're devious bastards. People get lazy and careless – that's how we trap most of our weirdoes.'

'How do you mean?' Reilly frowned.

'First of all, most networks are used as efficiently as possible, which means they put their email traffic over the same backbone – in other words, over the same cables. If it were possible to look for information transfer that was out of character – for example, at the wrong time, or in this case, the wrong season – then it might have been useful.'

Reilly was getting excited. 'That would only happen if there was someone on the site and still involved.'

'Exactly. And if there were, we would track the destinations of the messages.'

'And who sent them?'

'Unfortunately not. An encryption box was used, so we found the destination but not the sender.'

'Okay, I give in. What didn't you manage to discover?'

'We didn't discover that someone is sending emails from the Meyrin site to the Institute of Astronomy in Cambridge. It, in turn, didn't forward them to two ex-Soviet states before they finally didn't arrive at Atyraū in Kazakhstan. That's where the control is coming from.'

Reilly snapped his fingers. Magic – what a result.

CHAPTER 31

Willis was in the shower when the phone rang. His leg was still giving him gyp, but he was determined to go out for dinner. If he didn't get out, he would go stir crazy.

'I'll get it.' Sophie picked up the phone. The spray from the shower beat against his ears: as a result, Willis had no idea what Sophie was saying. A few seconds later, she approached through the steam. 'It's for you.'

Willis grabbed a towel and stepped out, took the phone and kissed Sophie on the cheek.

'Hello.'

'Brad, it's Reilly. I've got some news for you. There's someone at Meyrin working for the other side, but we've no idea who it is, so be careful.'

'We managed to work that out for ourselves. The other side knows everything that's going on here, even down to when Professor Yeung would be in his office out of hours.'

'How is your leg?'

'Getting better, thanks to an excellent nurse.'

Sophie stopped what she was doing and came over and kissed his cheek.

'And I have some better news. I have a source in the London Met. He's used their computer system to track where the transmitted data went after it left CERN. You'll never guess where it went…'

'How about Kazakhstan?'

'How the hell…'

'Never mind how; I have another job I need you to do. I have a mobile phone I need to track. The owner is here in Switzerland, but it's a Kazakh number.' Willis read the number from the scrap of paper. 'This is the hired thug that demolished Sophie's office – and he'll try to get at us again. I need to stay one step in front of him. Will you text me every time he moves?'

'Sure thing. As soon as I locate the mobile, I'll send you a message. What is your plan now?'

'We will need some new papers to get us into Kazakhstan in case they recognise our names at the border.'

'Our names?'

'Yes. I will take Sophie Fenwick with me. I will need her to recognise whatever we're looking for.'

'Take a commercial flight to Almaty. It's where most of the commerce and social life takes place. We have an agent there with a private plane that will get you to Atyraū.'

'Good. I've already checked – there's a Lufthansa flight via Frankfurt to Almaty tomorrow at 1.50 p.m. Tell your man to meet us from Flight 648. Will you arrange for papers and a passage through security?'

'Okay. The papers will be waiting in Frankfurt. I'll text you when I've discovered the whereabouts of your mobile owner.'

Willis dressed, and they prepared to go to lunch. Sophie had chosen the restaurant: it was close by, only two streets away from her flat.

The meal was excellent – quite different from that at the Crowne Plaza. The restaurant was small and only had space for about twenty seats. Sophie said she went there often; it was her local.

'We have come a long way, food-wise, since those early days at university,' she said. She leaned across the table and took Willis's hand.

'You are being naughty,' he said.

'Do you ever think of those days?' Sophie asked.

'Of course I do.' Willis thought of them often – the long afternoons and evenings they had spent making love in their room. They would take turns visiting each other's rooms. They were young, and their lovemaking had been very physical and always protracted. On the first full day they had spent together, they had formed an unusual habit. Halfway through the day, they had the sudden urge for food, any food, and the easiest option was to get a pizza delivered. They often had to cut short their embraces to answer the door to the pizza delivery boy. From then on, whenever they collapsed after making love, exhausted, laughing and begging for a break, they always referred to it as a 'pizza break'.

Although Willis wanted to believe that Sophie was softening to him, he didn't dare believe it could be true, but their reminiscing about their university days was giving him hope.

They summoned the waiter, paid the bill and were on their way back to Sophie's before the dessert trolley arrived.

The central light in Sophie's room was off. Two weak uplighters illuminated the pale walls. The lights of traffic passing outside made sweeping patterns on the walls and ceiling. Willis turned to Sophie. She was so close that he could only see her left eye. It was well out of focus, but he imagined her smile. Out of the corner of his eye, he watched her spinning her hair around her finger.

'Stop playing with your hair. What are we going to do when this is all over?'

'Why do you want me to stop playing with my hair?'

'Because it drives me crazy, and my leg is too sore for us to have ... pizza.' Willis kissed her nose. 'Answer the question.'

'Don't you mean, what will we do if we survive all this?' Her face fell, and she looked away.

'Stay with me, and we will get through it.' Willis grabbed her and pulled her as close to him as possible.

'I'm still not sure about us, Brad. You disappear, get married, never contact me, so what do you expect me to think? You're involved with intelligence services in faraway places. If I were able to trust you long term, things might be different, but in the meantime, I want to keep our relationship on the back burner.'

Something was wrong.

His pulse rose.

He was sweating. His hands shook. Sophie seemed to sense it and backed off from his embrace. Willis recognised the symptoms. It was happening to him again. His words became slurred, and his gaze darted backwards and forwards; he was unable to focus. These symptoms manifested themselves whenever he felt particularly emotional. His doctor had diagnosed it as PTSD, but Willis didn't believe him. It was just grief at losing Carole. Willis put a finger over his mouth to let Sophie know all was well, then covered his face with his hands. Sophie took the hint and lay back on the bed. Willis lay back too and let his emotions take over.

The memories flooded back. He had been driving that night. The night was calm. A slight breeze ruffled Carole's hair. The moon cast long shadows on the road ahead. Music filled his ears: music from the red convertible that was driving straight at them. Oh my God. It was going to hit them. Oh, my G—

After the impact, there was a second of silence that felt like minutes. The revving of the red car's engine broke the silence as it reversed from the tangled mess of Willis's car and then sped away. He turned and looked at Carole. Her eyes were open and empty. She had left him forever.

He envisaged her smiling, looking lovingly at him. Smiling, beautiful eyes. Carole's eyes. Tears welled in Willis's eyes. The past three years had been good times. Happy times. Then a hit-and-run driver had ended Carole's beautiful life. One short moment of inattention – and two lives ruined forever. He would never be with her again. Never hold her in his arms and tell her he loved her. Never kiss her lips and taste her flesh or feel her intimate touch. Images of Carole filled his thoughts. He didn't want her face to haunt him tonight. Her lips moved. She whispered, 'It wasn't your fault, Brad. It wasn't your fault.'

About fifteen minutes passed. All thoughts of Carole had gone, but adrenalin was pumping through his veins.

'There's something else you need to know. I've been diagnosed with PTSD. At least, that's what the doctors call it, but I don't think it is. It's nothing like normal PTSD. It started after Carole's death, so my theory is that it's grief, only grief.' He shrugged. 'I can fly off the handle and behave irrationally if I get stressed. So, there you have it. I can be dangerous.'

Sophie was silent for several minutes, then said, 'If the doctors have diagnosed it, then it must be a medical condition, and it will be treatable. What treatment have you had?'

'I attended a dozen or so therapy sessions at King's College Hospital in London over several weeks. It didn't help, so I gave up.'

Sophie looked thoughtful. She opened her mouth to speak.

But Willis wasn't listening. His brain was still racing. He sprang from the bed onto the floor. He picked up his case from a chair near the window and opened it. He threw the contents on the floor and, with Sophie's nail scissors, he cut the lining in the base. From inside, he produced a .38 Smith & Wesson revolver and a matching holster. He attached the holster straps around his chest and adjusted them until they fitted snugly. He checked the safety catch on the pistol and thrust it into its holster.

'We will need this soon.'

Willis picked up his mobile and typed in the number he had scribbled down in la Plas's office. He hit Connect.

A voice said, '*Da*? Yerkin.'

'This is Brad Willis, you murdering bastard. I am coming to get you.' Willis disconnected the call.

'Shit,' said Sophie, 'you've gone too far. That was *not* a good idea. Your so-called PTSD will be the death of us.'

Willis fell to the floor and lay there, motionless.

CHAPTER 32

'Just because you've got a plaster on your leg doesn't mean you're getting off with anything, pal.' Willis had rung Palmer as soon as he had finished his porridge. 'I'd like you to do us a favour. Sophie and I are leaving for Almaty this afternoon. We have a name. The guy who tried to kill us calls himself Yerkin – at least, that's how he answered his mobile.'

'What accent did he have?'

'I have more info than an accent. He speaks Russian, but he may be Kazakh. Their second language is Russian, so we have a name and probably an area of origin. Will you tell Baker and Reilly? Either British or US intelligence must have a file on him. If they don't, we will contribute a few entries if they want to create one.'

'Listen, Brad. I owe you an apology. I was well out of order. I'm sorry. It was my American stubbornness getting the better of me. I hate to take orders, especially from a Brit. As a civilian, I'm not used to taking orders, and this is the first time I've been in a situation where I've needed to. You're one of the good guys. I'm truly sorry.'

A weight was immediately lifted off Willis's shoulders. 'I'm pleased you told me. Let's forget about it – we have a job to do.'

'And thanks for dragging me out of the burning corridor.'

But Willis didn't forget it: Palmer's negative attitude had been bothering him, and he had avoided dealing with it. Now it was no longer necessary. Although Willis was confident in many ways, he was a coward when it came to confronting those he worked with. He'd known this for some time. He smiled ruefully. No one was perfect.

***

Palmer wanted to ensure that Willis got as much support as he needed. He decided to search the files and find out all he could. Anything he could find, he would report. He felt guilty and wanted to make it up to Brad for not being supportive before. His leg ached like hell, but he put it out of his mind and knuckled down to work. He and Willis agreed to use the code word 'ultra' to signify urgency in any message and agreed that Willis would call Greg 'Palmer' if he thought someone else was listening. Greg picked up his phone and dialled.

***

They arrived at Almaty without incident. Lufthansa Flight 648 had landed five minutes early, at 17.25. Reilly had done a good job. Willis and Sophie picked their papers up at Frankfurt, as he had promised. Sophie had giggled at the idea of being Mr and Mrs Callow. The new passports were American; even Willis's trained eye could not fault them. He checked the dates and location details of the immigration stamps and committed them to memory, then checked that Sophie's details matched his before making sure she too memorised her past itinerary.

Almaty Airport was small. Willis remembered the airport because two-thirds of it had burnt down in 1999 in a fire that started in the kitchen. The national dish was beshkarmak, a stew made from horseflesh and mutton. The chefs had likely burnt the kitchen trying to make the grey meat edible.

Again, Reilly had done them proud. He had arranged VIP tickets for them. Without these, it would be a nightmare to clear immigration and customs at the airport; with them, everything ran more smoothly.

According to the information Willis had picked up in Frankfurt, Reilly's contact would meet them at the Aksunkar Hotel at the airport. The Aksunkar turned out to be a small hotel with only forty-eight rooms. So far, everything in Almaty had been small. The building looked tired. Its sandstone bricks were weathered and darkened by pollution. The front door was dark brown and creaked when they entered. The hall carpet showed signs of wear. They approached the reception desk and introduced themselves.

'Sleep well, Mr Callow. I have changed your room to number eleven on the first floor.'

Sophie had complained about sleeping in a standard room – she still insisted they slept in single beds – and Willis had managed to negotiate the last of the hotel's double rooms. The other three had already been taken.

Checking in had been slow as their names, addresses, passport and visa details all had to be entered into the hotel's computer system. Willis yawned and stretched. The idea of a soft bed was becoming more attractive the more he thought about it.

'Please would you check to see if there are any messages for us?'

The receptionist drew his fingers over the numbers and stopped over the appropriate mailbox.

'No, Mr Callow, nothing.'

Sophie and Willis carried their bags to the lift. Considering what the hotel looked like from the outside, they were pleasantly surprised by their room, which looked very comfortable. It had two enormous beds covered with green and yellow striped quilts and wallpaper printed with yellow flowers and green stems.

Until their contact had touched base with them, Willis decided it would be better to stay awake and fully dressed. 'Let's not unpack yet,' he said. 'We should meet our man tonight. We might have to move on.'

But no one materialised. At around two a.m., they decided that sleep was more important. Willis took his pistol from his suitcase and put it under his pillow.

Within minutes, Sophie was sound asleep.

Willis lay awake, wishing he hadn't been so reckless with Yerkin on the phone last night. He had planned to unbalance the assassin. Willis knew that Yerkin would want to be in control. He would expect to set the agenda, the time and the place of his bloody deeds. Willis reasoned that if Yerkin thought he had become the prey, he might be unsettled and make mistakes. It might make him less careful. But now, Willis was not so sure. Yerkin might even change his phone number.

Why hadn't Reilly's agent shown up that evening? Willis wondered. What had happened to him? Had Yerkin intercepted a message that had been left for them? Ideas were dancing through his brain. He wanted to sleep, but his mind wouldn't rest.

Then it came to him in a flash. I must be more tired than I realised, he thought. He jumped out of bed and put on enough clothes to make himself decent.

'What's the matter?' Sophie was stirring.

'Go back to sleep. I'll be back in a minute or two.'

Sophie was still semi-awake, but she lay down and was soon sound asleep again. Willis opened the door and closed it quietly behind him.

He was back within a few minutes.

'Sophie – wake up now. We need to go out. He only searched in the wrong mailbox, didn't he?' He threw a sheet of paper onto the bed. 'He checked room eleven, but he had changed our room number, hadn't he? We were originally in thirty-four – and that's where the message was waiting.'

'Who … who searched in the wrong mailbox?' Sophie was fighting to wake up. She picked up the piece of paper, turned on the bedside light and screwed up her eyes to read it.

I am in Bay C, Row 8 of the car park, in a Lada Classic.

'That's useful – the car park will be full of Lada Classics. Why couldn't he have met us in the hotel? Let's go and meet him.'

Sophie threw on the clothes she had worn the previous day in Geneva, opened the wardrobe and reached in for her coat.

A blast pushed her into the wardrobe before she could do anything to stop herself. She lurched forwards, then backwards. Willis caught her, groaning as her momentum made pain shoot up his bruised leg. From somewhere above them, the sound of screams and smashing glass filled the room. A fire alarm sounded, but it was muffled and barely audible. The sprinklers cut in and sprayed everything in sight. Willis could only see outlines through the mist. He opened the door and checked the corridor. People were running around, the hall sprinklers adding more urgency to their panic. Some were shouting in Kazakh; others yelled in Russian. It made no difference; Willis understood neither. At the end of the corridor, the stairwell was filling with thick dark smoke pouring down from the floor above. Willis packed all his belongings, including his pistol, into the two cases and tossed them out of the window.

'Come on, let's get out of here.' He grabbed Sophie's arm and pulled her out into the corridor. It had got quieter in the short time it had taken him to fill the cases, but the smoke was even thicker, moving towards where they stood.

'Put this over your mouth and nose and run with me. Stay low. Keep your eyes closed and take my hand. Don't speak.'

The run to the stairwell seemed to take minutes. In reality, it was only a few seconds. Willis's eyes burnt and stung, but he had to keep them open to guide Sophie. They eventually reached the stairs and raced down and into the welcome cold night air.

A crowd of coughing people had gathered by the road at the front of the hotel. Willis and Sophie joined them. It was some time before they stopped coughing.

Three members of the hotel staff stood shouting in a mixture of languages. Finally came one Willis understood: 'Please stand in one place, please – we need to count to discover if anyone is missing.'

The man who had checked them in was standing with the guest book. 'We have ninety-two residents.' Another two hotel staff continued to count. They counted to ninety. They counted again. Ninety again. The hotel receptionist shouted out names from a sheet of paper. When he got to Newcombe, there was no answer.

He shouted again.

Still no answer.

'What room are they in?' shouted Willis.

'Room thirty-four.'

The crowd turned back towards the hotel, where flames spewed from a room two floors above reception.

'That is room thirty-four.'

Four minutes later, flashing blue lights filled the road. Three fire engines screamed to a halt, and uniformed officers took on the thankless task of trying to organise everyone.

Willis was wringing his hands. 'If our contact is going to meet us, he'd better be here now. If he's not, we need to make our own way to Atyraū without him. Staying here will be dangerous.' In the confusion, Willis took Sophie's arm and led her to the middle of the car park. It was well lit, so C8 was easy to find. The Lada was parked below a streetlight that cast harsh shadows around the other cars. Dew on the roof of the black Lada reflected the light from above it and made the saloon look like a soft top. By contrast, its inky black interior seemed ominous – and rightfully so. They were almost at the car before they saw the outline of a figure at the wheel. Willis stepped forward, tapped on the window and then opened the door.

The lifeless body toppled out onto the concrete. Sophie screamed. The lights reflected off the man's vacant eyes. A neat round hole decorated the centre of his forehead, and a thin line of blood had trickled down his face and collected on his chest. It was just like Ernst Yeung.

'What do we do now?' Sophie's eyes were swollen and red from crying and the smoke. Willis held her close. His heart was racing, and his breath wheezed in and out.

These bastards had to be stopped. He would be the one to do it.

CHAPTER 33

They hadn't been to bed for over twenty-four hours, but Willis was wide awake; the adrenalin that was pumping through his system eliminated any chance of sleep. The police were questioning guests. This was not a good time for him and Sophie to be around.

He collected their suitcases from where they had landed and moved them to the front of the hotel. He placed them with the other guests' cases. The majority were in good condition; the only obvious damage was due to smoke.

The suitcase closest to the hotel reception was the most damaged. Its clasps had burst open, and a gaping hole in its lid gave testament to its proximity to the flames.

Willis moved over to the case and placed his case alongside it. He picked up the address tag and read it. As he suspected, it read: 'Mr and Mrs J Newcombe, Baltimore, USA'. He prised open the lid and sifted through the clothes and toiletries until he found what he was looking for. Between pyjamas and a bundle of travel brochures, he found an A4 manila envelope. The address on the front was the Newcombes'. He pulled out the contents: two US passports, flight tickets to Astana, Kazakhstan's capital city, and a wallet containing credit cards. He slipped the envelope into the compartment on the outside of his case and placed Mr and Mrs Callow's passports in its place.

Nausea welled up in his stomach. Doing this to a dead couple was bad, especially since it had been Sophie's decision to change rooms that had cost them their lives. They couldn't be hurt any more. He made a note to make sure their family found out what had happened to them. In the meantime, he had to make it clear that the Callows had died as planned. Willis was relying on the booking clerk's confusion. If the clerk remembered that guests had swapped rooms thirty-four and eleven, his plan would be flushed out into the open. Eventually, the clerk was certain to notice, but by that time, Willis and Sophie would be well away from the burning hotel and relaxing somewhere anonymous where no one could find them.

In the confusion, no one seemed to notice them slip away and head back to the airport.

Willis bought another set of VIP tickets for the day. With the tickets belonging to the Newcombes, and another fifty dollars, he convinced an Air Astana official to swap their tickets. He now had two Air Astana tickets to Atyraū. Flight K883 was due to leave at 5.25 a.m. They arrived at the gate in ample time. He'd heard plenty of horror stories about Kazakh air safety – perhaps it would be safer if he stayed and took his chances in Almaty. As it transpired, he needn't have worried.

'Excuse me, sir, would you please come with us?' The two men might have passed for Sumo wrestlers. Both wore dark, heavy coats slung over their shoulders, leaving their arms free.

'Sorry? What's the problem?'

Willis wasn't expecting a reply. The men stared at him.

Willis kept up the charade, hoping the men didn't know who they really were. Putting on an American accent, he protested, 'We are American citizens. We have approved visas.'

It was ridiculous trying to play the dumb tourist, but it was worth a try. His stomach gave a twinge of complaint – for the second time that day.

The man on Willis's left moved forward and barged Willis out of the line of passengers. Willis staggered backwards. His slight frame offered no resistance to this irresistible force.

'It might be better to do as the gentleman says.' Sophie's voice shook. Willis needed no further convincing. He was busy reading the word 'Viking' on the side of the Yarygin PYa Russian pistol that protruded from under the goliath's coat.

Willis started to worry. How could anyone else have known that they were heading for the airport, especially this early in the morning? They walked back in the direction from which they had come. As they passed the check-in desks, Flight K883 had a 'boarding' sign flashing next to its number. Passengers were being directed to the leftmost gate. The old terminal building only had four stands for planes. The men led them down a flight of stairs onto the fringe of the runway, where they boarded a small electric bus.

At first, it seemed as though they were heading for a parked fire truck, but as they got nearer, it moved, revealing the sleek fuselage of a private jet. Willis recognised it as a Dassault Falcon 2000DX. The sleek two-engined jet had more punch than most commercial liners. He had no idea where they were going, but it was more acceptable than their planned flight with Air Astana…

He kept making eye contact with Sophie to try to reassure her that everything was okay. He had no idea who the men were or what they wanted of them, but if they had planned on killing him, they would have done so by now.

Inside the Falcon, a tall, thin man with a thick black moustache welcomed them. Willis had difficulty in keeping a straight face: as soon as the man spoke, he was transformed into Borat of TV and movie fame.

'Mr G has requested that you make yourself comfortable and have a drink.'

Willis had never suspected there could be a Kazakh with all the same characteristics as the television creation. He was fictional, after all. He had to look away. When he caught Sophie smothering a smile, he had to cover his mouth.

There was a thump, and the cabin shook as the door slammed shut. They were there for the duration.

Sophie and Willis each chose one of the rotating leather seats beside a cocktail bar.

'A whisky with ice, please, and the lady would like…?'

'I would like a dry white wine, please.'

'Borat' delivered the drinks and vanished.

Willis and Sophie took the opportunity to look around their prison. The walls and furniture were stark and white; the only relief from the starkness was thin black lines that outlined the edges of the furniture. On the floor was a thick dark blue carpet. Two mirrored doors that 'Borat' had closed hid the spirits and wine bottles above the bar.

A man strode through a door from the front of the cabin. He had jet-black hair and wore a white suit, a white shirt and a dark blue tie. 'Good morning, Dr Willis. Good morning, Dr Fenwick.'

'Good morning to you. I am afraid you have us at a disadvantage. Why have you kidnapped us?'

The man smiled, moved over to the bar and poured himself a large vodka. 'I always like to have the advantage, Dr Willis. Anyway, that is no way to speak to the man who saved your life.'

'Saved my life? I had no idea my life was in so much danger. Kazakh Airlines might not have a great reputation, but pulling passengers off a flight is a bit of an over-reaction.'

'I wasn't referring to the flight-worthiness of the plane you were about to board, Dr Willis. I was referring to the gentleman who had joined the queue four places behind you.'

'Who might that have been?'

'I believe you have met Vladislav Yerkin on at least two previous occasions, not including this morning's close encounter.'

'Yerkin was boarding our flight?'

'Oh yes. His advantage is that he knows what you look like. All you have is his mobile number.'

'You appear to know a lot about our activities, Mr…'

'My name is unimportant. But I believe we share a goal.'

'Why should we be interested in what your goals are?'

'You don't have to, Dr Willis. But if I hadn't intervened, your bodies would have been found after the passengers had alighted at Atyraū Airport. Yerkin is a professional. He has failed in his mission twice so far. He won't be pleased – and he won't fail a third time. You are free to go if you so wish, Dr Willis.'

'How exactly can we help each other?' Willis's phone vibrated twice in his shirt pocket. He pulled it out and unlocked it. It had switched over to the K'cell network. He pressed the message shortcut key, and a text flashed up on the screen.

Yerkin located in Almaty. Take care.

'Crap,' Willis said. 'You're only five hours too late.'

'Dr Willis, no doubt that is Mr Reilly telling you Yerkin is in now in Almaty.'

Willis replaced the mobile in his shirt pocket. 'Okay. I'm impressed. Tell me who you are and how we can work together.'

CHAPTER 34

'I am sure I read somewhere that the Kazakh *bratva* is more anonymous than their Russian brothers and don't flaunt their wealth? You're way over the top.' Willis smiled at 'Borat' as he offered a tray of drinks. He followed his host's example by taking a small white china cup of vodka. Sophie did likewise.

'That would be from the CIA's World Fact Book, no doubt. British intelligence does let you read it, of course?'

Willis caught Sophia looking at him, confused. His heart sank. Like him, she would be wondering how their host knew of his involvement with British intelligence.

'In any case, Mr Willis, Dr Brad Willis, your premise is false. I am not a member of the Mafia; everything you can see around you I earned legally. I enjoy my wealth, and I enjoy showing it off.'

'And how did you "earn" all this wealth in a country with an economy like Kazakhstan's?'

'It is exactly that economic profile that has made me rich. That and the greed of the British, of course, especially British Petroleum. And let's not forget our American cousins.'

'You made your money in oil?'

'Oil, and a few other things. I have diversified, as every good businessman should. It was the generosity of the Western oil companies, clambering over each other to give our country free oil lines, that got me started.'

'Somehow, I never imagined Kazakhstan as being good for business start-up opportunities. How come the autocratic rule here lets you get away with this?' Willis gazed at his host, challenging him to answer the question. The men were testing each other. Willis's luminous blue eyes contrasted with the deep brown eyes of their host. Willis didn't know whether he could trust his host or not. He decided to find out as much as possible about this man, who was giving him information by the bucketload.

'Your sources will have told you that Nursultan Nazarbayev, our glorious leader, lost his planned successor when he ostracised his brother-in-law. Now that some of the nepotism has gone, things have got a lot easier. It means that people like me can start legitimate businesses. Unfortunately, it also makes the *bratva* stronger. Ever since the Andijan massacre in 2005, the USA has been getting further from Uzbekistan and closer to us.'

'Alright, but I still don't understand how we can work together, Mr G.' Willis watched for his reaction. Only the slightest twitch of his host's left eyebrow registered any surprise. He hadn't been in the room when 'Borat' had used that sobriquet.

A smile spread over Mr G's face. 'I must remind myself never to play poker with you.' He signalled to 'Borat', who immediately produced a white briefcase and laid it on the table. 'Sabit is a trusted friend. He anticipates my needs. He is also the only person who ever refers to me as Mr G. It was a good try, Mr Willis.' He opened the case and took out a folder of papers. Willis stared at their black edges. They looked like death notices. G's idea was to promote an image by making the papers match the furnishings in the cabin. Willis thought the whole thing absurd.

'You are correct about one thing, of course: I haven't always been a legal businessman. I used to belong to VVZ. You might have read about them. It stands for Vory V Zakone, and it translates loosely as "thieves in law". We were a bit like your Robin Hood but nowhere near as noble. We did have standards, though, and we always kept to them. Not like the Mafia. But that is all in the past. A group of businessmen like me, all legitimate, are trying to change things. That is, despite our government and without outside influences. Kazakhstan is on the new Silk Road of the twenty-first century, and we are at its crossroads. Eastern Asia, Russia and the West's oil supply systems will all pass through here. Some people would like things otherwise.'

Willis was starting to like the guy. True, he was doing a good selling job on himself, but there was something about his character and attitude that appealed to Willis. Both men were starting to relax. Willis knew that could be dangerous, but he was in no immediate danger. 'Okay. What do you want me to look at?'

Their host selected a photograph from the pile of papers he had taken from the briefcase, spun it around and placed it in front of Willis. Willis picked it up and said nothing. Instead, he passed it to Sophie.

'This is Villiers's electro microgram of the holes in the ATLAS detection chamber. How did you…' Sophie put the photograph back on the table. As she did, a draught from the air vent caught it and spun it over. Willis read the label: it had American spelling. 'Color copy for the attention of G'.

Shit. How much information did this guy have? He even had photographs of the magnet – how had he managed to get hold of those so quickly?

'What does the "G" stand for?'

'George. Nearly every country in Europe has a George who slays a dragon.' He grinned. 'That is what I intend to do, Dr Willis. I do not intend to be evasive about my identity, but the less you know about me, the better it will be for both of us.'

'What don't you know about this picture…' Willis paused, then added, 'George?'

'I know what it is and where it came from. I don't know what caused the tunnelling effect in the metal.'

'You are not alone. It is puzzling us too. We have a theory, but it involves brand-new physics – none of the physicists at CERN gives any credence to it. May I ask where you got this copy?'

'It was taken off the corpse of a Mafia member after he tried to kill one of my colleagues.'

'You are not entirely against murder, then?'

'It was self-defence, exactly as you might have done with the Smith & Wesson you have under your arm.'

It was Willis's turn to hide his surprise. 'And how can you help us? Not that we're ungrateful to you for saving our lives this morning.'

'You need to get to Atyraū. I can fly you there. It can be difficult to board planes with the wrong photos on your passports, especially if you're carrying a gun. I can also get new papers for you – and I will give you any logistical support you need. My men will be in the background. All I want from you is to know the significance of the holes shown in the photograph – and what the Atyraū group is planning to do with what they have discovered. I am sure it won't be good, whatever it is.'

'We haven't eaten this morning,' Willis said, changing the subject. 'Any chance of some food?'

George signalled to Sabit, who exited via another white door.

'In the meantime, please make yourselves at home. You can have the guest room. All the facilities of the plane are at your disposal. After you have eaten, relax and let me have your decision.'

Sabit appeared again on cue and ushered them to the guest room. 'Mr G likes his guests to be comfortable.' He opened the door into a five-star room. Flowers were displayed in specially stabilised vases designed for flight. What Willis liked most was the fact there was not a bit of white anywhere. He switched on his mobile and read the message from Palmer. He brought up his contacts list. He pressed Palmer's number and waited for his friend to answer.

CHAPTER 35

It had been twenty-four hours since he had last spoken to Baker. The brigadier sounded sullen and serious when Palmer answered the phone. They exchanged the usual pleasantries about Palmer's damaged leg, then got on with business.

'There's not a lot on file about Yerkin, but what is there is bad news.' Baker was calling from Langley, Virginia. He had been forced to go to General Hayden, Director of the CIA, to get the information. 'Yerkin is an independent agent. He specialises in tidying up loose ends for whoever pays him the most. He did a lot of work for the Solntsevskaya Bratva, a Moscow-based brotherhood of the Mafia. That is, he did in the late nineties.'

'Are you saying the Russian Mafia might be involved in what is happening here?'

'Who knows? But he has gone quiet since 2000. Either he has dropped out of the scene, or he's getting better at not being associated with his deeds.'

'And I guess he specialises in assassinations and murders?'

'Well, he doesn't value life. He has turned up in Uzbekistan and Kazakhstan a few times since then, and he spends most of his time in the latter. There have been suspicions that he was responsible for the fires at Almaty Airport in 1999.'

'Fires?' asked Palmer, emphasising the 's'.

'Yes, fires – at least five separate fires caused the damage. The kitchen suffered the biggest fire, and that's the one everyone remembers, but it was no accident.'

'Who claimed on the insurance?'

'Intelligence says it wasn't an insurance job ... They believe it was some kind of fallout among "business associates".'

'That has Mafia written all over it.'

'Maybe, maybe not.'

'He gets involved in big jobs, but they have to be challenges for him. He loves his work.'

'I have a report here that says exactly that.' Baker was rummaging through what Palmer assumed was a pile of papers. 'Goddamned woman – I told her not the move anything on my desk.'

Palmer took the opportunity to change chairs and swing his plastered leg over a coffee table. He had discovered that it hurt less when he lifted it to waist height. He'd also discovered that a stiff Scotch was a good analgesic, so he poured himself a double.

'Ah, here it is.' Baker read it aloud. 'Studies have shown that Vladislav Yerkin is a near perfectionist in what he does. He does have, however, one major flaw in his personality: he needs to get a perverted buzz from what he does. As a result, he constructs elaborate plans, sometimes overly elaborate, to achieve a simple outcome.'

'Like starting five fires to burn down an airport or driving a tanker through a room to demolish it?'

'Depends on how you interpret it. Either it's overly elaborate, or he designed it to be foolproof and not fail?'

'Well, it did fail, or I wouldn't be having this conversation with you.' Although Yerkin had failed on this occasion, he might not have; he was a consummate professional. Simply thinking about what might have happened made Palmer feel sick.

'When will you next speak to Willis?'

'We usually text. I will text him and ask him to ring back. What else have you got on Yerkin?'

'That's about it, I'm afraid, but he's a ruthless killer. It is on record that he killed at least one CIA agent in 2009, but that was long before he moved east to work for the stans. When he's caught off guard, and he has to improvise, his favourite weapon is a knife.'

'Where is he now?'

'He's in Almaty. I texted Willis. I hope he got it in time, as he hasn't acknowledged the message yet.'

After Baker had hung up, Palmer poured himself another whisky and lay back on the bed. The throbbing in his leg was still perceptible. What had begun as drumming had subsided, to be replaced by an unbearable itch. He couldn't make up his mind which was worse: the pain or the damned itch. The only way he would conquer it was to take his medicine like a man, so he poured yet another Scotch. While his leg ached and itched, it could have been a lot worse. Palmer shuddered.

'Succeed' and 'successful': the words played over in his mind. Why had Yerkin been so careless? Why had he allowed him and Willis to live? If he was as clever and as competent as Baker's intelligence believed he was, why had he screwed up in such a spectacular way? It was an elaborate enough plan – and it had been a heavy-duty plan, as the CIA personality profile from Langley had predicted. Had it all been to feed Yerkin's psychological need, or had it been intended to be successful?

Could it be that Yerkin had succeeded, and his and Willis's presence in the room was just a coincidence? Had he succeeded in killing his intended target after all? Palmer's brain was fighting the effects of the alcohol and the pills the doctor had given him. As he wondered if the alcohol and the pills would interact, he fell into a deep sleep.

When he woke, he was unsure how much time had passed. It was raining outside, and the effects of the whisky had worn off enough to let the throbbing invade his plaster cast once more. His mobile was playing Robert E. Lee, Willis's name illuminated on the screen.

'Hello, Brad, and before you ask, my leg is a lot better, thank you.'

'I got your text.' Willis sounded cold and business-like. 'What did Baker have to report on Yerkin?'

'Apparently, our friend has quite a reputation. He is a cruel, sadistic bastard who rarely makes mistakes. Thankfully we are still here, so that proves he isn't perfect.'

'Who has he worked with? Has he had any dealings in Kazakhstan before?'

Palmer gave Willis a précis of Baker's report and finished off by saying, 'They believe he has been in Kazakhstan since early 2014. Before then, he was an independent operator, but now they think he's employed by a single group of criminals. Baker says he has no known associations with the caviar or oil Mafia groups in Kazakhstan.'

'Good, that's what I expected. Strangely enough, it was what I was hoping to find. I can't explain now, but I would like you to tell Reilly that we're still in Almaty, and we're safe.'

'What are your plans now? Are you flying to Atyraū?'

'Eventually, but not immediately. I would also like you to ask Reilly about a group known as VVZ – their full title is Vory V Zakone.' Willis spelled out the words to him. 'Put this request to him ultra-fast. Understood?'

'Roger, Willis, fully understood. Is that all for now?'

'Yes, Palmer, over and out.'

Once Willis had said it, Palmer congratulated himself on remembering the code they had devised, but this was no time for self-congratulation. He had to contact Reilly as soon as possible to pass on Willis's message.

Palmer waited for Willis to end the call, and then he immediately dialled Reilly.

'Hi, Greg. You got me as I was leaving the office.'

'Willis has been in touch. He used the code word "ultra", meaning that his request was urgent. He wants you to find out about some people known as Vory V Zakone, and he called me Palmer – which means he was not alone. Someone was listening in.'

'Excellent. It looks like he's making progress already.'

CHAPTER 36

Yet again, Vladislav Yerkin was happy with the outcome. At Almaty Airport, he had picked up a copy of the early edition of the English language newspaper the *Kazakhstan Monitor*, which reported most of the news about foreigners in the country. The headline read 'Fire at Almaty Airport Hotel kills American Couple'.

He thumbed to page four, where the front story continued. The second paragraph confirmed what he knew: 'Mr and Mrs Callow from Maryland, Baltimore, USA, were killed in the fire.' A limousine was due to pick him up as soon as the flight had touched down. There was no sign of it yet, but he wasn't worried; the traffic around the airport was heavy at this time of the morning. It was still early as he had gained an hour flying west from Almaty.

The bar was already open, even at this goddamned time of the morning. He signalled the bartender for a double measure, but he waved him away from the cognac bottle, which was the usual drink of Kazakhs, towards the vodka bottle. The vodka tasted good. It was a fitting way to celebrate his success, and he swallowed the drink in one gulp. For a few seconds, his face twisted from the taste of the raw alcohol. He sat back and lounged in the comfortable bench seat facing the exit while a wall-mounted television showed a daytime game show.

Missing his target at CERN had disappointed him. It annoyed him that he had made an oversight. He hadn't screwed up like that since he was twenty-three and much more impulsive than he was now. He had planned well, but not well enough. However, his performance at the Aksunkar Hotel had made up for that. The timing device in room thirty-four had worked faultlessly. Having to eliminate the driver in the Lada Classic had been a surprise, but it pleased Yerkin that he had handled it in such a timely manner before it became a problem. All in all, the outcome had been good. Even if his masters were aware of the partial success at CERN, they would be pleased with his latest result.

The neon lights inside the terminal reflected off the sliding doors that led onto the walkway outside. The dawn sky had begun to lighten enough for him to make out the shape of the dark limousine outlined against it. He drained the rest of the vodka, picked up his case, and walked towards the doorway.

The limousine had stopped in the 'no parking' section. A Kazakh policeman, standing metres away from it, ignored it. That was the culture here. A policeman was lucky to earn the equivalent of six hundred American dollars a month, and he would know who owned the unusual car. He was unlikely to upset the money source that had often thrown crumbs his way, so he turned away and challenged another driver several spaces away.

The limo slid away and joined the line of traffic leaving the Arrivals area. As the policeman had done, the line of traffic acknowledged the status of the car and slowed or pulled over to let it in.

Yerkin relaxed in the plush leather seat and helped himself to a drink from the built-in bar. This is the life, he thought. He reminded himself that he had made the right decision by joining his new business masters. He was now getting easy commissions from all the surrounding stans and most of Central Europe. Ever since he'd changed the country he worked in, he'd started to enjoy himself more. Finding more challenging and dangerous tasks to undertake made his talents shine, and this attracted new customers in need of his services.

He was so intent on self-congratulation that he failed to notice the limo turn left at the airport junction rather than right. It wasn't until he saw the lights of an industrial estate that he paid attention. He leaned forward and tapped on the dividing glass between him and the driver. Immediately a loudspeaker crackled into life, and the driver responded. 'Yes, sir?'

'This isn't the correct way to my meeting.'

'No, sir. I have instructions that the meeting has moved to the estate for security reasons. I believed you knew this, sir.'

'Security reasons? Okay. I should have been told in advance.'

'Sorry, sir.' Although he was always ready for any eventuality, Yerkin didn't like surprises, and this was certainly a surprise. He steeled himself for whatever was to come. He removed his pistol from inside his case, checked its ammo clasp and safety catch then slid it into his left jacket pocket.

The limo kept going into the industrial estate. A guard at a pair of iron gates beckoned them in. The driver let the car coast up to a set of triple loading doors, then pressed a button under the dashboard. The roller mechanism squealed through lack of oil as the huge door opened. Before the door had fully opened, the car was inside and parked beside two identical limos. Yerkin recognised both cars and relaxed. The chairman had arrived before him.

He took his case from the back seat, folded the newspaper and tucked it under his arm.

A guard met him at the end of the loading bay. 'Please go straight to the main meeting room and join the others. It's towards the front of the building, through a set of swing doors.'

Yerkin was the last to arrive. Twelve suited men turned towards him as he entered. The chairman gestured towards the bottom of the table, where the last empty seat was. Yerkin removed some papers from his case and placed the folded newspaper on top of them.

'I have heard that the exercise at CERN was a failure.' The chairman lifted a brown folder from the table and removed a sheet from it.

'That is correct. It was only partly successful – that is why I followed them to Almaty and finished the job there.'

'You finished the job?'

'That is correct. They used false passports and travelled under the names of Mr and Mrs Callow. The local paper reported the fire, and it reported the deaths of Mr and Mrs Callow. I have the newspaper here.' Yerkin handed the paper to the man on his left, who passed it on until it reached the chairman at the top of the table. 'The report on page four confirmed they burnt to death in room thirty-four.'

There was silence while the man at the top of the table read the article. He then turned to the front page and shook his head. 'This is the early edition, Mr Yerkin. The later editions report a different outcome.' He took the sheet of paper he had removed from the folder on his desk and passed it down the table.

Yerkin read the paper with disbelief. It was a scanned page from the *Almaty Herald*, the second of the free English newspapers.

He scanned the lines like a madman, the veins on his forehead swelling. The headline read 'Bodies of Dead Americans Misidentified'. The article explained that it was a Mr and Mrs Newcombe who had died in the fire. Mr and Mrs Callow, whose passports had been found at the scene, were still missing.

'They must have changed rooms and swapped the passports!' shouted Yerkin. He pounded the table with his fist, making a glass of water spill over his papers.

'They are now aboard the Dassault Falcon. You have failed.' The chairman stood and dropped his papers on the table. 'You are dismissed. Sergei, please show your former partner to the door.'

'Please, Pythagoras, I will fix this. I will go back and eliminate them. There will be no charge until I finish the task.'

'We have the matter in hand now. Thank you very much for your services.'

Yerkin stood up and swept the papers into his briefcase. The horror of the situation overwhelmed him. Fired. He, Yerkin, had been fired. His pulse raced so fast that it made him dizzy. He must avenge the insult of this incident. He stared daggers at Sergei as they walked together towards the door. Even as he followed his companion into the corridor, he couldn't accept what had just happened. Nothing like this had ever happened to him before in his professional life.

'I declare the meeting closed, gentlemen,' said Pythagoras. 'I will report back when the problem has resolved itself. Desperate times demand desperate actions.'

There was a rustle of paper as files returned to briefcases and the men vacated the table.

A series of deafening cracks filled the room. The men in suits threw themselves to the floor, dropping their briefcases. Only the chairman remained standing.

Sergei re-entered the room. 'It is done,' he said, placing a semi-automatic on the table.

'You are in charge now, Sergei. I will not tolerate failure. I declare the meeting closed a second time, gentlemen.'

***

Willis had finished eating, and he and Sophie were relaxing aboard the Falcon. As he sipped the last of the Bordeaux, his mobile vibrated again. It was another message from Palmer. He read it aloud to Sophie: 'Reilly reports Yerkin is in Atyraū. He says it looks like he is now stationary.'

CHAPTER 37

'So, Yerkin is in Atyraū?' George had been visiting the pilot of the Dassault Falcon and now re-joined Willis and Sophie at the table. 'He didn't spot you at the airport. Otherwise, he would never have boarded the plane when you joined us. Now is the moment of truth.' He looked straight at them. 'Are you coming with me to Atyraū, or do you want to get off now? You are free to go if you wish, but I cannot wait around the airport much longer. Even I shouldn't abuse privileges.'

Willis hadn't received any answers to his questions from Palmer. He was not sure who this man was – or whether he was ready to trust him with his life. He stared back at George, matching the intensity of the big man's gaze.

'I still don't know very much about you. You haven't given anything away. You're a huge risk,' he said, shaking his head.

'So be it, Mr Willis. I do need your help, but I don't want to coerce you. You are free to leave.' George waved to

Sabit, who opened the hatch door. 'There is a limousine waiting to take you wherever you want to go.'

Willis signalled to Sophie, and they walked towards the open exit. He stopped, turned, and said to George, 'Thanks for saving our lives at the airport.'

He didn't know whether he was making the right decision. Would George let him leave? He screwed up his eyes at the brilliance of the sky as he walked through the open hatch. The limousine was standing a few metres from the bottom of the steps, exactly as George had promised. It contained only the driver and seemed non-menacing. He proceeded down the steps until he was out of George's direct line of vision. Then he turned to Sophie. 'We have nowhere we want to go. Have we?' He took her hand, turned and led her back up into the cabin.

'I fear I will have to trust you.' Willis sat down across from George. 'I believe we can work together – for a while at least.' Although Willis was sure he had made the right decision, in the short term, at least, he still had a nagging doubt. Could he trust his apparent new ally?

'That is all I ask. When we have spent some time together, I will earn your trust.' He tossed a copy of the *Almaty Herald* onto Willis's lap. He had circled several paragraphs in red.

'Sabit brought this on board while you were eating. You and Sophie are now considered missing persons.'

'And you were willing to let us go when you knew they were searching for us? They would have taken us and arrested us since we have no passports.'

'Only arrested, Mr Willis. The local police are friends of mine. I would soon have "rescued" you and so gained your trust.' George swung back in his chair, laughing and drinking another large cognac. Then he pressed a button on the wall beside his chair. A male voice answered. Willis didn't understand the Qazaq language, but he recognised one word. *Gurjev*. This he knew was an alternative to Atyraū. He also thought he picked up *tort*, meaning 'four', which he assumed referred to their arrival time at Atyraū. He only spotted this due to the Turkic language's use of vowel harmony: the final syllable of each word is emphasised, making the words stand out. He faced George. 'Thanks.'

Willis had lost some of his newly found confidence. If this was how George would act, then he would need to take greater care. Within minutes the jet engines of the Falcon had fired up. It swung around and began to taxi towards the runway. Willis mused that George's instant access to a take-off slot was another example of the privilege he had referred to.

The two Pratt & Whitney jet engines, each capable of 7000 lb thrust, were soon at full power. The Falcon 2000DX lifted into the Kazakh sky, pushing Willis into the lushness of his white leather armchair. The 2000DX had all the comforts of a large jet and the economy of a small one. With six passengers on board, it had a range of 3,250 nautical miles and could reach Mach 0.8.

Sabit returned as soon as the Falcon had reached its cruising altitude, supplying George with another cognac while Willis and Sophie opted for black coffee.

'Our friends in Atyraū started life as part of the caviar Mafia.' George sipped his drink and relaxed. 'They made their money by controlling the price and the supply of caviar to the insatiable Russian market. They get upwards of five thousand dollars a kilo for the finest beluga caviar.'

'Aren't there strict controls on the export of caviar?' said Sophie.

'Oh, there are. It's the illegal market that makes the most money. The latest estimates reckon it's twelve times bigger than the official one. Some of the beluga catch goes to pirates on the Caspian – they attack and raid the fishing boats. Our friends have fingers in all that.'

'I bet the workers on the Ural River don't get much of the money,' said Sophie.

'No, they don't. They are stressed people. Environmentalists say the beluga could be extinct in ten years at the current fishing rate. Families who have relied on the trade for generations will no longer have a source of income.'

'What are these guys doing with their wealth that interests you?' asked Willis.

'They have started a new line in business investment. They look for ways to drive commodity markets up or down, then make sure they buy and sell at the right time. It is screwing up honest businessmen and investors big-time, and we've decided to do something about it.'

'Who is "we"?' asked Willis.

'We are a group of people who are trying to make business work in the country. You could consider us vigilantes. We apply the same standards that worked well when we were the VVZ, but all we are asking for now is that there are rules. We are not crime fighters; we are protecting our interests.' George reached out and took an iPhone from Sabit. Willis could see the screen well enough to tell it was displaying a web page.

'You ask me what they do – have a look at this.'

Willis looked at the image in front of him. It was Villiers's image of the damage to the ATLAS detector, with the holes highlighted. He scrolled down and read the accompanying commentary. It described the discovery of 'a new form of cheap energy that will replace oil and gas'. It went on to describe the diagram and explain that the holes had been made by a combination of subatomic particles, the Higgs boson and the inflaton. It continued: 'A spokesperson at CERN in Switzerland, where the discovery was made, has been quoted as saying that the Higgs boson has proven to be easily controllable and will be a new source of sustainable energy within three years.'

'They know as much as the physicists at CERN do … and then a bit.' Willis handed the iPhone back to George. George pressed a few buttons, then handed it back to Willis. It was showing the Bloomberg financial news pages. Willis read aloud for Sophie's benefit. 'Oil prices worldwide have dropped fifteen per cent in three hours. The values of oil companies have reduced by as much as thirty-four per cent as countries announce their intention to reduce reserves. London awaits the reaction from the US when Wall Street opens for trading in a few hours.'

'What a mess,' Willis said to George.

'And a mess our friends in Atyraū will no doubt enjoy when they invest heavily in the falling prices of shares and commodities. Millions will be wiped off pension funds worldwide as their fund managers panic and sell off the plunging shares.'

'So it's already too late? They will clean up in forty-eight hours as soon as they announce the hoax.'

'It would seem so,' said George. 'What we need is—'

A klaxon went off in the cabin, cutting George off in mid-sentence. The aircraft lurched to port, and Willis was crushed against the bulkhead. Sophie was pushed against him, squeezing the breath from his body. George was thrown out of his chair: he flew eight feet across the cabin and crashed into the cocktail bar. Willis felt an intense pain in his chest as the air was sucked from his lungs, and he struggled to breathe. *This is the end.* Willis's mind was fogging up. *All is lost. There's no way out of this.* The plane was in freefall with the nose of the Falcon pointing towards the earth. Oxygen masks fell from the ceiling. Willis leaned forward to grasp one. It swung away, and he caught a glimpse of open sky through the bullet holes that riddled the side of the plane. He turned and held Sophie close. She looked into his eyes with resignation. He could imagine her terrified thoughts: this was surely the end. She and Brad would perish together. It was all over. Tears ran down her cheeks, and she buried her face in his neck.

He had to fix this. Somehow.

Willis reached out one more time for an oxygen mask. He missed. His sight blurred and everything around him took on a pink hue as the drop in cabin pressure forced blood into his eyeballs and retinas. Darkness flooded in. It came from the edges of his vision at first, then finally, all-pervading darkness covered him like a closing coffin lid.

He fell forward onto the table. Now he felt comfortable. The excruciating pain in his lungs had gone, and he was at peace.

CHAPTER 38

Willis had no idea how long he had been unconscious. It might have been minutes or seconds. He strained against the rushing air in the cabin of the Falcon. George lay against the opposite bulkhead, his legs outstretched and arms akimbo, like a limp teddy bear. Sophie was still in her seat, which was safely facing aft. She clung to its arms. He assessed that she was as safe as she could be – in the short term, at least. There was no sign of Sabit. The plane was dropping, but not quickly enough to allow the air pressure in the cabin to recover.

Willis's pulse was racing. His back was sodden from the sudden sweating that had enveloped his trembling body. Adrenalin flooded into his veins. He was in control of the situation. Thank God for PTSD.

The plane was still falling earthwards, but it had levelled off to about a 10-degree drop. Fear filled Willis's mind. His hands were soaking wet. His breath came in gulps. He let himself fall out of his seat and used the fixed legs of the tables and chairs to pull himself towards the cabin door. He was half falling, half crawling as he forced himself towards the cockpit. Lactic acid was building up in his leg muscles, but he forced them to drive him forward under the anaerobic conditions caused by the thinning cabin air. Thankfully, the flight deck door was open, swinging on its hinges, when he reached it. He had no idea how far below him lay the grassy steppes of Central Kazakhstan; how far away was the impact that would smash the fragile jet to smithereens?

He struggled forward, not thinking about what he might find when he got inside the cockpit. Whatever he might have imagined, it could not remotely have resembled what he saw. The pilot sat in his seat, slumped to one side, still strapped in. A bullet had penetrated the side of his skull. Death would have been instantaneous.

Willis tore at the seatbelt to undo it and let the corpse lean towards the floor. He took no notice of the limp body in the right-hand seat. With a mammoth effort, Willis pulled the pilot's body free of the controls so he could slot into the dead man's seat, then he pulled back on the stick. It resisted. Autopilot was still engaged, but it was only partly effective.

'How the shit do I disengage the bloody thing?' he shouted. Willis had only ever flown one jet before. That had been a Hawke trainer – very different from a Dassault Falcon. He pulled on the stick. If given enough force, it would fight against the autopilot and give him control. As he pulled, the nose lifted slightly. He pulled harder, and it gave a little more. The horizon skewed in front of him, 30 degrees from horizontal. There was no way for him to tell how far below them the steppes were or how fast they were approaching the ground. His arms were tired. The stick was pulling back too strongly for his arms, which were starved of oxygen. He searched for the altimeter on the electronic display. It was racing down; the right-hand digit turned relentlessly. A sick image rushed through his mind. It reminded him of a bomb timer counting down. The analogy made him nauseous. He flicked a switch near a computer trackball in the centre panel. The Falcon's upper Multi-Function Display Unit changed the image it displayed. He grabbed the trackball and moved the screen cursor across the screen, and clicked. This was as easy as playing a flight simulator. The nose responded immediately. It rose a full ten degrees and stuck again. Willis pushed both throttle levers forward another three inches. The airspeed increased. He lifted the nose gently, and the Falcon levelled off. Willis pulled back on the throttles again and let the plane slow down. Only then did he look at the crumpled body in the co-pilot's seat. A hail of bullets had hit the poor bastard's chest.

'He's alive. He's still alive.' George was behind him. 'We need to get him some help.'

Was the fact that he was alive an advantage or not? Willis was playing with the controls and changing the displays. A moving GPS map took over the screen. 'What's that to the south? It looks like an airport.'

George was shouting to be heard above the wind blowing through the bullet holes in the side of the plane. He stopped shouting and placed a plastic tray against the cabin wall. The vacuum sucked the tray against the holes and the leak reduced to a trickle. The decompression of the cabin would slow long enough for them to reach a safer altitude. He took a breath and said, 'That is the Baikonur Cosmodrome. It is a Russian space facility. But Krayniy Airport is just outside the town of Baikonur, which is south of the Cosmodrome. We will land there and get help for Anatoly.'

Anatoly's eyes opened, but they were empty. George was holding his hand in an effort to comfort him. Anatoly's lips were moving. George bent close and placed his ear against his mouth. He breathed a few words in Qazaq, then fell back, exhausted.

Willis held out little hope of getting help for him in time.

'The plane won't turn,' Willis said. 'The blast must have damaged some of the electronic controls to the tail.'

'I am surprised we're still in the air. Anatoly just said they spotted a fighter jet firing on us before they lost control.'

'Check on Sophie, please, and fasten her up. This is going to get rough.' Willis increased power to the starboard engine and eased off on the port engine. The plane vibrated and turned in the desired direction.

George was back behind the co-pilot's seat, pressing buttons on the audio panel. 'Hello, Krayniy. Mayday. Mayday. We are attempting to land. Our pilot is dead, and the co-pilot is injured. Mayday. Mayday. Can you hear me?'

'Hello, this is Krayniy. Please circle until we make safe for landing.'

'Negative, Krayniy. We have no tail control, steering by trimming engines. It is now or never. Over.'

The voice from the control tower sounded panicky. 'We are clearing runaway. Please delay landing as long as possible.'

'What the hell is that supposed to mean?' Willis said. 'It's all academic anyway. I can't get enough torque from the engines to face Krayniy.'

'Well, you sure can't land in the steppes. The land is too uneven for a jet to put down.' Then George's eyes grew wide. He took a deep breath. 'No, you can't. You can't land there.'

'Watch me.'

Baikonur Cosmodrome had two airfields. The Falcon was descending towards one of them.

'Hello, civilian flight. You do not have permission to land. This is a restricted area. Turn around immediately. Over.'

'Sorry, Baikonur. Unable to comply. Mayday. Mayday.'

'If you do not divert, we will shoot you down.'

'Tell me, George. Right or wrong? President Putin ordered all military personnel out of here early in 2008, right?'

'I'm not sure whether that happened, but there are always delays with military movements.'

That's odd, thought Willis. He would have expected George to know the status of Baikonur Cosmodrome. He knew about every bloody thing else, so why didn't he know this?

'Well, my new friend, George, you are about to find out.' Willis leaned forward and switched off the audio. 'No point in letting him get us stressed. Is there?'

Willis increased the power of the starboard engine. The chassis began to vibrate.

'Can I remind you that the hull is compromised? It is riddled with bullet holes. It might not take the strain.'

'Tell me about it. But do we have a choice? Now would be a good time to shut up and let me concentrate. Go aft and get strapped in.'

Willis played some more with the throttles but to little avail. He eased back on both to reduce airspeed. His gaze darted over the multi-purpose display panel, looking for a display that told him where the air brakes were. He knew the specs of the 2000DX well enough to recall that it used Nordam's single-pivot thrust reversers. If he couldn't find the necessary control in the display, he would have to land without brakes.

Landing gear. Shit. Willis had forgotten to drop the wheels. He did so. When a thump confirmed that they had engaged, the nose swung to starboard. He was going too far left. He pushed on the port throttle to straighten up. An almost horizontal windsock showed a low-altitude wind blowing him to port. Damn, missed that too, he thought.

The runway was in sight. He pulled the throttles back to almost off and dropped the flaps. The ability of the Falcon fleet to fly at a very slow speed was near legendary, but Willis was testing it to the extreme.

Four jeeps swerved along the runway in front of the plane, two from the left and two from the right, zigzagging to prevent it from landing. Willis made the only decision he could. He ignored them. He was banking on the driver's self-preservation instinct being stronger than their desire to stop him.

He was nearly right. Three of the jeeps swung off the runway, but the fourth held its course. As the wheels touched down and squealed on the concrete, he lowered the nose and immediately applied the thrust reversers in an attempt to miss the jeep.

When the Falcon landed right behind him, the jeep driver swung to the right, but he was too late. The plane's starboard wheel hit the back of the jeep. The nose of the jeep rose as though ready for lift-off. It flew into the air, then crashed to the ground, nose first, bounced and rolled over several times before coming to a halt, right side up.

The Falcon was still careering forward. The end of the runway was approaching. The plane's speed was dropping, but was it falling quickly enough?

The jet was travelling at no more than three miles for an hour when its front wheel tipped off the end of the runway and buried itself in a sand trap. Willis leaned forward and cupped his head in his hands.

'Now the shit will hit the fan.'

CHAPTER 39

George went to find Sabit. He was in the toilet, shocked and dazed. Blood trickled down his forehead, perhaps from hitting it against the washbowl. Both men came back to the cockpit and tried to comfort Anatoly. Sabit wiped his face with cold water. Blood had collected on his shirt and jacket. Each breath made more blood leak out. He was pale and drawn, his breathing was shallow, and he was drifting in and out of consciousness. Willis doubted whether Anatoly would make it. There was enough blood collecting around his chair to supply transfusions to an army of injured soldiers.

Willis backed up into the cabin to check on Sophie, who was trembling and sweating but otherwise unharmed. He planted a quick kiss on the top of her head and then headed back to the open door.

Outside the aircraft, blue lights flashed. Three fire tenders had positioned themselves strategically around the fuselage. Ambulances formed a semi-circle around the damaged plane.

No one approached the Falcon. Willis could see guns glinting from the open windows of vehicles. Willis pushed open the door and let it settle on the edge of the runway. The Falcon's nose was sitting low because the front landing gear had sunk in the sand trap. This made the emergency chute scrape the ground before it opened fully. As a result, its integral steps were also skewed. Willis stepped carefully onto the first level of the chute and bounced on it to test its strength. Immediately there came a wave of sound as weapons were cocked and readied.

'Who is in charge here?' Willis shouted.

There was no reaction.

He took another three or four steps and shouted again.

Still silence.

'We have wounded men on board. We need medical help. Who is in charge?' he asked again. He slid down the chute, shouting, 'Can you send in paramedics or a doctor? Our co-pilot is seriously injured. He needs help. It is an emergency.'

A soldier stepped forward. 'You were told not to land. This is a secure base, and you have no permission to be here.'

Willis's knuckles tightened, and an overwhelming desire to flatten the soldier swept over him. He clenched his teeth. 'I have every right to be here! Have you not noticed that there are bloody big holes in the side of my aircraft? You are obliged to allow aircraft access in an emergency.'

'This Cosmodrome is under military control. The convention does not apply to military secured bases.'

'This is not a military base.' Willis was taking a chance. 'President Putin reclassified Baikonur as a civilian operation. He published that internationally – are you telling me that hasn't happened?'

'You must leave the base immediately.'

'We will be happy to get off your base as soon as you make it possible – or perhaps you would like to explain to my newspaper why you are letting my pilot die?' Willis lifted his left hand, in which he had been concealing his mobile, and put it to his ear. 'Have you got all that? They're happy to let our pilot die.'

Willis held the mobile out to the soldier. 'You tell my editor why you can't help us.'

The soldier lifted his hand and issued a command in Russian.

Within seconds two medical vehicles had squealed to a halt at the bottom of the steps. Men with medical crosses on their arms wearing what Willis assumed were paramedics' uniforms got out of one; from the other, a stretcher crew jumped out.

Anatoly was soon in the ambulance. Sabit accompanied one of the paramedics to have his cuts cleaned and dressed. An ambulance raced by to attend to the unfortunate driver of the jeep.

A diminutive army officer stepped out from behind what Willis assumed to be a staff car. His oversized plate-like hat made him look even smaller. The front bent skywards, as Russian military hats do. Russian military hats always struck Willis as funny. If things had been different, he would have smiled. The soldier stood in front of Willis, eyeball to eyeball. 'I am afraid we got off to a bad start. We have been accustomed to challenging anyone we don't recognise.'

Willis held his hand out to him. 'Let me buy you a vodka – or would you rather have a local cognac?'

The man wearing the general's uniform smiled and shook his head. 'There will be much time for that later.'

Willis introduced himself, George and Sophie, and let General Boris Korolev introduce himself.

'Korolev? You aren't related to…?'

'Sergei Korolev? He was my great-uncle. He was father of the Russian space programme, and we are very proud of him. Did you know that he helped design Sputnik too? He worked here years ago when it was known as Tyuratam. I like to think that we're like two beans in a pot.' Korolev's English was excellent, but now and then, he used words in a manner that made Willis smile.

'So why are you still at Baikonur?' asked Willis. 'Shouldn't you have moved to the Vostochny Cosmodrome on President Putin's orders?'

'Oh yes. Sometimes the military can be quite slow, but the site is almost one hundred per cent civilian now, and private contractors are working here too.'

Their dinner was excellent; the conversation was even better. Discussion swung from politics to the economy to science. Korolev's knowledge of science impressed Willis. He was also au fait with the areas of science that the teams at CERN were investigating. He didn't fit the physical stereotype of a Russian. He didn't have the large bushy eyebrows of the early generals or the mouse-like features of Putin. He would have fitted in well at Sandhurst or even in the Metropolitan Police. He was an excellent listener. His dark gaze darted around, never lingering at any one place but taking in everything around him.

'Why do you know so much about science? Is that a prerequisite for working at Baikonur?' Sophie asked.

'My role here is security. I need to think like a scientist and technologist if I am to understand what goes on here. We still have problems, even with civilian people.'

'But nothing too serious, I suspect,' Willis said. 'A bit of petty crime … theft?'

'Sabotage, more like. That's the real reason I'm still here. If only I could go home to my family, but there is not likely to be a solution soon. We have a Proton rocket launching a geological survey satellite in two days, and it had better go smoothly. But I have no idea who is making the sabotage.'

'Are you here as a policeman?' asked Willis, pleased with his assessment that Korolev was really fulfilling the role of detective.

'More like your English Sherlock Holmes, but I have said far too much. Let us have some more wine.' He glanced around the room and smiled. There was a hint of embarrassment on his face that signalled he had let his guard down too much.

'General, I will bet you a box of those Havana cigars you are smoking that it is only commercial projects that are having problems?'

'I had never considered that before. Most of our projects today are commercial.' He paused. He had emphasised 'most'. Willis could almost see the gears whirring in his brain. George was also leaning forward. He nodded at Willis.

'Tell me, Mr Willis – Brad – why do you suppose that to be the case?'

It was Willis's turn to exchange a glance, this time with Sophie. She seemed to understand his intent and smiled.

'Is it possible to go somewhere more private and speak off the record?'

Korolev led them to a secure area deeper inside the building. The room was large, with acoustic tiles on the walls. It was windowless, not dissimilar to the room Reilly had taken Willis to in London. Korolev opened two thick mahogany doors at the end of the room. They revealed layers of polished titanium lining a cabinet. A small box with several coloured lights sat on a shelf. On each side stood a high cabinet housing a host of acoustic apparatus. Microphones, speakers and various other sound equipment lay on either side. When Korolev threw a switch on the wall, it crackled into life.

'This is something we built based on US stealth technology.' He grinned mischievously. 'Instead of negating the effects of radar, it disables sound. It works within a radius no larger than this conference table. It operates like a huge noise-cancelling microphone, but better.'

Once it had been explained to Willis, the idea seemed simple – so straightforward, in fact, that he wondered why no one had dreamed up the concept sooner.

'I'm impressed,' he said.

They sat down at the table, and Korolev handed them all a rubber mat. They placed the mats in front of them on the table.

'What do these do?' asked Sophie.

Korolev invited everyone to lean forward into the centre of the table. 'You won't be able to listen to others speak, and they can't listen to you unless your mouth and ears are inside the area outlined by the mat. Otherwise, all sound is cancelled out.'

Like a group of schoolchildren, they experimented by leaning forwards and backwards over their mats. Their giggles were cancelled out whenever they leaned back in their chairs.

'I hope you have switched off your mobile phone this time, Mr Willis?'

'It was never switched on, General.'

Korolev smiled. 'I am becoming to like you, Mr Willis. Right, let us get going. You first.'

Willis gave Korolev a quick summary of the incidents at CERN and the other European and US locations. He described the data loss from CERN and how they had traced it to Atyraū. Then he brought him up to date with their experience at Almaty Airport.

'There is at least one connection between my problem and yours, my friends, and that is Vladislav Yerkin.' Korolev tossed a pencil onto the table. 'He is major suspect. We suspect his involvement in many incidents on the base, but where do you come in, George?'

George looked surprised. Willis noticed and thought it was odd. George explained what he hoped to achieve in Kazakhstan, and, to Willis's surprise, he also described his organisation.

The general shook his head. 'I am well aware of the VVZ. They are still very active in Moscow, but they are only a lowly band of criminals who claim to have code of conduct. The code only helps other members of the VVZ. You have no place here.'

Willis sensed a link between the two men that went beyond the knowledge of the VVZ: both men were doing a poor job of acting as if they were strangers.

'That is true, General,' said George, 'but there is also a higher level of VVZ that is trying to get things done despite the government's "help" in Kazakhstan. You can think of us as criminals if you wish, but that was in the past. Today we are trying to protect Kazakhstan from within.'

Korolev rose and walked over to a second set of mahogany doors. George looked nervous and glanced questioningly at Willis, but Korolev simply produced two bottles and a selection of glasses.

Back at the table, Korolev leaned over his mat. 'Let us drink to an informal partnership. Unfortunately, it has to be informal. I have no authority in Kazakhstan, only on this base.' He placed the vodka bottle on the table, accompanied by four glasses. 'Vodka for this toast, I think – it is an important one. Maybe I will even get home sooner than I had thought.'

CHAPTER 40

'We will drag your aircraft out of the sand and hide it in a hangar. If you want to email the Dassault technicians, I will get contractor passes for them. They should be able to repair the cockpit glass, but the hull might be more of a challenge.' Korolev chewed on his cereal and spoke to George with his mouth full.

'There is a Dassault maintenance facility in Le Bourget, France, for the 2000EX… They might be able to repair the DX if the structure of the hull hasn't been compromised.' George sipped some pineapple juice. 'I can never face food this early in the morning. If you can get me permission to fly in another Falcon, we will get out of your way.'

At that point, Willis and Sophie turned up and helped themselves to some bread rolls and black coffee. 'George and I are talking about repairing the plane and getting you on your way again,' said Korolev. He turned his attention back to George. 'They track all flights into and out of Atyraū

Province. It is better if you don't fly on your own. I can arrange a flight to Russia with a stop at Atyraū if you want. The flight plan will look like a normal trip for staff on leave – the plane will take some of our boys back home to their families.'

'That would be ideal, but what about passports?' Willis looked at George.

'Those are in hand. They will be waiting for you when you arrive in Atyraū.' George smiled. 'I have access to an excellent forger.'

After the pause that inevitably followed the comment, Willis turned to Korolev, put his hand gently on his arm and asked, 'How is Anatoly? When they carted him into the ambulance, he didn't look too bright.'

Korolev frowned and shook his head. 'As soon as you finish eating, we will meet on Runway Two.' He stood, gulped an orange juice, and left.

By the time they met outside, the dregs of an overnight fog had thinned. Rows of taller buildings were still half-submerged in the mist, which hugged the ground.

It would take the rest of the morning for Korolev's men to move the Falcon to a secure hangar. At one end of Runway Two, a TV crew was making a documentary celebrating the new civilian nature of the Cosmodrome. Korolev explained that they would taxi to the other end of the runway so as not to disturb them.

A single electric bulb hung from above one of the hangar doors. The light breeze that was helping to disperse the mist made the bulb swing on the cable that supported it. Willis and Sophie kept moving to keep warm. At the same time, they tried to ignore the moving lights and shadows the bulb created in the swirling mist. It was taking longer than they had expected for the shuttle bus to pick them up, and they were getting colder as time passed.

Then it happened.

There was a bright flash. Willis flew through the air and then was aware of nothing else. He and the others lay unconscious on the concrete apron.

Willis was the first to regain consciousness, but his brain was running in slow motion. At least he was alive – at least, he guessed he was. The air was heavy with a metallic stench that made Willis cough and spit onto the concrete floor. He could see nothing; inky-black darkness surrounded him. An ache at one side of his head suggested he had fallen and cracked it. His hand went instinctively to it. The bump was smooth and shiny, but it was dry, so it hadn't drawn blood.

He rolled onto his side and raised himself onto his left elbow. As he did so, he collided with another body. The invisible form let out a groan and a few curses. As they weren't in English, Willis assumed it was George or Korolev. He reached out to touch the shape in front of him. The lack of bulky buttons and the feel of silk confirmed it was George. What did his white suit look like now?

'You okay?' asked Willis.

'I think so, but I hurt all over. What happened?'

'No idea. It might have been a stun grenade. We need to find out where we are. I suspect we're inside the hangar.'

Willis shouted out to Korolev and Sophie. No reply. They must still be unconscious, he thought. A slither of light came through a narrow crack in a door. He sat up, then got shakily to his feet. The first step was fine, and the second, but with his third step, he kicked a body lying on the floor. It was Korolev. His groan of complaint signalled that he was also alive. When Willis reached the crack of light, he pushed. The door swung open, and the light from the bulb flooded in.

The light was feeble, but it illuminated the inside of the hangar well. As his eyes had fully adjusted to the dark, Willis knew they had spent more than a few minutes in the darkness. George was there; Korolev was sitting up.

One of Sophie's shoes protruded from beneath her coat. Willis walked over and lifted the coat, but that's all there was – a coat and a shoe. There was no sign of Sophie. His heart sank as he looked around the hangar. It was empty apart from a couple of damaged wooden cases and a wooden pallet. There was nowhere she could be concealed. Sophie had gone. Tears welled in Willis's eyes as the nightmare pervaded his murky brain. Had he lost her? Had he lost her too? The idea was too terrible to contemplate.

'They've taken Sophie!' he shouted. But Korolev was already on his phone, instructing all gates and exits to be sealed and saying that no one was to leave the Cosmodrome. 'They've captured Sophie, and they will hold her to try to force us to stop our investigation. I'm going to kill the bastards.'

Inside his head, Willis tortured himself. Why had he allowed Sophie to get into danger? If it hadn't been for Willis's insistence that she accompany him, she would still be safe in Geneva. At this point, the shuttle bus arrived much later than expected, and they headed back to the main building to organise the search for Sophie.

***

Back in Korolev's apartment, Willis was tending to his bruises. George was trying to salvage some respectability from his tatty white suit, scrubbing it with a brush and soapy water, but only succeeding in making it look worse.

'She is still on base.' Korolev sounded adamant. 'No one entered or left through the gates, and no vehicles left between breakfast time and the time I alerted the base. Having said that, my men can't find her on-site either.'

'Where could she have been taken? Are all the old military facilities still here?' Willis asked. Korolev nodded. Willis continued, 'How many missile silo sites are still here?'

Korolev opened his mouth to speak, but before he could say anything, Willis had carried on, 'And don't tell me the information is classified.'

'It doesn't matter how many there are,' said Korolev. 'There are too many. It would take days to search them all. It's like a rabbit warren beneath the surface.'

'How about security cameras?'

'There are security cameras all around the base, but I doubt very much whether we will find out anything from them.' Korolev lifted his phone, said something in Russian and dropped it back into its cradle. 'They are low lux cameras, hardly the latest technology. They can detect almost anything in the dark, but the combination of low lighting and the mist will have taken away any contrast they had.'

At that moment, the door opened, and a spotty boy in uniform, who looked no older than eighteen, entered. 'Here are the tapes you requested, General,' he said in Russian. Korolev took the tapes and said something in reply, sounding annoyed. The young soldier bowed his head and walked out backwards.

'They never wait for permission to enter.' The general moved to a machine in the conference room and loaded the tapes. He fast-forwarded the tape to the time when they had left the building, then let the tape run for a few minutes. 'See? I knew it. The mist is screwing the images up.'

'Let it run for a bit,' Willis said. 'We can make out our outlines, so that's something.'

They could see themselves walking up and down, but there was no sign of anyone else.

The image on the screen went blank. Several seconds passed, and all it showed was white. Slowly the image returned, but even worse than before.

'The intensity of the flash has saturated the electronic chip on the camera. It will take several hours for it to recover, so the tapes are useless. I will have the images processed, but I fear that no amount of image processing will get anything out of this mess.'

'Are you listening, Brad?' asked George.

Willis was in his own little world. 'Sorry, I was miles away. Something is very strange here. You say that these cameras are surveillance-quality cameras?'

'Yes,' said Korolev.

'If these cameras can't deliver good results, what was the television crew hoping to achieve in these conditions? What were they up to?'

CHAPTER 41

The 10.30 train to Norwich had left on time, but overhead electrical problems at Manningtree had added twenty minutes to the journey. Reilly cursed his stupidity for taking the train on a Sunday – a car would have got him there much more quickly. He had already missed the 11.50 connection to Lowestoft.

His wife had been less than pleased that he had to go out, as he had promised to take her to visit the newest of their three grandchildren. She would now have to wait until next weekend, as she had trouble walking, which prevented her from travelling on her own. He had delayed updating the Prime Minister for as long as he could. He had avoided several appointments at Westminster and Downing Street, so when the PM summoned him to Rectory Cottage, his unofficial weekend retreat, on a Sunday, Reilly knew he couldn't delay any further. He was usually called to Chequers to make his reports, but when the PM wanted personal time, he always came to Suffolk. He remained in contact, of course, but only for emergencies. Part of Reilly knew the meeting would be a waste of time, but another part welcomed the opportunity to discuss the mess with someone else. The Foreign Secretary was in the Middle East – that was a bonus. Reilly didn't want anyone to go off half-cocked and put Willis in danger. Leaks from government departments were, unfortunately, common.

The arrivals and departures screen at Ipswich Station showed that all trains were delayed. Then a tired voice came over the public address. A Lowestoft train was waiting to depart. Reilly managed to catch about sixty per cent of the message – of course, the vital information was inaudible, like the time and platform number. He shouldn't be too negative, he told himself. At least a train was waiting – whether it was the original held back or the next train was of no importance.

He settled down at a table seat as far away as possible from other people, avoiding a young family out for the day and a group of shrieking teenage girls. Once he was sure of reasonable quiet, he opened his mobile and dialled a number. 'Apologise to the PM for me, please. Tell him his crap national rail service has let me down, and I'm running about twenty-five minutes late.' There was a pause as someone said something at the other end. 'Yes. I will be getting off at Halesworth Station.' Another pause followed. 'Yes, a car would save us all time. Thank you. Goodbye.'

The car would take at least thirty minutes off his travel time, but it would leave more time to chat with the PM… He hadn't expected a limousine, but he hadn't expected what was waiting for him at the station either. It was an R-reg Vauxhall with more coloured panels than his granny's bed quilt.

'Sorry, I'm a bit on the drag, boi. Traffic is heavy for a Sunday,' said the driver.

'What was the original colour of this old bus?'

'I don't rightly know, boi.' The rich Suffolk accent had a colour of its own. 'We don't need anything too fancy as long as it gets us where we're goin.'

'It's reliable then, is it?'

'Sure is. Done all the repairs myself. You like Adnams?'

'Adnams?'

'It's the best brew in the land, is Adnams. Suffolk's own brew. It's made just up the road in Southwold. Maybe we'll manage a jar later.'

Reilly wasn't sure if the question was rhetorical or not. He treated it as such.

'Hold on to you' seat, boi cos this lane is a bit bumpy.'

He was right. Reilly's rear end spent most of the time in the air and the rest crashing down onto an iron strut that supported the thin cover of the seat. The lane was no more than a hundred yards long, but he was grateful when the pink wattle-and-daub cottage came into view.

'Mind your head.'

Reilly did as the Prime Minister told him and ducked as he stepped through the low front door.

'Thank you for the car, Prime Minister. If I had known, I would have taken a taxi.'

'That was the taxi.' The PM latched the door behind him. 'He's my next-door neighbour but one. I couldn't have got anyone else around here on a Sunday – not anyone who would know how to find this place, anyway.'

'When are you going to get those trains fixed?'

'Speak to the Minister of Transport. Sundays are always bad: that's when all the engineering work takes place, but it's getting better. Anyway, sit down. As you're not driving, may I offer you a whisky?'

'I was told I should treat myself to an Adnams.'

'Old DG is always trying to get someone to buy him a pint. You would never guess he owned this half of Suffolk. I have some Adnams if you'd like to try it.'

'Okay. I'll try it. I'll pretend I'm on holiday.' Reilly opened the can and sipped. 'Not bad at all. DG gives good advice.' He had expected a hostile reception, but the PM was being pleasant, so he relaxed, ready to enjoy his drink. He leaned back in the comfortable armchair and admired the view from the cottage's tiny window. But it was not to be.

'You might as well be on holiday for all the good you've been to me. Where have you been hiding, Mike?'

'I haven't been hiding, and I don't have much more to tell you. Things are changing by the hour. I've been waiting for something solid to develop that I can tell you about.'

'Something solid? Your man is in a jet that crashes in Kazakhstan, and that isn't a development?'

'How did you find out about that?'

'I'm supposed to know everything, remember? It would be better if I'd heard it from my side rather than from the Americans.'

'Sorry.'

'I get your email updates, but they don't give me a flavour of what's happening. Now, I need to know everything, Mike. I've been told about the oil price in the markets, and I would have liked it to have dropped for other reasons.'

'The possible new energy source discovered at CERN caused that drop.'

'My advisers tell me it is a scam.'

'Possibly. It's not my line of expertise, but I have some of the evidence on electron microscope images.'

'It must be a scam. They published it on the internet to drive the price down. Someone's trying to influence the markets – and they're succeeding. I gave my assurance at the House of Commons that this wasn't happening.'

'Some people don't believe it's a scam, or the energy prices wouldn't be so low. It would be useful, Prime Minister, if we could discover who had profited from these price swings: for example, who sold immediately before the internet exposé and who bought immediately afterwards.'

'That would mean finding out what transactions are doing on the Russian market, the MICEX, and the Kazakhstan market, the KASE.'

'Surely it's a form of insider trading, with criminal intent to defraud? They would want to assist with that.'

'It's not as easy as that. If the Exchanges suspect something, they will stop trading the shares, and for oil and gas, that's unthinkable. I will have an exploratory conversation with the Chancellor. The Treasury might be willing to watch the trades.'

'Should I update Baker on this or wait until later?'

'I will speak to the US President tomorrow. When I do, I want to be up to speed. Tell Baker to call and update the President too. This could make Enron's management team look like a bunch of choirboys.'

When Reilly saw DG's multi-coloured 'taxi' come to collect him, his heart sank a second time, but going with DG would be better than remaining with the Prime Minister and being exposed to further questioning.

CHAPTER 42

'I tell you, we didn't run film shoot this morning.' Korolev was translating the film producer's aggressive reply. 'We couldn't even get early morning mood lighting effects today, because the mist was too thick. We are supposed to be promoting the new civilian status of the base, so we must show it in bright conditions, not through thick mist.'

'*Someone* had your trucks out this morning, and *someone* cleared it with base security to have them on Runway Two.'

Willis followed up equally aggressively. 'Who has the keys for the filming truck?'

'All the keys are together.' The producer waved his hand in the direction of the building behind him. 'They were in a lockable box in the dormitory, supplied by the base. I had locked it.'

'Was it forced?'

'No. Whoever took the keys also had a key to the box.'

'It is exactly as I feared,' said Korolev. 'The security on base is non-existent – the enemy is inside and active in major way.'

They left the dormitory and walked back to Korolev's block.

'Do you believe the producer?' asked Korolev.

'I do,' Willis said.

'I do too,' said George. 'If they wanted to lie, they would have come up with something a little more convincing.'

Willis had wandered away to one side and was taking an interest in one of the film trucks. 'What's that?' he said.

'What's what?' George asked.

'This.' Willis pointed to red mud embedded in the treads of the tyres. 'I haven't seen any red mud around the parts of the base I have visited so far, and it hasn't rained. Was this morning's mist damp enough to cause mud?'

Korolev shrugged. 'There is plenty of red soil around the base, but out where the launch silos are. Hold on – there is some loose gravel here too.' He bent down to inspect the tyres more closely. 'We are filling in some of the old silos we used for ICBMs during the cold war. It is still large area, but it is manageable. Let's get some men and go over there.'

***

The Russian equivalent of a US military Humvee rolled to a halt. Any dampness left by the morning's mist had long since evaporated. A thick cloud of red dust billowed behind the vehicle. Willis and the others slipped out and stood in the dusty landscape. A light wind lifted clouds of dust into mini dust devils across the plain. One of the soldiers took six automatic rifles from the back of the vehicle and distributed them.

The area – once the location of scores of intercontinental ballistic missiles – was sad and lifeless. Concrete silos, where the huge rockets had stood, were crumbling. Grass grew through the cracks. Crude observation huts dug into the soil for protection were overgrown with weeds. About half a dozen silos were still maintained. These allowed Baikonur to act as backup and support for the newer launch facilities at Vostochny Cosmodrome in Russia.

Somewhere in this desert of dust and concrete was Sophie, but where would they look first? Willis hoped she was more useful alive to her captors than dead. It was his fault. He was the one who had put her in danger, and he could imagine her staring at him accusingly. He had no idea why they had chosen to kidnap her – or who had taken her. Few people knew they were here.

His thoughts were interrupted when he glimpsed six other Humvees in the distance. Korolev's radio crackled, and he confirmed to the leading driver that he was to stop and wait there until told. Stealth would be a useful weapon; surprise would be on their side.

Willis looked behind the truck at its freshly formed tracks. They had already been almost completely obliterated by blowing dust. Tracks from earlier this morning would be long gone by now.

'We are filling in six silos on the southern side. We should start there,' said Korolev.

Willis and George agreed and followed Korolev in silence. Willis's initial assessment of the diminutive general had changed some time ago. The man was full of courage and determination. Willis wondered why he was here. He should have delegated the task to somebody else. Perhaps he had even less confidence in his security team than he had already hinted at.

The observation bunkers had been built to keep their occupants safe in the all-too-common event of a missile blowing up at launch and also to give occupants a view of the launch pads. Their doors faced away from the launch pads. Two slotted windows faced the silo, making them easy to approach, unseen, from the side. The other walls were blank, with no openings.

Two soldiers closed in on the first bunker from one of its blind sides. Then they swung around to the rear door, weapons ready for action.

The bunker was empty.

Shit. At this rate, they would run out of time, putting Sophie's life in even more danger. They had to find her soon.

The adjacent silo would not be so easy to search. The silos had been designed to divert exhaust gas and heat away from the rockets. Any unplanned rise in temperature would ignite the rocket's volatile propellant and the oxidant needed to burn it. The silos were huge holes in the ground – about thirty-five metres wide. A large tunnel diverted the main exhaust to the side away from the base of the rocket. Spreading out from the bottom of this was a set of smaller tunnels to dissipate gases in other directions. Ramps on the floor of the main hole below the engines acted as guides to ensure the gases took the intended route.

They split into two teams. The general and two soldiers took the tunnels running clockwise. Willis, George and the remaining soldier took a similar route but anticlockwise.

The two teams met again at the opposite side of the silo. Willis and Korolev shook their heads. They had found nothing. It had taken twenty-five minutes to check out the silo and another five to check the observation hut. They had another five to check, and time was ticking away.

It was getting dark by the time they had reached the last silo. It seemed that the red soil on the tyres had been a red herring.

'What's over there?' Willis pointed to a low building separate from the silos. 'What was that building used for?'

Korolev strained in the fading light to look where Willis was pointing. 'That's where some of the lifting equipment is stored to lift rockets onto their ends. They are usually transported horizontally.'

'If a truck was there and wanted to get back to the dormitories, it would have to cross the gravel area.'

'You're dead right,' said Korolev, 'especially if they wanted to take the shortest route back.' He signalled for them to move forward. He didn't take them the direct route but instead took a long sweeping path to the left of the building. They needed to approach from its far side.

The reason for his tactics soon became clear to Willis: this wall lacked windows. Korolev lifted his hand, and they all came to an immediate halt. He waved and pointed to his ear, suggesting they should listen. They could hear voices coming from inside the building.

Korolev waved to his men to group around him, then whispered instructions in Russian. He then moved to where Willis and George were crouching. 'Let the professionals do this. You wait here.'

Willis had no intention of arguing. Although the British Special Forces trained him after he teamed up with Reilly, he never felt comfortable putting his new skills into practice. But these guys were recently trained, and they knew the site and the language.

Korolev and three soldiers moved towards the building. A signal from Korolev sent two of the men around the back to approach from the other side while he and the remaining man moved towards the near side. Once all four were in position, he signalled again, and they stormed the door. The door gave way easily against the weight of the first two soldiers. Korolev rushed in and released a burst of fire into the roof. As he did, he shouted instructions in Russian.

Willis rushed in, only seconds behind him.

The occupants froze on the spot. One held a mug high above him. Its contents poured out over his shoulders; the other held a rag. Two automatic rifles lay on the table in front of them.

Korolev and the soldier to his right swung around together in response to a movement from the far corner. A third man was raising a weapon. The soldier and Korolev fired together. The man danced as bullets riddled his body. His finger still on the trigger, he blasted the ceiling with gunfire.

A second burst of bullets followed. Korolev's other two soldiers were firing on the two men in front of them. A third man had entered from a door at the rear. Their guns were no longer on the table. They had bet on the distraction and lost. When the gunfire stopped, they collapsed over the workbench behind them.

'Damn. I wanted them alive.' Korolev's gaze darted around the room, looking for Sophie.

Willis rushed into the small room from where the third man had come. Nothing.

A sickening sound rose from the floor. One of the men was laughing and drowning in his own blood. 'You will never find the bitch.'

'Where is she?' demanded Willis.

The man's laughter faded to a gurgle … then silence.

CHAPTER 43

Korolev went over and emptied the dead man's pockets.

'His name's Sergei. He's a nasty piece of work – he worked with Vladislav Yerkin. He's known in Kazakhstan as an eliminator. At least we don't need to worry about him any more.'

'I recognise him,' Willis said. 'He's one of the two men in black coats we spotted following us. He's been trying to kill us.' The dark red birthmark over Sergei's left eye had confirmed his suspicion. 'Anyway, let's stop worrying about him and keep looking for Sophie.'

The group went out to search in the nearest silo. It was dark and dreary inside. Crystals had formed on the concrete walls due to the immense heat from the exhausts of the launches of Soyuz and then Proton rockets. The smallest noise was amplified by the tunnels. They shouted, 'Sophie!' then stood in silence, waiting for a sound in return. Nothing came back.

'Let's try the next silo,' Willis snapped. They moved on.

They repeated the routine for the third and fourth silos with no result. In the fifth tunnel, Willis thought he heard a low rustling noise. 'This way!' Willis shouted. They ran towards where the rustling had originated.

'It's getting louder,' he yelled as they turned the next bend.

'There she is,' shouted Korolev.

In the distance lay the dark outline of a huddled figure. Willis ran up to it. 'It's her!' He ripped at the material, trying to untie the sacking that shrouded her body. Once her face was clear, he removed the gag from her mouth.

'You're alright now,' Willis said soothingly. 'They're all dead. They won't bother you any more. God, I might have lost you. I couldn't have survived losing you.' He took her in his arms and held her tight. As he hugged her, the worry fell away, making him instinctively relax his grip on her, but he shuddered, thinking about the dark cloud of what might have happened to his darling Sophie.

'Thank God you got to me. One of the men said they were planning to come back and get me. They would have if you hadn't come for me.' She was shaking, and her voice trembled. Her face was swollen and red from crying. Willis wiped her cheeks with his sleeve, then held her tightly until she stopped shaking.

Korolev came forward. 'They would have left you there till tomorrow when the next Proton rocket was due to launch. This is the silo that is due to accept it. Sorry, I should have realised and searched here first.'

Sophie got to her feet unsteadily. With Willis and George's help, she staggered along the short tunnel, back to the surface and fresh air.

***

Back at Korolev's quarters, they took some time to relax and gather their thoughts.

'These guys know what they're doing.' Willis spat the words out. 'They know everything we're doing almost before we do it. We have to get an advantage soon.' He looked at Korolev. 'Let's get that flight to Atyraū if it is still possible?'

Korolev picked up his phone and relayed something in Russian. It was presumably instructions to ready the plane.

'I'll remain here until I can get the jet repaired,' said George. 'I'll join you in Atyraū as soon as possible.'

'A plane will be ready in about twenty minutes,' said Korolev. 'We had better go and collect your cases now.'

***

The plane circled Atyraū International Airport, waiting for permission to touch down.

'At least the flight has gone smoothly,' Willis said. 'I'm getting accustomed to explosions or other interferences getting in the way of whatever we're doing.'

After landing, Korolev gave instructions to the cab driver to take them to the hotel he'd booked for them. The hotel was located on the European side of Atyraū on Qanysh Satbayev Avenue. According to its online brochure, the Renaissance Atyraū Hotel boasted an indoor pool, a gym and a sauna. The cab dropped them at the main door of the hotel. The hotel had a white marble façade with long narrow windows arranged in regular rows along its length. A curved entrance opened into a high-walled hall decorated with gilded cherubs and angels. They walked up to the reception desk and booked themselves in.

'Let's freshen up first and meet later for supper,' said Korolev.

They agreed and dispersed to their rooms.

Once in his room, Willis rang Reilly. 'What is Yerkin's latest position?'

'He hasn't moved for some time. I suspect he's holed up somewhere, taking it easy and waiting for you to arrive in Atyraū.'

'Do you have co-ordinates for him?' asked Willis.

'I will text them to you within the hour. I will send a tracker to your phone that will update you in real time. I will also text you tomorrow in case he gets on the move again.'

***

They met in the foyer later, as arranged. They were hungry and finished off a quick supper in no time. Willis told them the details of his conversation with Reilly.

'Once I've received Yerkin's co-ordinates, we can set off early tomorrow morning,' Willis said. 'The plan is to find him before he has time to find us. I'll get the hotel to rent a car for us. We'll set off shortly after eight o'clock. If we can get ahead of Yerkin and find out where he's travelling to, we will be one step ahead of him, which will be a welcome change.'

The group acquiesced, and they all parted for their respective rooms.

'Sophie, you look tired,' Willis said.

'I guess I've had a hectic day.'

'Then I suppose there's no pizza tonight then?'

'You never give up trying, do you?' Sophie gave a half smile.

'How much do you remember about your kidnapping?'

'I was unconscious at first, but when I recovered in one of those concrete buildings in the middle of nowhere, my head hurt, and I couldn't breathe. I thought they were going to kill me…' Sophie threw herself at Willis and hugged him tightly. 'According to Boris, if you hadn't rescued me, I would have been roasted alive in that silo when the rocket was launched tomorrow morning.'

'You're safe now, but it must have been terrible for you. I dread to imagine.'

'Those men knew my name. They spoke in Russian, but now and then, I could hear my name – and yours too. A guy with a bad eye gave the orders, and he spoke about how his employers had traced our movements. How could they have done that, Brad?'

'At least one of their contacts we know about, within CERN, was Yeung, but I'm sure there were others. Maybe Villiers was one of their informants. I'm praying they haven't cloned our phones, but just in case, we ought to switch them off. When we arrive, we'll buy some burner phones to replace them.'

'Promise to keep me close, Brad. Keep me safe.' As they walked to the bed, Sophie buried her face in the nape of Willis's neck, drying her tear-soaked eyes against his warm skin.

'You need some sleep, sweetheart.'

'You've never called me sweetheart before.'

'No… I haven't. When I was young, my grandfather gave me a piece of advice that I'll never forget. He told me when I met the right lady that I had to keep her close to me and make her my sweetheart. And he said he'd failed to do that and regretted it all his life. I'll look after you, my sweetheart.'

'That's a lovely story, Brad. It makes me feel special.'

Brad leaned down to tell her she was special, but her eyes were closed. She was fast asleep.

CHAPTER 44

At 7.30 a.m. the car was waiting for them. It was just as well, as Reilly had texted Yerkin's co-ordinates as they were finishing breakfast. Yerkin was on the move. They needed to leave immediately. Willis and Sophie left Korolev eating but took the opportunity to thank him for all the help he had given them. Willis said he would call him to tell him whatever they discovered. Then they went to find the car.

Willis turned right and right again onto the one-way system that was Qanysh Satbayev Avenue. The Ural River was on their left. It was hidden by the buildings of Tco Dostyk village as they joined Abulkhair Avenue and continued west. The further they travelled, the more industrial the landscape became. The blip on the tracker, sent by Reilly, bleeped on the phone in Sophie's hand. It was travelling at a moderate speed, but they were gaining on it with every minute that passed. They were heading back towards Atyraū International Airport. While they tracked the limo, Willis allowed himself to appreciate the wonders of modern technology. Thanks to it, a tracker could be loaded onto a mobile phone that contained more circuits than the moon lander.

A sleek black limousine came into view ahead. As they got nearer to it, the signal confirmed it was the right car. Two concentric circles appeared on the phone's screen, superimposed on the city road map, like a satnav. The circles flashed slowly, emitting a low bleep with each flash. Soon they were right behind the limo, and flashes and pings filled the cab with light and sound. The signal was bouncing off surrounding mobile phone towers, and its distance from each tower was used to work out its location. Sophie pressed a button on the mobile to reduce the volume. Willis dropped back and let a truck overtake him in case the driver of the limo became suspicious. There was no need. As the limo passed the Sultan Palace Hotel, it turned left into the car park of a disused warehouse. Willis drove past and did a three-point turn on the first small street on the left. He then drove back and came to a halt before the entrance to the warehouse.

Two men got out of the car and unloaded a roll of material from the boot. It looked heavy. Was it a rolled-up carpet? Willis wondered. They dragged it to a dumpster at the side of the building and got back into the car. The limo exited onto Abulkhair Avenue and turned back in the direction from where it had come.

'Yerkin's no longer in the car,' said Sophie. 'The signal isn't moving.'

The reality of the situation dawned on Willis: the men had dumped Yerkin's body, along with his phone, and were driving back to their base, wherever that was. Willis let out the clutch and took off after the receding car.

Vehicle registration plates in Kazakhstan use black letters on a white background. They have a Kazakh Flag and the country code, KZ, on the left. A two-digit area code is on the right. The limo's code was VP. That meant it was an Almaty municipal car, so it would be easy to track. Willis took a mental note of the rest of the registration plate in case he lost the limo.

The limo continued along Abulkhair Avenue. It then turned into Zeynolla Ghumarov Street and drove along until it joined Mukhtar Auezov Avenue. When it reached a T junction, it turned left. Just after was the turning to an oil refinery. The limo swung into the refinery gates and stopped briefly at the security box. It then drove to the right of what looked like the main building and stopped.

Willis turned right at the T-junction, then first left into a small road that ran parallel to the refinery. The black limo was visible through the wire fence. He stopped the car when it was level with the limo, and they got out. They followed the wire fence until it reached a small gate designed for pedestrians. A lock and chain secured it to its metal pillar.

'What now?' asked Sophie.

'We'll need to get in somehow,' Willis said. 'Hold on. I'll be back in a minute.'

He returned to the car and came back with the wheel jack from the boot. He positioned the jack's lever behind the chain and then walloped the other end of it with the body of the jack. On the third hit, the chain slackened and fell to the ground. The door swung inwards.

'Sophie, you go back and wait in the car. If I'm not out in thirty minutes, ring the hotel and alert Korolev.'

'Alright, but I'll do that after twenty minutes. Thirty minutes is too long.'

That decision gave Willis a warm, fuzzy feeling. Now that Sophie was considering his safety for a change, it made him feel as though he might be as important to her as she was to him. He smiled, then left.

A security camera pointed to the left on the wall above the loading bay. Willis circled to its right, crossed the access road and opened the door that the limo had parked beside. Inside was a large storage unit, cases and crates lined up along its shorter wall. Willis slipped behind a stack of crates and listened. Distant voices came from his right. They were faint but discernible. He edged forward in their direction. They seemed to be coming from a glass-walled office in the far right corner. Willis ducked down and shuffled forward until he was below the office window. Twelve men were sitting around a large table, conversing in English.

One had an American accent. 'Fermilab is okay – there's no trace at Fermilab of any data audit trail, so therefore, there's no need to take any action.'

'It would be safer if we did, Pythagoras,' said another man, who had a strong Russian accent. 'We will get Sergei to sort it once he returns from Baikonur. It's better to be safe than sorry. We've come this far, and we must not take any risks.'

'Okay, agreed,' said the American. 'I have a man who can sort it. I will contact him tonight and instruct him to get it done. He can have it finished in twelve hours.'

Willis stretched higher to get a better look at the men. When he did, he took a mental note of their faces. One of the men put something down on the table. Willis stretched even higher to see what it was.

Willis glimpsed the shadow of an arm swing above him and the glint of something shiny … and that was the last thing he remembered.

***

When he came to, the inside of his brain was throbbing like a jungle drum. He opened his eyes, but everything was blurred. He shook his head to clear his vision. His feet were tied to the legs of a chair, and his arms were tied behind the chair. His head hurt, and blood trickled down his face.

'Our visitor is awake,' the American said, walking over and standing beside Willis. 'Welcome, Mr Willis. It's disappointing to meet you. I expected that Sergei would have taken care of you by now.'

'If Yerkin didn't manage it, what makes you believe his evil twin might?'

The tall Russian who had been sitting at the table rose and approached Willis. 'What will we do with him, Pythagoras?' He drew back his hand and punched Willis in the face. Willis could taste blood. He shook his head for the second time.

'You will tell us what we want to know!' the Russian yelled.

'Okay,' Willis said. 'Tell me what you want to know.' He had no idea who the men were, but he might learn more from their questions than they would learn from his answers.

The tall Russian lifted his foot and drove the heel of his boot into Willis's crotch. Willis winced. The room spun like a merry-go-round. The pain was so intense that Willis struggled to retain consciousness. He closed his eyes, hoping the pain and spinning would subside. He had an urge to bring his thighs together, but the rope securing his legs to the chair prevented him from doing so. 'Okay. I admit it. That hurt like hell, but what the fuck did it achieve other than demonstrate your football skills?'

Shit. What had he got himself into? He was out of his depth on this adventure. Unless Sophie managed to contact Korolev and quickly, he would be a goner for sure.

'What's an astronomer doing visiting CERN?' the footballer asked.

'Well, the two sciences are similar,' Willis said. His voice was strained. 'At the beginning of time, they were identical. I was at CERN to promote that idea and find out what more we had in common since my last visit.' The ropes tying his arms were digging into his wrists. How long had he been unconscious? Would Sophie have alerted Korolev by now?

'Don't take us for fools, Mr Willis. That much we know. You didn't need to travel to Switzerland or France to impart that knowledge. That's what scientific publications are for. Now tell us the real reason you were there.' The Russian smashed his fist into Willis's face again. It didn't hurt as much as the first time. His face was numb from the previous impact; blood flowed freely down his chin and neck.

'I was there as a health and safety officer,' said Willis. 'There has been a spate of accidents in all our major scientific institutions. I was there to try to get to the bottom of the incidents.' Willis reasoned they'd be aware of this much already if they were involved, and he wouldn't be telling them anything they didn't already know.

'And did you find out?' Pythagoras asked.

'I found out quite a lot. Let's compare notes.' Willis cringed. "Pythagoras?" This is turning into a bad James Bond movie, he thought.

'Why would we do that?' said another Russian.

'I'm intrigued.' Willis spat a mouthful of blood onto the storeroom floor. 'You have no plans to let me out of here alive, so I'd like to know why you've been sabotaging data centres all over the globe.'

'You should have worked that out by now,' said the American, more like a question than a statement.

'Oh! We did. You were trying to hide the critical results you had obtained from CERN. I guessed that Ernst Yeung had sent them to you.'

'Very clever, Mr Willis. How did you work that one out?'

'That was easy. Yeung had Yerkin's number on his phone. It was still working after his "accident", fortunately for us. But why did you have to kill Yeung?' Willis was flying by the seat of his pants, ad-libbing and trying random ideas. The first one had worked a treat.

'Yeung was making demands for his services. Financial demands. That wasn't in the playbook,' said the American. 'He wasn't a member of the team.'

'This guy is a risk, he is no longer useful, and he's given us all we needed. Let's kill him.'

Willis had been bluffing, but it had paid off. 'So, what are you planning to do with all this free energy you will be generating? Are you hoping to disrupt the world's oil markets and make a killing on the commodity markets?'

The American gave a bemused grin. 'That's all bullshit, but we are certainly planning on making a killing in the markets. The disruption of the data centres destroyed all evidence relating to our imaginary new energy source. By the time the markets realise it's a scam, we will have bought up most of the world's oil shares at a fraction of their true value.'

Now Willis was puzzled. Had they seen the picture of the holes in the ATLAS magnet? Or did they believe this was part of the scam arranged by Yeung? How could Yeung have created so fine a pattern of holes?

'The markets are still falling,' said the American. 'Once they stabilise, we will invest. There's nothing anyone can do to stop us now. It's too late—'

'Hold on,' interrupted Willis, 'where is all the cash coming from to finance these purchases?'

'The organisations behind us are the American and Russian mafias – but we don't need cash if we buy and sell oil in the futures markets.'

The taller Russian took a step towards Willis. 'There's nothing more he can tell us. We should dispose of him now.' His boot came up again and landed a second kick in Willis's groin. Willis's head swam, and he thought he might pass out. He needed more time to let the cavalry arrive

– that is, if it was ever going to arrive. Pythagoras took a pistol from his pocket and pointed it at the centre of Willis's forehead.

'One more thing,' Willis said, 'before you kill me. How did you manage to create the picture of the holes in the CERN magnet?' He was playing for time now: this was the only thing he could think of to stall them a little longer.

The shorter Russian spoke first. 'That was fabricated in the lab using a miniature laser devised by the South Koreans. It was a tiny piece of metal imaged up close, and the scale altered. There are no holes in the CERN detector; it is all part of the scam.'

'It will be months before the oil markets recover.' Willis shook his head.

'Damn the fucking delay,' said the taller Russian. 'The markets will recover. Even so, we will have to wait a little longer, but it will be worth it in the end—'

'I've had enough,' Pythagoras interrupted. 'He's told us nothing. Let's kill him now.'

There was a noise behind Willis. He tried to turn towards it.

'Let go of my arms!' It was Sophie. Her voice sounded muffled, and the reason soon became clear. One of their captors was manhandling her into the storeroom, one hand covering her mouth.

Then the Russian holding her pulled his hand away. 'Ah, fuck!' he yelled. Sophie had bitten his hand. Pythagoras, who had been threatening to shoot Willis, walked over to Sophie and pressed the barrel of his pistol into her cheek.

'What have we here? A lovely lady might loosen his tongue.'

'Leave her alone, you bullying bastard.'

'Ah, we might have ourselves a negotiating chip.' He swiped at Sophie's cheek with the pistol. It split her skin open, and a rivulet of blood ran down her face.

Willis tore at his bonds, which only dug deeper into his flesh. He struggled, but it was in vain. 'I'll see you in hell, you bastard.'

Pythagoras closed one eye and aimed the MP-443 Grach pistol once again at Willis's forehead. 'Any last requests?'

Willis saw a shadow move behind the Russian. 'Yes,' whispered Willis. 'Look over your shoulder.'

The four Russians spun around, their pistols raised. There was a hail of gunshots. Bullets slammed into the thighs of the four standing Russians. They fell to the floor like a poorly choreographed ballet.

'You arrived just in time.' Willis sighed in relief.

'No, we didn't.' Korolev smiled. 'We've been here for some time. We heard everything.'

CHAPTER 45

'You are lucky to have good Russian friend like me.' Korolev grinned. He was puffing on an odious Russian cigarette he had produced from somewhere. 'About another minute and you would have been, how do you say … goners?'

'That is true, my dear Boris,' Willis said. 'We will forever be grateful to you and your six buddies. At last, we're making some progress: we finally know who some of the men are.'

They were back in the hotel, relaxing. Willis's wrists hurt from chafing caused by the ropes. His jaw smarted even more, and his other pains were too sore to contemplate. And his mouth hurt from the punch.

'I'll make it better later,' said Sophie, smiling.

Willis caught the end of the smile. Should he be optimistic…?

At that moment, George made an unexpected entrance. 'I bet you didn't expect to meet me again so soon.

That's French service for you. They flew a spare jet over for me while my one is being repaired. It should only take about a month, they say.' He sat down and joined the group. Soon there was a cluster of drinks on the table, and everybody was getting more relaxed and chattier.

The comfort of the Renaissance Hotel's main lounge helped them to forget the events of the day, and they imparted the story to George in great detail. Willis was trying to relax, but something was bothering him. His attention kept wandering to the maroon velvet wallpaper that adorned the room. He puzzled over the Kazakh symbols that made up its elaborate circular pattern, and his thoughts kept drifting back to the storeroom and the twelve men that Korolev and his six buddies had captured.

'It isn't right.'

'What isn't right?' asked Korolev.

'Those twelve couldn't have masterminded all this by themselves. There must be something larger than them to make this all come together.'

'They did volunteer that two Mafia groups were helping, but we'll hear no more until they get out of the hospital and their real interrogation gets under way.'

'They won't talk even then. I'm not sure they know the full extent of what is happening around them. We have part of the plan, but not all of it.' Willis brooded alone with his thoughts for at least half an hour. Their drinks were drained and replaced several times. Everyone was getting tired.

As they chatted, he was working out all the possible combinations of events that he could think of, starting with the possibility that these men were rogue members of the Mafia. After that, he even wondered whether George could be a plant inside his group sending information to the opposition.

George was the first to weaken. 'I'm off to bed now. Sleep well, everyone.' He went towards the lifts. Korolev followed soon afterwards.

Soon only Willis and Sophie remained. 'What time is it in England?' asked Willis. He glanced at his watch; they had been drinking until 2 a.m. 'England is four hours behind us.' Willis answered his own question after checking Google on his phone. 'We ought to speak to Palmer, bring him up to date with the day's events, find out if he has anything of interest for us. I am intrigued by George: he is very keen to be in our company and on the flight, he knew a helluva lot about what had happened at CERN. He even knew about the pictures of the holes in the magnet before we told him. I asked Palmer to find out what he could about the man's background.'

Willis tapped the screen of his mobile. Ten seconds later, Palmer said jokingly, 'You're making a habit of disturbing me late at night, Willis.'

'It's not late at night; it's only ten o'clock. I did check. Anyway, it's a lot better than after midnight. How's your leg mending?'

'It's coming along, but it still stiffens up a bit after I've been sitting for a while. What are you after?'

'Have you uncovered anything on our friend George yet? Finding out his real name would be useful,' Willis said.

'Well, you do set me some difficult tasks, young man. There's nothing in the company files, according to Baker and his friends at Langley. He's like a ghost. No bank accounts. No credit cards. No known address.'

'That doesn't surprise me in the least,' Willis said.

'I did manage to get a trace on his jet, however. It's registered to a Grigori Fauler. That's according to the Federal Air Transport Agency, otherwise known as Rosaviatsiya – it's the equivalent of the Civil Aviation Authority in the UK. I suspect they would need someone's real name for registration, although it's possible that George used the name of one of his company directors or the company secretary to register the jet.'

'That might be right, but it's a coincidence. Grigori and George both start with G, so I think it's more likely to be his actual name. It is a long shot, though.'

'Anyway, based on the theory it is him, I did a full search on Grigori Fauler.' There was a short pause. Willis could hear Palmer shuffling papers.

'And?'

'And I've discovered a group of companies identified with the name. Grigori Fauler's companies didn't exist five years ago, but the group now has a multi-billion-dollar turnover. He has fingers in most pies, including the energy markets. Oh, and commodities. In my opinion, his company has grown far too quickly to be one hundred per cent kosher. There must be something shady in its operations to have enabled it to have grown so much.'

'That points to it being his real name. He has been, so far, too mysterious about everything to be one hundred per cent kosher, as you suggest. What else did you manage to uncover? You've done well,' Willis said.

'He has a brother, Karl. He isn't officially employed by Fauler's group of companies – he might well be the black sheep of the family. Grigori is squeaky clean, but Karl has quite a list of felonies. I wondered if he might be involved with Grigori's more dubious activities.'

'Okay,' said Willis, 'we ought to put a tail on Karl, and even Grigori, if that's possible. It will at least help us to identify whether we have the right person or not.'

'I will ask Baker if we can put some people on this,' said Palmer.

'Thank Baker for me.'

Palmer replied in the affirmative. He hoped Willis would sleep well, and Willis returned the sentiment.

After they had hung up, Willis turned to Sophie. 'Don't say a word to George or Grigori, or whatever his name is, until we get more confirmation from Greg Palmer.'

'Alright. And let's have one more drink,' said Sophie, 'before we go to bed. We're all wound up now – it will help us to relax, and maybe we'll even get some sleep before morning.'

Willis ordered glasses of his favourite cognac. They downed them in one, then walked towards the lifts. As they reached them, Willis said, 'I have an idea that might trick George. Don't look surprised by anything I say at breakfast.'

When they got out, Willis and Sophie turned left at the end of the corridor and went to their room.

'That was a cryptic remark, Brad. Where the hell are you coming from?'

'Wait until tomorrow morning. It's a sneaky ploy, but it might work.'

***

The next morning, Willis and Sophie arrived at the restaurant first. On Willis's instructions, they grabbed the end seats at the table. Willis was munching on scrambled eggs on toast when Korolev arrived.

'Good morning, Brad,' said Korolev.

'Good morning, Boris,' said Brad. At the same moment, George put in an appearance. He sat down opposite Willis.

'Good morning, Brad,' said George.

'Good morning, Grigori,' said Brad. 'Would you like some coffee?'

'That is an excellent idea,' replied George without flinching. 'Please pass me the cream.'

Willis leaned forward and handed over the cream. Sophie sat next to him, her mouth wide open. The rest of the meal continued without incident.

CHAPTER 46

After they had finished eating, Willis, Sophie and George remained at the table while Korolev retired to his room to pick up some cigarettes.

'Why would someone fire at your jet?' asked Willis, looking at George.

'I had assumed it was because you were on board. The two men realised they had missed you at Almaty Airport, and they needed to take more drastic measures.'

'That was my reasoning, too,' Willis said. 'They certainly have resources at their beck and call. Not everyone has access to – what? A fighter jet?'

'I agree. These people, whoever they are, have huge resources. They have people everywhere and almost unlimited intelligence. As a result, they can find out what has happened almost as soon as it has. What are we planning now?'

'I need to take a few days out,' Willis said. 'I need to go to a dark energy conference in Munich. It's of the utmost importance, and I committed some time ago to go.'

Sophie sent a puzzled look in Willis's direction. He returned it with a minuscule shake of his head.

'I'll take Sophie with me to the conference, but I'll keep my room and meet you here when I return. Assuming you will still be here, that is?'

'Yes, I'll be here. I need to sort out a few things in the company, and I could do with a little R&R. I'll help Korolev prop up the bar until you get back.'

Although Willis had planted the seed in George's head, only time would tell whether he had taken the bait or not. Willis would have to be vigilant while he was in Munich to see if he had been followed.

Willis and Sophie went to their room to pack after asking George to give his apologies to Korolev. As they got out of the lift, a tall man with dishevelled hair bumped into Willis. He had an odd insignia on his T-shirt that was shaped like an elaborate triangle. Willis paid little attention to it; he went straight to his room and threw his suitcase on the bed.

Sophie went to get her case. 'What is this all about? There's no conference in Munich.'

'Yes, there is. I booked myself on it some time ago and had forgotten all about it until now. But that isn't important. This is a ruse to smoke George out. If he's crooked, he will follow us to Munich to find out what's going on. He won't be able to resist it.'

'That's a bit of overkill,' said Sophie.

'Yes. It is. But we need to flush him out somehow.' Willis continued to pack. He opened the pocket in the lid of his suitcase and removed an MP-443 Grach pistol. It had one previous owner: a tall Russian. He put it on top of the wardrobe. 'They won't let me on the plane to Munich with that.'

***

They picked up a cab outside Franz Josef Strauss International Airport in Munich. Willis asked to go to the Marriott Hotel at Das Galileo at the KongressZentrum, the new Science Congress Centre at the TUM Campus, Garching. When they got out of the cab, they stared in awe at the magnificent building. Its white exterior walls were designed to be randomly covered in windows, reminding Willis of a science fiction film from many years ago. The Centre had a futuristic, modern outlook, and Willis considered it to be a masterpiece of architecture. It had, in his opinion, been designed to attract scientists from around the world.

Once in their rooms, they unpacked and read the conference programme that had been left on the desk by the organisers of the conference. They found out that it didn't commence until 10 a.m. the following day. They had expected this. As was usual on the first day of conferences, the later start would allow more local attendees to travel on the first morning instead of the previous day, thus saving money.

After they finished unpacking, they went down to the restaurant for supper. Willis loved Bavarian cooking. Eagerly he sank his fork into the *Schweinshaxe* he had ordered for himself and had recommended to Sophie. It fell off the bone and dissolved in his mouth just as easily. He dipped a piece of the pork into the delicious but unhealthy gravy that surrounded it. Not only did he love Bavarian food, but he also enjoyed the almost unlimited choice of beers in Munich. With pork, he especially enjoyed Dunkles Weiss Bier, a cloudy, dark brew. Sophie chose a bottle of Crozes-Hermitage. Willis had told her it was his favourite tipple.

'Aren't you vegetarian?' she asked.

'I am, mostly, but I like to eat meat about once a month. I had whitebait not that long ago and a steak with you and Palmer. That way, my stomach won't forget how to produce the enzymes I need to digest meat.'

'Ah. Are you a biochemist, too, now? You are a poly…'

'The word you are looking for is a polymath,' joked Willis, a huge grin on his face. 'And I'm not a polymath; I didn't read enough at school. Do you know something? I love Shakespeare. I always wanted to act in *Hamlet.*'

'Every actor wants to play Hamlet.'

'Oh, I didn't want to play Hamlet. I wanted to play Polonius, Hamlet's wicked uncle's adviser. I love his speech where he sends his son abroad. "Never a borrower or a lender be." That's more or less how it goes, but he gets killed anyway.'

'Doesn't everybody get killed?'

'Oh, shut up and eat your *Schweinshaxe.*' He was grinning again to let Sophie know that he was being playful.

They sat in silence for a while, enjoying the peace and quiet after the previous few days' excitement. After their meal, they ordered brandies and sat in the lounge sipping them.

Since there was nothing to do now but wait, it made sense to relax and enjoy themselves. If anything untoward was about to happen, it wouldn't be until after the conference started the next day.

'So, what do you expect to happen now?' asked Sophie.

'Just about anything. Maybe George will turn up, or he might delegate the task to someone in his organisation. In any case, he will need to find out what we're doing in Munich, especially at a conference that's so relevant to the matter at hand.'

'Well, we could have an early night. How are your bits today? Could we order pizza at this hotel?'

'It might be possible, as long as the pizza isn't too hot.' Willis glowed with anticipation.

Just then, a tall, dark-haired man walked through the lounge. There was something about him Willis recognised, but he couldn't quite put his finger on what it was. Maybe it was the T-shirt that looked familiar. He wasn't sure.

He pushed him out of his mind. He had something much more important to think about.

***

Back in their room, Willis kicked the door shut. He took Sophie in his arms and kissed her. The kiss flushed his brain with memories, and it felt as though they had never been apart. He was transported back to their university days when everything in the world had been rosy.

One by one, he unfastened the buttons on her white blouse and let it slide down her arms and onto the floor. Moving slowly, he repeated the process with each remaining piece of clothing. At no time did they break eye contact. Their expressions were serious. The occasional smile flashed across their eyes.

Willis pushed Sophie gently back onto the bed. He found her body was pliable and submissive. He trailed a line of kisses down her neck, and her breathing deepened and became erratic. His tongue played with her nipples, sucking them into hardness. As he scratched his nails across her taut stomach, he felt Sophie arch off the bed and sigh with pleasure. He watched her open her mouth to scream, but nothing came out. He moved his body gently over hers. As he penetrated her, Sophie shuddered and screamed. Her low groans by his right ear sounded like a hurricane.

Afterwards, she grinned and stared into his blue eyes, then tipped her head to one side and raised her eyebrows mischievously. Sure enough, there it was – that same grin. He was smiling too. They used to call it their 'filthy' grin, but it was anything but filthy. It was part of the warm, fuzzy feelings they enjoyed when they were together.

They lay on the bed for what felt like hours. 'We have a lot of catching up to do. Do you fancy another pizza?' asked Sophie.

'I'm full – I couldn't eat another thing.'

'I wasn't talking about food, dummy.'

'I know you weren't, but haven't you noticed? My leg is a problem, and it's already been given the once-over.'

'I'm sure we'll find some way of overcoming that little problem.'

They were both sticky with sweat, but Willis loved that smell – the natural perfume her body exuded after sex was intoxicating. He took a deep breath and held it, enjoying every piece of her perfume his nostrils could capture. Sophie was still breathing heavily. Her warm breath softly brushed his cheek as she rose and knelt astride him. This was heaven. He hoped it would never end. Willis had forgotten the pain in his leg – for now, at least. Sophie rocked backwards and forwards, her arms stretched above her head, making her pert breasts lift and sway. Her fingers tangled in her hair, lifting it and then dropping it again.

Willis closed his eyes and let sensation wash over him. He was in paradise. Sophie was humming. When he opened his eyes, she was smiling down at him. Her left hand was absentmindedly wrapping her hair around her index finger.

'More pizza?' said Sophie.

'I'm making this one last.'

'I want you now.'

'Come here, then.'

Sophie slid down the bed and let her legs straighten and tighten around the outside of Willis's thighs. She squeezed his legs together and pushed down hard on his groin.

'Tell me if your leg hurts.'

'I will. I will.'

Willis rolled over on top of Sophie. Her eyes sparkled. She pressed her lips tightly to his. He forced them apart with his tongue, and she surrendered by parting her lips. He plundered her mouth like a man starved. His tongue moved down Sophie's cheek and stopped at her neck, where he let his teeth take over. They scraped along her shoulder to her breast. Sophie's sighs blew over Willis's neck. His head rose for a tantalising moment before his lips fastened around her left nipple. He teased it with his tongue, making it stand erect. Sophie raised her shoulders off the bed as he thrust into her wet, hot heaven. They fell back on the bed, exhausted, and then Morpheus took them from their new world of love and engulfed them in sweet unconsciousness.

***

They stayed in bed late the following morning. It was eight forty-five when the waiter delivered a cooked breakfast to their room. Willis made quick work of his bacon and eggs. Sophie was rushing to catch up. Afterwards, they changed quickly and rushed out to join the conference.

When they walked into the Congress Centre, a chart was displayed in the foyer that pointed them to the first plenary session of the day. Sophie and Willis held back until the main lecture theatre was almost full, then waited another ten minutes to let any latecomers arrive. They stopped to collect their badges after Willis had explained to the receptionist that Dr Sophie Fenwick was a late registrant. The girl on the desk was having problems finding Sophie's badge. Willis took the list of attendees and scanned the names, selecting a delegate who had not yet arrived.

'Here it is,' he announced. 'She's standing in for Dr Schmidt. It was a last-minute change. Please hurry, the welcome speech is about to start.'

Flustered, the receptionist picked up a blank badge and printed 'Dr Fenwick' on it by hand. She gave it to Sophie, and they proceeded into the theatre.

'That was quick thinking, Dr Willis,' said Sophie.

'It's an old trick I learned when I was a PhD student. It got me into conferences I couldn't afford to pay for. The secret is to wait and try to spot a possible "no show" then pick that name out.'

'You are very cunning.' Sophie hugged his arm, staring into the dazzling blue of his eyes.

'Interestingly, I also checked the list of attendees for any names we might recognise. There were many, but there was also a Dr Fauler attending. I'm not aware of him, and it's not a common name. It can't be a coincidence that it's Grigori's family name. His name was also pencilled in on the list of attendees, which means he registered late.'

'Let's look out for him,' suggested Sophie. 'We'll wait until the coffee break and do a quick scout around and see if we can spot him.'

The tea break arrived. By that time, Willis had questions he wanted to ask the previous lecturer, but they would have to wait. He didn't want to be distracted from the real reason they were there. They collected two cups of coffee and split up, looking at the names on delegates' badges.

After ten minutes, Sophie came up to Willis. 'We've been doing this all wrong,' she said. 'All the time I've been searching, there's been a man following you. He's looking for you too. If you stand still for a moment, I'll go and find out if I can read his badge.'

Sophie left Willis and walked back into the crowd. He gave her a few moments to dissolve into the mass of scientists when he spotted her speaking to a rather untidy-looking delegate. That wasn't particularly unusual; scientists could be scruffy. He recognised the man as the one who had passed them in the hotel lounge the previous night. He held back and let Sophie continue her conversation.

An announcement came over the public address system to inform the delegates that the tea break would end in five minutes. Sophie said goodbye to her companion and went back to her seat in the auditorium. When she got there, Willis joined her.

'It's him,' said Sophie. 'It's a Dr Fauler. I tried to find out his area of interest, and he was very evasive. I suspect he is neither an astronomer nor a particle physicist.'

'I guess you're right. I saw him in the lift last night and thought I recognised him. But that isn't unusual – after all, the hotel serves the Congress Centre.'

Willis glanced over his shoulder. Dr Fauler was sitting two rows behind him to his right. He was staring straight at Willis. Willis held his stare but then turned around to talk to Sophie. The man rose from his seat and almost ran for the exit.

Willis jumped to his feet and followed him, uttering a string of apologies to the other delegates in his row as he bustled past them, making them drop their papers and shift their laptops from their knees. They were even less pleased when Sophie followed, a little slower but with as many apologies.

By the time Willis had left his row and reached the door, Fauler was gone.

Sophie and Willis rushed back to the hotel and enquired at the desk for Mr Fauler. 'You've just missed him,' said the receptionist. 'Mr Fauler has just checked out.'

'Well, that's blown it,' Willis said. 'We had better ask Grigori why his brother has been following us.'

CHAPTER 47

Willis had reluctantly dragged himself away from the conference that he would have loved to stay at, and they arrived at the Renaissance Hotel later that evening. Willis phoned Grigori and Korolev and asked them to meet him in his room as a matter of urgency.

When the men arrived, Willis asked them to take a seat. He waited. The awkward silence lasted for minutes. Willis let it continue, watching Grigori's reaction. He didn't look particularly uncomfortable. God, he's a cool customer, Willis thought.

'Alright,' Willis said finally, breaking the silence. 'George, I know your real name is Grigori – Grigori Fauler. Can we cut the crap? Tell me why your brother Karl followed us to Munich.'

'You are very smart, Mr Willis. Okay, I'll be straight with you. Yes, my name is Grigori Fauler, and yes, I have a brother named Karl, but I can assure you that Karl was nowhere near Munich yesterday. He is at the family home in St Petersburg. I know this for a fact because I spoke to him last night when I asked him to go to Munich and shadow you. He's probably arriving in Munich as we speak.'

'Why should we trust you? You have been devious and duplicitous since we met. You know everything there is to know about us, but you have told us nothing about yourself.' Willis was almost shouting, and beads of sweat peppered his forehead. 'You haven't shared with us a single piece of information. I was wrong to trust you. Why would another man named Dr Fauler run away from us when we spotted him?'

'Well, there's a lot more to my story, Dr Willis. I do odd jobs for the Russian Federation, similar to those you do for your country. In return, Vladimir Putin rewards me by pushing business my way. I suppose you could call me an agent, a spy, but I am a philanthropic spy, not unlike yourself. True, I make a lot of money being philanthropic, but it's difficult not to. After all, I'm dealing with so much of it. Our country's economy is struggling, and people like me – who find things out and get things done – help it in a major way.'

'So, what's your interest in us?' asked Willis.

'That should be obvious to you by now. Russia is a major producer of oil on the world stage. My interest lies in looking after one of my country's greatest assets. If the price of oil were to crash, then it would be an economic disaster for the Federation. I'm here to make sure it doesn't happen – and I imagine that is your objective too.'

'It is, Mr Fauler, but I have not been trying to conceal my objectives from anyone. That's something I can't say about you.'

'Don't blame me entirely. It's part of our country's culture to be secretive. When the Soviet Union collapsed in 1991, the country experienced a feeling of shame. Part of

Putin's goal was to put pride back in our country. Anything I can do to assist with that, I will.'

Korolev cut in. 'I can identify with everything Grigori has said. This is important to us, and … although I don't know the man personally,' he added after hesitating, 'I do understand his motivation.'

'Grigori? Isn't that a name for the Fallen Angels?' Willis said cynically. 'Is that what you are, Mr Fauler? A fallen angel?'

'It's interesting that you should make that connection. That's one of the meanings of Grigori, but it also means watchful or vigilant. I could name many more things that have related to Grigori through the ages. No, Mr Willis, it's just a name. It has no more significance than it's the name my father chose for me.'

'Where do we go from here? I don't know if I can trust you. Until I can, there's no way forward for us.'

'I have helped you a lot. If I'd chosen to, I could have killed you at any stage of our relationship – but I didn't. That surely must count for something?' Grigori paused, waiting for a reaction from Willis. It didn't come. 'I'll tell you what I'll do. Would you trust me if I found out who the Dr Fauler was you crossed paths with in Munich? And what he was doing there?'

Secretly, Willis realised that he needed Grigori's help – but that's how he'd play it, secretly, because there was no way he wanted to give the impression that he was reliant on him.

'That would go some way to helping me trust you.'

'Consider it done.'

***

Willis was edgy for the next couple of days. He communicated with Grigori but in a half-hearted way. He didn't know if Grigori was as philanthropic as he claimed to be. He was right, though; he could have harmed them but hadn't. Why would he want to if he was above board? But neither had he given them any useful information. Willis was cornered and couldn't figure out the best way forward. He had no other ideas about how to resolve the mess he was in. If Grigori was genuine, then Willis needed his help, and he needed it soon. If it hadn't been Karl in Munich, then finding out who Dr Fauler was would be critical to discovering the next move to make.

Grigori left the restaurant and retired early to his room, saying he was still working on the problem. No doubt, if he were playing it straight, he would be on his mobile getting his lackeys to do the digging for him. Since Willis had returned from Munich, he felt uneasy. A feeling of distrust was building up between him and Grigori, and he wasn't sure how much information, if any, he should share with him.

Korolev came over to the couch and sat beside Willis and Sophie. 'There is bad news about the twelve men we took into custody. They have no criminal records we can find, so there are no fingerprints on file. We have no way of finding out who they are. I didn't feel comfortable questioning them until their injuries had been wrapped up.'

'That is bad news,' Willis said. But he forced a smile at Korolev's choice of verb despite grinding his teeth at the news.

'There's even worse news. There was a breach at the prison yesterday morning. After they'd had surgery to repair their bullet wounds, three of the group – Pythagoras and his two strong men – managed to break out. I need to return immediately and order a full investigation. If I find out anything of interest, I will let you know. Corruption in prisons is rampant, but we have no idea who or where the missing prisoners are now.'

'Can things get any worse?' Willis asked himself. He went into the bathroom and closed the door, then immediately called Reilly. 'Can you get some background for me? It's on a Grigori Fauler. He claims to be a Russian businessman but also admits he is also an agent of the Federation.'

'I know all the big players in Russia,' answered Reilly. 'I've never heard of anyone called Fauler, but if he is an agent, then we will find him. Someone must have come across him at some time. Is there anything else you need from me?'

'I asked Palmer to contact Baker in the States and find out anything he can about Fauler's brother, Karl. I did this before I knew about Grigori having links with the Federation. Could you act as my middle man and find out what Baker has discovered? That way, I only have one call to make. I'll ring you this time tomorrow, if I may. Oh … I'd also like as much detail on the rest of Fauler's family as you can manage to find out.'

'I'll get on to it. I'll speak to you tomorrow.'

By the time Willis returned from the bathroom, Korolev had left. He had said his farewells to Sophie and said he would fly out the following morning.

Willis wanted to question Grigori some more. He told Sophie he would be back in a few minutes and strode towards the door. When he reached Grigori's room, he knocked but got no reply. He was about to leave when a maid approached. He indicated to her, using complicated arm movements, that he had forgotten his room card. She shrugged and shook her head but swiped her master card in the door and let him in.

The room was a mess. Grigori had left in a hurry; his suits had gone, but dirty socks and clothes littered the floor. There was no sign of his passport or anything else that might identify him.

He had gone. Grigori had absconded.

CHAPTER 48

Sophie and Willis were now alone. The next morning, they didn't surface until after eight-thirty. They decided to have breakfast, speak to Reilly, and then go back to Geneva.

'I'm disappointed with myself,' Willis said. 'I should have anticipated that.'

'You should have,' said Sophie. Her comment wasn't in the least encouraging. She sighed. 'But he's such a convincing character. I can't blame you. I liked him.'

'He had me fooled.' Willis sounded despondent. 'Where do we go from here? We might find a trail of sorts in Geneva, but I doubt it very much. Maybe Korolev can uncover something about our escapees from his military prison?'

They went down to the restaurant, ordered breakfast and ate without paying attention to anything around them. Neither of them said a word.

They went back to their room to call Reilly. As Willis opened the door, he stopped abruptly in his tracks. The room had been ransacked: clothes and paper were strewn over the floor.

'What the…?' Willis gasped. He raced forward and rummaged through the bedside drawers. 'At least our fake passports are still here.' He checked the case. So was his money. But what was missing, from its hiding place on top of the wardrobe, was the MP-443 Grach pistol.

'They know all there is to know about us. They're in the hotel and spying on us. Pythagoras must have people everywhere, and they must have done this.' Willis sank onto the bed and put his head in his hands. 'I might as well give up, tell Reilly and get it over with.'

Willis had to wait a few seconds for the call to connect. He told Reilly the bad news about Grigori and the escaped prisoners. 'What do I do next? I have no idea.'

'Well, I've traced Grigori Fauler,' said Reilly. 'He's a very rich man. He owns a raft of high-value companies, including energy consortia, which do most of their business through the Russian Federation. I have checked out the Federal Security Service, the Foreign Intelligence Service and the Federal Protective Service; there is no trace of anyone named Fauler. I've also checked the GRU to cover the military intelligence angle as well, but nothing. If he's a member of any of these organisations, he is hiding it well.'

'Thanks, Mike. I had already had an inkling of his wealth from Baker through Palmer, but it surprises me that nothing has shown up on the security side. I have no option but to go back to Geneva and hope something pops out of the woodwork.'

'Okay, Brad. I'll keep looking, but our computer system is quite robust in how it does searches. If something hasn't shown up now, I doubt it will.' They said goodbye and hung up.

No sooner had the phone disconnected than it rang again. It was Palmer. 'Sorry, Brad. I know you wanted all communication to go through Reilly, but this is important – the doctors have given me permission to fly. They say the chances of thrombosis in my leg have reduced. I'll be leaving for the States this evening. I'm no good to you here anyway until my leg is fully mended. You can still contact me on my cell – shit, I nearly forgot. We did a bit of research into your friendly Russian, General Korolev. It turns out he's a member of the GRU or, as it's known nowadays, the GU, the military arm of the federal secret service.'

'Bloody 'ell,' Willis said in a subdued tone. 'Is anybody who they say they are? Our whole team is leaky. No wonder all our activities have been circulated far and wide.'

'He's quite senior. He's held positions all over Russia, but currently, he's the head of security, based in Baikonur, responsible for most of the armed forces. But in the past, he's been responsible for investigating the Russian Mafia.'

Slowly the seriousness of the situation sank in. Even if Willis had used his cover as a researcher to hide his true objectives, he didn't think that was in any way duplicitous – not compared with what Grigori had done. And he wasn't secretive.

'Well, we have been led up the garden path by our apparent friends. But I shouldn't complain. I knew Grigori was dodgy from the start, but Korolev…' Even more despondently, Willis said, 'Thank you once more. Have a good flight.' He turned to Sophie. 'We had better stay in our room as much as possible, so we're less likely to be overheard. At least, I want you to stay in our ro—' He stopped speaking and put a finger over his lips. 'Shh …' He searched everywhere that someone could possibly have planted a bug. Five minutes later, he held a tiny microphone. After showing it to Sophie, he replaced it behind the picture frame where he'd found it.

Willis stood near the picture and said loudly, 'We'll stay in our room for the rest of the day. Is there anything worth watching on telly?' He selected a pay-per-view channel, chose a movie at random then turned up the volume. He kissed Sophie on the cheek. 'I'm going to visit that oil refinery again. There must be more to it than meets the eye.'

'That would be foolhardy,' Sophie whispered back. 'Remember what happened last time? There's no Korolev to rescue you this time.'

'Maybe, but I have to try.'

Willis studied the view from the window. To the right was a steel fire escape. He walked out into the corridor and went over to inspect the fire exit door. It was, as he had expected, alarmed. He went back into the room and opened the bedroom window.

'I'm going out,' he explained. 'I can't risk anyone spotting me leave, or I'll be in trouble. Don't answer the door to anyone except me. I will shout through the door when I arrive, so you're sure it's me.'

He stepped out onto the window ledge, which was only a few inches wide. He estimated it was a six-foot jump to the fire escape. There was a railing he could grab. After bouncing on his sore leg a few times, he decided that the jump was worth the risk. If he judged it well, he could land on his strong leg. He looked down, then wished he hadn't. Some bins and a waste skip lay about fifty feet below. He took a deep breath and jumped. He caught the railing, but his foot missed. He scraped his shin against the iron edge of the step. It hurt like hell. He managed to swing back and pull on the railing at the same time. On his third attempt, he succeeded in getting his foot on the step. He swung over the railing in one fluid movement. God, his shin hurt. He limped down four flights of steps and crossed the backyard into the car park. Was he making the right decision by going to the refinery on his own? He had no choice. He had to take the risk.

The rental car was where he had left it. The engine burst into life on the first turn of the key. Now all he had to remember was how to get back to the oil refinery. He got on the right road after remembering to make three right turns onto Qanysh Satbayev Avenue. It would be plain sailing from here: all he had to do was to keep driving west, and he would find it. Zeynolla Ghumarov Street loomed in front of him. He turned and drove to the T-junction at the end of the road. Straight across from the junction stood the oil refinery.

He turned right, then left and stopped beside the small iron gate again. The chain hadn't yet been replaced. The gate opened, and he swerved once again to the right to miss the security camera above the loading bay. The door into the storeroom was still unlocked. He entered and surveyed the space. The crates were in the same positions. He dodged from crate to crate to stay out of sight. At the far end of the storeroom, he turned right, so he was facing a glass-panelled door. He moved stealthily forward until he was level with the glass panel.

This was déjà vu. It was the same office, the same door, and some of the same men inside, but this time there were only three. The first he recognised as Pythagoras, the second was the American, and the third was the tall Russian who had kicked him in the crotch. The same three men who had been arrested, imprisoned, and had broken out the previous day.

A hand landed on Willis's shoulder. Oh crap. His heart sank. This is taking déjà vu a little too far, he thought. He froze, waiting for the blinding light that had dazzled him the last time. It didn't come. Slowly he turned and studied the hand that gripped his shoulder. He recognised the ring on one of its fingers. He looked up. It was Boris Korolev, a finger over his lips.

They sat for a while, listening, but the voices were too indistinct. They were speaking English, but they could make out only a few words. Among them were 'tomorrow', 'noon' and 'jeep'.

Korolev shook his head and pointed with his thumb over his shoulder. Willis followed him. They left through the door where Willis had entered and closed it behind them. Nothing more was to be gained by hanging around and risking being caught again.

'You have a gun. Why didn't you use it?' Willis said, his face flushed and his eyes wide.

'Because, I think the saying goes, there are bigger fish to fry.' Korolev jerked his head to his left, indicating he wanted Willis to follow. Willis's knuckles were white as he followed. They exited through the wire gate and got into Willis's rental car.

'I'm sorry to have deceived you, Brad, but I arranged for the three men to escape yesterday morning. They're not aware who freed them; they assumed it was someone in their organisation who'd helped them.'

'And what organisation is that?' asked Willis. 'And what about us working together?'

'That, we don't know yet. That's why I had the idea of letting them out. But we are planning to discover that tomorrow, fingers crossed. My car is on the main street in front of the refinery. Let's return to your hotel. I will meet you there and explain everything.'

***

Willis arrived first. He didn't bother to use the fire escape to get back in. He went straight to his room and signalled to Sophie that he was at the door. She unlatched it and let him in. She had tidied the room since he left and restored everything to its correct place.

Willis led Sophie out into the corridor, away from the bug in the picture frame, and told her what happened and Korolev's story about releasing the men. 'He hasn't told me yet that he's a member of the GU. I will ask him about that when he comes.'

Once they were back in the room, there was a knock at the door.

'Who is it?' asked Willis.

'Korolev.'

Willis opened the door and let him in. Korolev took the chair next to the desk. He rushed to blurt out his story, but Willis stopped him by pointing to the bug. To continue their conversation without being overheard, Willis guided them into the bathroom and closed the door. Korolev started to explain, keeping his voice low. 'We put the main three men in a room together yesterday before we took them to prison. They chatted and chatted without realising we had bugged the room, and we were recording every word they said. We let them escape from custody before they were taken to jail. It turns out that they're part of something much bigger – we haven't discovered what yet. Something is due to take place tomorrow. I plan to get some men ready and surprise them in the act.'

'We are closing in on them,' Willis said. He was still unsure whether or not to trust Korolev. 'I would like to be part of whatever transpires tomorrow.'

'You will be, my friend.'

'If I'm your friend, why didn't you tell me you were part of the GU?'

'I am a policeman, Mr Willis, no more, no less. I never admit to being part of the security forces.'

'And Grigori Fauler has fled the coop. His room is empty.'

'That man will be the death of me,' complained Korolev. He didn't show the least surprise at the revelation. 'Let's go to dinner. There's plenty of time to get things sorted for tomorrow. We don't want to alert the spying bastards in the hotel to the fact we're on to them.'

CHAPTER 49

A thin blade of light cut in through the narrow window, illuminating dust motes floating in the air. Greg Palmer sat, one hand over his eye, following a fleck of dust with the other eye as the sunlight warmed the air, causing the dust motes to rise. He followed his chosen mote until it rose and vanished into the shadow of the window frame. Jesus H. Christ, he was bored.

After he returned from Europe, his leg on the mend, he'd become restless. His consultant's words echoed in his ears: 'Remember, no physical exercise until I tell you to. Favour the damaged leg. Keep it elevated so that your tibia is higher than your femur. That means keep your calf higher than your thigh. And do the physio exercises that I have given you to make sure your muscles don't get weak. Three or four times a day. More, if you're up to it.'

But Palmer wasn't about to take his advice. His leg had mended. After all, he had travelled from Europe and that hadn't caused any problems, so why couldn't he do a little careful exercise? Jorgen Jensen was a Danish colleague whose office was next door but one. Jorgen was a keen Nordic walker and convinced Palmer that if he borrowed his poles, he could walk without straining his leg. Fortunately, because the men were a similar height, the poles were the right length to suit Palmer's size and stride. He decided to go ahead and use them rather than wait for permission from his consultant, Chuck Morrow. His theory was that the poles would take part of his weight, enabling him to walk sooner and a little faster. He was wrong. After less than a mile, his leg ached and throbbed, forcing him to limp back home. The next morning, his leg was double its size. Pains shot through it every few minutes, so he got very little sleep during the night, despite drinking several medicinal shots of Jack Daniel's. The Tennessee liquor had helped him grab brief snatches of shut-eye, each lasting barely ten minutes. Now he sat with his leg elevated, exactly as Chuck had advised.

Palmer wished that he had taken Chuck's advice from the beginning. The leg was in no hurry to mend this time. Getting around was a rigmarole. Putting two hands under his thigh, he lifted his leg and lowered it to the floor as gently as he could. He groped for his crutch. As he raised himself from the chair, his right leg took his weight. After tucking the crutch under his arm, he hobbled into the corridor and towards the water cooler. A colleague passed.

'Hiya, Cassidy.'

Another: 'There goes Hop Along.'

It was gradually wearing Palmer down.

Glug, glug. As he balanced precariously, the noise of the double bubble that formed inside the cooler every time he filled his glass made him think of a mechanical laugh, constantly jeering at him. He hobbled back to his desk and placed the glass on one corner. The chair complained as he dropped his full weight heavily into the seat. With the intention of trying to lift his leg onto the desk, he put two hands under his thigh and heaved.

'Shit, the glass.'

He let his leg lower again so he could move the glass. This was a pain in the ass. Jorgen's Nordic poles stood in the corner, mocking him for being so stupid.

While he sipped the water, he watched the screensaver on his PC swing and dance as the green and blue spirals intertwined and separated again, finally replaced by red and green swirls. Such was his boredom.

While the Astronomy Building was being refurbished, he had been moved to this temporary office. The smell of burnt wood still lingered, even after all this time. Even in this remote corner of the astronomy building. Palmer could also smell the fresh paint that had been applied to the doorframes.

Willis was probably having fun in Kazakhstan. Palmer bit his lip and slapped the desktop in envy. But he knew he had no right to envy Willis – he had saved his neck, after all. Still, he longed to get out of the office and be part of the world again.

Since his return to Berkeley, Palmer had acted as a relay point for Willis's messages to Langley, Virginia. Langley was a metonym for the CIA. Palmer had formed a strong working relationship with Special Agent Charlie Dexter from Fairfax County. All Willis's messages were routed via Charlie. This meant Palmer had to stay up late to compensate for the twelve-hour difference between California and Kazakhstan. It made sense for Palmer to communicate directly with Langley; he didn't need to stay up as late as his counterparts in Virginia would.

He hit his mouse, and the screensaver disappeared, to be replaced by his email screen. An email flashed up. It was from Charlie. He hovered the cursor over the mail and clicked. It was a message about nothing:

Extra information expected soon about Brad Willis's contacts. Will email as soon as I hear more.

It was an old message; he had read it at ten that morning. Palmer stared at the message, wishing it would come alive and reveal more. Of course, it didn't.

Charlie Dexter – was that a guy's name or a gal's? Palmer couldn't make up his mind. Some phrases in the emails suggested that Charlie might be female. The writer had a penchant for correct grammar and never used abbreviations. But it could be a guy writing too. How could he find out? He could hardly ask outright – or could he? Palmer amused himself by devising subtle questions to ask that might result in Charlie revealing their gender.

The sun no longer shone into Palmer's tiny office. That meant it was getting late. He glanced at his watch. It was after 4 p.m. – it would soon be time to go home and be bored there. There was little to do, even at home. He wanted to be out and about. But his leg held him back. He wanted to be with Willis.

The previous day, Palmer had been given three hours of telescope time on one of the Paranal instruments. It had flown by in the wink of an eye. It was in the Atacama Desert, about seventy miles south of Antofagasta, but he had worked from his office computer. Since that was before he'd damaged his leg, he was able to sit comfortably with both feet on the ground. Writing up his results had taken him all of eight hours. They were now with other astronomers, being peer reviewed. Oh, for some more telescope time. What wouldn't he give now for another few hours of observing time… Even with his damaged leg, he could sit at a monitor and observe, but no more time was forthcoming. Not yet anyway.

He glanced at his watch again. 4.10 p.m. Sod Willis, he thought. I suppose he's doing something exciting – either that or enjoying spending time with Sophie. Lucky devil.

The swirls were attracting his attention again. He leaned forward and switched the power off to his LCD monitor. He dropped a pencil on the desk. The lead broke. Pushing the pencil into his electric sharpener, he sharpened it – for the third time that day. The sharpener's battery was close to giving up the ghost.

Time for more water. Palmer lifted his leg off the desk. This time, it slipped and crashed heavily to the floor. A searing pain shot up his leg, making him grimace and hold his breath.

While his eyes were closed, his computer pinged. He leaned forward. Damn. The power switch was just out of reach. He lunged forward, hitting his leg on the desk. His fingers hit the switch, and the screen burst into life. Another email from Special Agent Charlie. It was longer than the last one, so hopefully, it contained some important intel.

He read the subject line:

Background information on Grigori Fauler's cousin

He read on. As he read, his eyebrows rose. 'Holy shit. Willis isn't going to like this. Grigori has fed Willis fed a complete load of bullshit.' Another look at his watch. It was not quite 5 p.m. In Kazakhstan, it would be 5 a.m. Willis would be fast asleep. Palmer struggled to his feet, grabbed his crutch and headed for his car. 'Thank Christ I didn't buy the stick version of my BMW,' he muttered as he limped towards the car park. At 7 p.m. EST, he dialled Willis's number. A groggy voice answered the phone. 'Hello, Greg. I hope this is urgent.'

'I think it might be. Get a load of this…'

CHAPTER 50

Early the next morning, Willis was wakened by the sun shining through the window. The thin red and white checked curtains covered the room in a warm orange glow. The bright sunshine was accompanied by the persistent ringing of his mobile. It was Palmer. He sounded excited. He had news on Grigori – or, rather, on another member of his family, who neither he nor Willis knew existed. Grigori had a cousin who was as crooked as a seven-dollar note – and he was involved in this racket too.

Palmer was speaking quickly. 'We still haven't found out anything about Fauler being in the Federal Services, but we have uncovered a Klaus Fauler who is a cousin of Grigori's. He lives in Atyraū.'

'Why doesn't that surprise me? They're on our doorstep. They're all around us. It's no surprise that they can find out everything that's going on. What do you know about him?'

'Not a lot. He has a criminal record as long as your arm – even longer than Karl Fauler's – but we haven't been able to uncover any allegiances to any organisation. Believe me. We've tried.'

'Thanks, Greg, you've done well. That should help us get a lead on things. At least it will prevent a wasted journey to Geneva.'

'It's no bloody surprise. I've suspected that Grigori was dodgy ever since we met.'

Willis decided not to tell Palmer that his advice had come too late and that Grigori had already absconded. 'Thanks, Greg. If you hear anything else, let me know.'

Willis showered and shaved and was ready for breakfast before 7 a.m. Sophie had followed his lead.

'Let's eat,' he suggested. 'We will probably be the only people in the restaurant. It has only just opened.'

They picked up their key cards and headed for the door. Before they reached it, three aggressive knocks shook the door on its hinges. Willis grabbed Sophie and bundled her to one side of the door, against the wall.

'Who's there?' he shouted and stood back against the wall himself.

'It's me, Grigori. Let me in.'

Willis grasped the handle and opened the door a crack, keeping his foot lodged against the inside of the door. He squinted through the narrow gap and saw Grigori standing there with two huge men.

'C'mon. Let me in. I haven't got all day.'

Willis glanced at Sophie as though seeking her approval, but it didn't come. He opened the door wide. The three men strode into the room, and Grigori closed the door behind them.

Before Grigori had a chance to speak, Willis removed the bug from behind the picture frame, wrapped it in a pair of his socks and placed it in a drawer, covering it with some more clothes.

'Where did you go last night?' whispered Willis before Grigori had a chance to open his mouth.

'I told you I was going to find out who was behind this, and I have. Take a seat and listen.'

Willis sat and listened.

'I did this to give you confidence in me, although I doubt if what I have to tell you will, in any way, help the situation. First of all, the leader of the group we are familiar with is Klaus Fauler – my cousin Klaus Fauler. The group is called the Golden Triangle. Klaus is also a member of Solntsevskaya Bratva, one of Russia's largest Mafia groups. It might even be the largest, with some five thousand members. Its name comes from the district where it was formed. My cousin's little group is a breakaway group working independently and unknown to Sergei Mikhailov, otherwise known as "Mikhas" Mikhailov, who is the head of the main Solntsevskaya Bratva group. You must understand: I have had no dealings with my cousin or with the *bratva*. I haven't met or spoken to the man since we were at school together. His objectives are the exact opposite of mine. He is selfish.' Grigori ran his fingers through his hair and gazed down at the floor. He continued, 'He and his group, the Golden Triangle, are here in Atyraū.'

'In the oil refinery, by any chance?' asked Willis.

'I won't ask how you discovered that,' replied Grigori. Only Korolev had been at the refinery when the men were arrested. 'Now to the crunch. They are planning something today at the refinery. What they are planning, we have no idea, but we plan to surprise them anyway. That's all I have discovered.'

There was a long pause.

'Can we work together and beat this gang?' He waited for Willis to reply.

As Willis listened to Grigori's story, he felt more confident that the man could be trusted. 'Everything you've said has been backed up by what Boris Korolev and I discovered yesterday,' Willis said. 'We visited the refinery and managed to overhear some odd words through the glass door to an office where they were meeting. We established that something is due to happen today, but we didn't discover what.' Willis paused. 'On whether we have a deal, the answer is yes. I believe what you say.' Willis decided it was better not to tell Grigori about Palmer's phone call and his information about his cousin.

'Good,' replied Grigori. 'In that case, allow me to introduce you to Dmitriy and Aleksandr Petrov.' He indicated to each man in turn. Each stepped forward and bowed his head when his name was mentioned. 'These are my right-hand men, and they are brothers. They each have a team that will help us out today.'

Willis bowed back. 'You will already know that Boris Korolev is a member of the GU?'

'Of course. Boris and I go back several years. That I knew Boris is something else I ought to have told you. It is unfortunate, but sometimes we tend to get in each other's way. He and I need to talk a lot more to prevent this.'

Now, Willis was a lot more confident that he could trust both of his new associates. 'You will have the opportunity to do that later. Boris never left Atyraū, and he will be involved today too. We believe that whatever is happening is planned for noon.'

Grigori made a face. 'We had better find out what Boris is doing before we mess up each other's plans.'

'I'll ring him,' Willis said, going to his desk and picking up his mobile. He pressed some keys and put it on hands-free. To prevent the bug from picking up their conversation, Willis set the volume at minimum. 'Hello,

Boris, this is Willis. We have some visitors this morning. Grigori and his friends are here.'

There came what sounded like a long sigh from Boris.

Grigori spoke first. 'We need to lay out what our plans are so we don't screw up at the refinery.'

The three of them talked through their plan. They would enter the refinery and get the three men and their team out – alive. They all agreed that they needed any information the three principal members of the gang could provide. Boris added that their interrogation would not be as friendly as the one they had received when the men were first 'arrested'.

'You will need to put four men undercover around the periphery of the refinery,' Willis said. 'They can let us know if any activity kicks off before noon.'

'Agreed. We will meet at noon,' said Grigori. 'But now it's time for breakfast.'

After he had hung up, Willis turned and said to Grigori, 'Sophie and I need to be visible in the restaurant. Otherwise, they might get suspicious that we are on to them.'

Grigori nodded. 'We will go out the way we came in, unnoticed and unseen. We will pick you up at eleven-thirty and go to the refinery.'

After they had left, Willis suggested to Sophie that they ought to go for breakfast. It was eight-thirty, and by now, the restaurant would be almost full.

Once they had been seated and had ordered, Willis turned to Sophie. 'The same rules as before: lock yourself in the room until I return. Put a "DO NOT DISTURB" sign on the door handle and stay put. Sweetheart, you asked me to take care of you, and I will, but you'll need to stay indoors until we get back.'

When their food came, Willis made a noisy issue of sending his back, complaining that the eggs were undercooked. This was to ensure their presence was noticed by any interested parties. When they had eaten, they returned to their room and tried to relax. 'We have two hours to wait – for what, only time will tell. The difference this time is that we are well prepared. We will turn up with enough resources to get the job done.'

***

At eleven-thirty, with military precision, Grigori turned up at the hotel with three Ural medium-sized Russian cargo trucks. Any hotel spies would have long left to join their friends at the refinery. Korolev had contacted Willis to tell them the activity was already underway. They would need to approach the refinery with caution and remain out of sight for as long as possible.

Grigori's lead truck had swung out well to the right of the refinery. He planned to approach from its blind spot across the fields to its rear. From their vantage spot, they could watch the comings and goings inside the compound. Cars and trucks were arriving, along with what looked like a couple of army personnel carriers. Willis assumed that the soldiers were mercenaries: he didn't recognise the uniforms they wore, despite the cloth being the standard-issue Russian colour. Several surface-to-air missile launchers were unloaded. They all disappeared inside a loading bay to their left.

'What would they need rocket launchers for?' asked Grigori.

At that moment, Korolev's army car pulled up alongside Grigori's. Boris got out and came to the driver's side. 'Did you notice the missile launchers that went in?'

Grigori nodded.

'There's nothing here they might need missiles for,' stated Korolev. 'They must be planning an attack somewhere else.'

'Right,' said Grigori. 'Boris, you bring your men around the right side of the premises. I will bring mine to the left.'

'Let's ignore all the equipment the men are loading. We need to concentrate on getting the members of the Golden Triangle out and in one piece,' Willis said.

Korolev agreed. He removed a full face mask from his waistband and hooked it over his elbow. 'Don't put on your gas masks until we get near to wherever they are meeting.'

Twenty-four men had gathered beside the trucks alongside the two that contained Grigori and Boris. Those with Federation markings aligned on Boris's side and the rest on Grigori's side.

Willis's watch confirmed it was fifteen minutes past twelve. Grigori twisted towards the rear of the jeep and mouthed, 'Okay.' He got out of the jeep and waved his right arm, signalling to his men to advance. Korolev did likewise.

Two lines of men crouched and made their way in single file to the wire fence that surrounded the refinery perimeter. Wire cutters made quick work of the fence, and two six-foot-square holes allowed their ingress. So far, it had been easy. There were no windows on this side of the building, and they were out of sight, blocked by the wall. The men who entered through the left hole went to the left of the building, and Korolev's men went to the right.

'You'll need me up front,' Willis said to Grigori. 'I know where they are likely to be meeting. It's a small glass office through the door halfway along the wall on the left.' He stepped in front of Grigori and edged his way along the left wall towards the door to the storeroom. Once inside, he stopped and listened. It was ghostly silent. He worked his way forward from crate to crate until he reached the end of the storeroom. The glass-walled office lay on his right. Willis signalled for Grigori to wait as he worked his way up the office window. Damn. It was empty – even the table and chairs that had been there before had gone. He worked his way back to Grigori's side.

'The office is empty,' he whispered, 'but let's go through. There's a door leading out the other side.'

The men followed him. At the other end of the office, Willis grabbed the door handle and opened it a crack. He peered through, sucked in air through his teeth and then slowly exhaled. 'Have a look at this.' He swung the door open and signalled for Grigori and his men to follow. The room they entered was in complete contrast to the one they had left. It was exquisite: elaborately decorated with oil paintings on the walls. The floor was thickly carpeted. On the left was a lift, its walls made from silvered glass. Its double doors lay open, and its panel of pearlised buttons indicated the two floors it served. There were only two buttons: up and down. The gold arrow on the lower button was illuminated, indicating that the lift was ready to descend. Willis backed out of the lift. He followed Grigori, who was pointing to a narrow fire door with steps that led down to the basement.

Willis ran down, and Grigori followed. What they entered looked more like a palace than a refinery. Again, there were carpets and paintings. On the far wall hung an insignia of a triangle with a star inside it. They were in the headquarters of the Golden Triangle.

Willis, Grigori and his army crept forward into what was a reception area. Being quiet was easy since the floor was so thickly carpeted. They made their way along to a door. Willis and Grigori peered inside. It was a boardroom. On the walls was soundproofing like the sort Korolev had demonstrated at Baikonur. Around the boardroom table sat eleven men. Each wore a gold triangular badge with a star at its apex. Willis and Grigori recognised the three men from their previous encounter, but here, they merely seemed to be members of a larger team.

To the left of the door was a huge window. Through it, they could see scores of men dressed in military uniforms and loading military equipment onto transport trucks. Each man wore an armband displaying a yellow triangle.

'This gang has enough resources to start World War III. If they are alerted, we will be outnumbered.' Willis walked closer to the window and peered in.

CHAPTER 51

'That's blown it,' whispered Grigori. 'The least noise, and we'll alert them.'

Korolev had re-joined them. On Grigori's first command, the men donned their gas masks. On his second, they threw gas canisters into the boardroom. A noxious white vapour filled the room. The eleven men at the table turned around in horror. As the gas reached them, their eyes glazed over. Some staggered around, bumping into each other, then fell unconscious, one by one. Two soldiers threw the doors open, and Grigori's and Boris's men rushed in. At that instant, a twelfth man, who had not been at the table, entered through a door hidden behind a projector screen. He aimed his pistol, at random, at the crowd of soldiers rushing into the room. As soon as he fired, a hail of automatic fire riddled his body. He crashed against the back wall of the room before sliding down the wall into a sitting position with his head slumped against his lifeless torso.

'There's no point in being quiet now,' yelled Willis. Eleven military men chose one of the Golden Triangle group, picked up their limp bodies and threw them over their shoulders in a fireman's lift. 'Let's get out of here and back to the trucks.'

In their haste to get the men out, nobody noticed that Boris was leaning against the boardroom door. Blood streamed from his abdomen.

'God!' shouted Willis, indicating frantically to one of the team. 'Come and get Boris out of here. Now.'

'Let me be,' whispered Boris. 'I think I'm bleeding internally too. I feel so weak. It's no use. Let me be. Go and get these bastards out of here.'

But Dmitriy and Aleksandr appeared from nowhere, lifted Boris by the shoulders and feet and carried him up the stairs.

The gunfire had clearly alerted the soldiers in the loading bay. The window in the reception area shuddered as they blasted it with automatic fire, but its reinforced glass didn't fail immediately. It took several seconds before the glass crazed and shattered over the carpet. Three uniformed enemy soldiers climbed over the sill while another unloaded the clip of his AK-12 carbine into the room. Willis and Grigori ran to the narrow stairs, but they were blocked by Dmitriy and Aleksandr carrying Boris. Grigori turned back, produced a grenade and threw it at the hole. Willis grabbed Grigori's rifle and sprayed bullets through the smoke-filled room in the direction of the window. The air conditioning was clearing the air. Two of the men were hanging over the window ledge, and another three were clambering over their inert bodies. Willis let go with another burst of fire, and three bodies joined the other two. Other men pulled the bodies free from the window to gain access.

The stairs above then were almost clear. Willis and Grigori rushed halfway up. Grigori turned around and threw two grenades down the stairs. They took shelter behind the landing until the grenades blew. The walls collapsed and blocked any entry from below.

They emerged on the ground floor to a barrage of bullets coming from the roadway in front of the loading bay. A Kornet-D, a mobile anti-tank guided missile system, was being wheeled out of the refinery. Six of the team were hiding behind two Ural cargo trucks, returning fire. It was having little effect; a shot caught the driver of the Kornet, and he slumped over the wheel. Another man took his place, and the vehicle continued moving.

Two men ran up behind the Ural, pulling an 82-mm Podnos infantry mortar behind them. They set it up and fired two shots in quick succession. The Kornet, lifted by the blast, rolled over onto its side, neutralised. But the attack was relentless. Another two Kornets turned towards them, and two missiles raced towards them. One glanced off the side of the refinery and exploded; the other scored a direct hit on the Ural. It disintegrated, and the eight men behind it catapulted into the air.

Willis and Grigori ran. They ran along the side of the building and caught up with the men carrying their unconscious prisoners.

A deafening roar filled the sky. Willis could feel his chest vibrate in tune with the noise. A fleet of six Russian Mi-24 helicopters flew overhead, blocking out the sun. They had come from the south. Their bellies were scarcely twelve feet above the men's heads. Grigori shouted some orders in Russian. They ran past the men carrying the unconscious members of the Golden Triangle until they reached the two other Ural trucks parked on the field. It didn't take long. Earlier, they'd driven the trucks back, closer to the refinery. The men from the refinery shifted their attention away from them and focused on the helicopters. Mortars and gunfire surrounded them as they loaded Boris into one truck and bundled the Golden Triangle members into the other. They did an about-turn and raced back to the field. A mortar just missed them as the trucks sped away from the refinery.

When they were half a mile from the refinery, the trucks stopped in a copse. Willis and Grigori got out of the trucks and stared back in amazement. Missiles from the Mi-24s bombarded the refinery buildings. The sky went black again. Another four Mi-24s eclipsed the sun, only feet above where they stood. Wave after wave of missile attacks swept over the site and blasted all four buildings. One missile hit two of the condensation pipes leading from the crude oil tanks. A mushroom of black smoke filled the sky. The stench of burning crude oil caught in their throats. They choked and coughed uncontrollably.

The choppers took it in turns to sweep over the building, releasing their missiles in waves. Attack followed attack. A second blast erupted from the refinery. This time the crude oil had ignited on its own. Another three missiles hit the refinery buildings, which disintegrated into rubble. A fourth hit the main storage tank at the centre of the complex. Flames illuminated the darkened sky. The underside of the black plumes changed to deep purple as they reflected the light from the towering inferno. Survivors rushed into the fields surrounding the refinery. They were cut down by machine-gun fire from the choppers, which continued their relentless sweep of what remained of the buildings.

'Secure the prisoners,' shouted Willis, 'and let's get the hell out of here.'

The trucks followed Grigori's lead truck and disappeared behind the trees to the west. They were out of sight of the helicopters from there.

The caravan of trucks crossed the surrounding fields and went west past the airport and into the open countryside.

***

Grigori's truck finally turned off the road and drove towards a barn. Its doors opened as they approached, and the trucks vanished inside.

'Bloody hell,' Willis said. 'Where did the helicopters come from?' He went over to the Ural where Boris was and inspected his wound. It didn't look good; blood saturated his uniform and had collected in a puddle on the floor.

'We need help here,' Willis shouted to Grigori.

Grigori was by his side in seconds. He yelled into his mobile, 'One military ambulance – immediately.' He read out the co-ordinates from the truck's satnav system to the person at the other end of the line. 'Make that four ambulances,' he added as he spotted the other wounded lying in the back of the second vehicle. He threw his mobile on the seat and helped Willis with Boris. Willis had torn off Boris's tunic. Blood oozed from a bullet hole in Boris's stomach. Willis took his own shirt off, ripped it into strips, covered the wound, and then applied pressure to the wound with the palm of his hand. He glared at Grigori and shook his head. It was bad. Very bad.

Although Willis had been in many situations as bloody as this one, he had never seen so many horrendous injuries to so many men at once. As he looked at Boris, a pool of dark liquid bloomed on his chest, then spilled onto the leather seat of the Ural. If they didn't get him to a hospital quickly, it would be too late.

Three ambulances displaying the Kazakh logo arrived in under ten minutes, and the fourth came shortly afterwards. The paramedics whisked Boris and the others away.

Dmitriy and Aleksandr Petrov were helping to manhandle the prisoners into secure areas at the rear of the barn. The purpose of the barn was exactly this: it was part of Grigori's 'empire'. Only seven out of the eleven men had survived.

Grigori was busy with the tallest of the men they had captured. The man's eyes were full of fear.

'If Korolev dies, so will you.' Grigori drew the butt of his army pistol across the man's face, and he cowered away.

Willis was about to comment but bit his tongue. The family resemblance was clear: it was Grigori's cousin.

'You can kill me if you want.' Klaus spat out the words and defiantly returned Grigori's stare.

'Perhaps I won't kill you,' said Grigori. 'I will just hand you over to the Solntsevskaya Bratva.'

The blood drained from Klaus's face. His face turned sallow, and he began to sweat profusely.

'Your friends razed the refinery to the ground, expecting you, the traitor, to be in it. I wonder what they will do to you if we hand you over?'

Klaus had lost all his bravado. 'Okay, I'll tell you the lot, but as a family, surely we can come to some kind of arrangement?'

'There will be no *arrangement* between us. The best you can hope for, cousin, is to come out of this alive and uninjured.'

Klaus flushed. Sweat replaced his smug smile. His story spilled out. 'We set an explosion at CERN and fabricated photos suggesting they were about to announce a new source of power. We knew that the data distributed by CERN would soon disprove what we were trying to achieve, so we needed to destroy the audit trail by eliminating communication centres. But only the ones through which the files had travelled.' He was gabbling, telling his story as quickly as he could. 'We had several informants in CERN who provided us with information. We had to kill them to keep our plan from being discovered.'

'What about Mike Fecher?' Willis was as angry as Grigori was. 'You killed him in Prague, but he was no threat to you.'

'Oh yes, he was. He wrote a paper as part of the Supernova Cosmology Project. He suggested that the Higgs boson was unable to join with the inflaton particle. He had claimed the two particles were incompatible, so he had to go. He planned to resurrect his idea at the Royal Astronomical Society's Christmas lecture. If he had given the lecture, it would have blown the top off our scam. We tried to get the notes from Matt Quimby's briefcase but failed.'

'Why kill the other astronomers?' Willis was right in his face.

'That was merely a precaution. It added to the credibility of the story, and we couldn't risk any of them contradicting the information that we were spreading about the discovery.'

'Merely a precaution? Christ, life has no value for you mad bastards.' Willis held back from swinging a fist in Klaus's direction.

'This was a very elaborate setup,' said Grigori. 'It was bound to fail.'

'It would have been successful if Willis hadn't interfered and started asking questions. We had almost managed to drive the oil price down enough to make it profitable to play in the markets.'

'But the markets weren't falling fast enough for you, so you were forced to delay your dodgy *investments* and …' Willis left his sentence unfinished. He shook his head. 'That was the spanner in the works. You no longer enjoyed the advantage. Anyone could buy oil at the new slowly dropping price – your advantage had completely dissolved.'

'That must have been a great disappointment for you,' said Grigori. Klaus Fauler let his head drop. He looked defeated.

'What will we do with him?' asked Willis.

'His least favourite uncle will take him back to St Petersburg. He will be dealt with there. He won't cause any more problems.'

'But he is responsible for many murders,' insisted Willis.

'I know. He will be taken care of, Brad.'

Willis couldn't see an easy solution. He was unhappy about Grigori simply vanishing into Russia, especially with his crooked cousin, and he told Grigori so.

'This is the neatest and quickest solution.'

They agreed to disagree.

***

Willis and Grigori headed for Atyraū Hospital, hoping to find Korolev conscious. The rectangular black and white building was supported by black pillars over the entrance to its reception: they held up the overhanging structure that jutted out into the service road that adjoined it. The building was modern in every sense of the word. At reception, they were given directions to find Boris. When they got to him, he was only partly conscious. Tubes fed into his arms and stomach. A sign saying 'NIL BY MOUTH' in Kazakh hung above his bed. The nurse told them he was due to have surgery in the next hour and not to stay long.

Boris gave a weak smile when they entered his room. Grigori told him that they had rounded up the Golden Triangle group and how Klaus Fauler had confessed to everything. Boris smiled as he heard each new piece of information. Grigori admitted that there was one thing puzzling him. He said that he suspected Solntsevskaya Bratva's helicopters had destroyed the refinery, but he didn't understand how they had known the Golden Triangle was there. Boris gave a stronger smile and moved his thumb in his direction.

'You told them?' Grigori said.

Boris gave a faint nod.

'You cunning bastard.' said Grigori, a huge smile on his face. 'You saved our lives. We were all in deep crap until the helicopters turned up.'

The nurse came in and cut the meeting short.

After they had left, Grigori said, 'What if the Solntsevskaya Bratva had arrived while we were still in the building?'

'But they didn't. Did they?' Willis was grinning.

***

An hour later, Willis was back in the hotel. He was sipping vodka and telling Sophie the story that Grigori's cousin had told them.

'It all makes sense now,' said Sophie. 'In the short term, it might have worked. It might have lasted long enough to let them make quite a killing in the markets.'

'Shall we have a late dinner?' he asked. As he opened the door for Sophie, his mobile rang. He answered. 'I understand,' he said, his face serious. 'Thanks for telling me. Yes, I will meet you tomorrow.' He put his phone down and took Sophie in his arms. 'That was Grigori.' Willis buried his face in her shoulder and held her close so she couldn't see his face. He was hiding the tears that ran down his cheeks. 'Boris didn't make it through surgery. He won't be seeing his family after all.'

CHAPTER 52

Willis was up and about early again the next morning. Neither he nor Sophie had slept well following the news of Boris Korolev's death. They dressed and showered and were ready by the time Grigori arrived. They planned to have breakfast together. At seven-fifteen, they went to the restaurant in silence. The lack of conversation continued while they ate. It was Willis who spoke first. 'At least he knew we succeeded. He knew we had captured all the central members of the Golden Triangle. It is only a pity he won't be around to see their comeuppance.'

'Comeuppance?' asked Grigori.

Willis explained, 'What they deserved.'

'He saved our necks, well and truly,' said Grigori. 'I will be forever in his debt … and it's a debt I can never repay.'

'Since we caught the bad guys, he would consider that the debt repaid, at least in part.' Willis changed the subject.

'What will you do about your jet at Baikonur? How will you get access to it to have the repairs carried out?'

'That won't be a problem; I can pull strings in Moscow. Remember, I do a lot of freelance work for the Federation, just like you do for British intelligence. I will get a permit to allow the French company that made the Falcon get access to the Cosmodrome. The same thing will go for the Golden Triangle seven. I will get visas so the authorities will allow them into Russia.'

'What about the American in the group? I don't imagine the Americans will be happy about one of their people being taken to Moscow. There is no extradition treaty between Russia and the United States.'

'Good point. His name is Henry Carter. He works on the Berkeley campus, and it was he who alerted the group to Mike Fecher's paper. That resulted in Mike's murder in Prague. Do you have a contact in the States, one who could arrange for a couple of chaperones to come to Atyraū and escort Carter back to the US?'

'That won't be a problem. When would you like them to arrive?'

'It won't be possible to get him out for a couple of days. The refinery is still burning, and the smoke from the fires is drifting to the west. The airport will be out of service for a couple of days until the smoke subsides. No flights are allowed in or out of Atyraū at the moment. Ten fire engines are trying to control the fire.'

Willis told Grigori that they had scheduled a Zoom conference that afternoon. It would be between Willis's boss, the US and Atyraū. Grigori was welcome to take part if he wanted. It was set for four-thirty. Grigori smiled and declined. 'I need to keep a little anonymity with the UK and US.'

'I understand,' Willis said. 'I will get the escorts for Carter sorted out and tell you the outcome.' Finally, things were coming together. While they waited for the airport to reopen, they would be able to relax and enjoy their remaining time in this interesting city.

'We have a free afternoon,' said Grigori. 'Let me give you a demonstration of a selection of my favourite vodkas. We will also toast our dear departed friend Korolev.'

'Great idea.' They made their way towards the lounge bar.

***

Mike Reilly reached over and spoke into his laptop. 'Are we all here yet?' he asked, checking the small video icons that littered the screen.

'We're still waiting on Palmer,' replied Willis. As he answered, the last window blinked onto the screen. Palmer was adjusting a microphone on the front of his shirt.

'Welcome, Greg,' Willis said. 'Welcome to Kazakhstan – even if it's only via the internet.'

Willis and Sophie were in the main video conference centre of the Renaissance Hotel, Palmer was in Berkeley, and Reilly was hosting the Zoom from his office at Albert Embankment.

'Do you want me to kick off, Mike?' asked Willis after a suitable pause.

'Go ahead,' said Reilly. 'You are the most up to date, but we'll need everyone's contributions to get this sorted.'

'Thanks, Mike,' answered Willis. 'Well, most of you are up to date by now with what has happened. The seven surviving men we picked up in Kazakhstan were the main players in the operation. Klaus Fauler, their leader, has given us all the information we need. His three companions have done likewise. The three more junior members, who were providing the technical expertise, are talking their heads off too.'

Reilly interjected. 'The oil market is still in a mess, but thanks to your fast action, all is well. Everyone is now on a level playing field as far as investing is concerned. We had a tentative plan to close the markets for futures worldwide, but that won't be necessary now. It would have been impossible to put it in place, in any case. The smaller countries couldn't have resisted making a play on the market.'

'We don't have enough solid evidence to get them or anybody for the murders. But we can charge them with attempting to control the markets, and we can rely on our Russian friends to ensure that a kind of justice is handed out. At least we have prevented anyone from making any ill-gotten gains from what's happened.' Reilly believed what he was saying. Willis secretly grimaced.

'Some of the murders have been taken care of,' Willis said. 'The Golden Triangle killed Yerkin, and Boris Korolev's men finished off Sergei. By the way, would it be possible to put a commendation forward for Boris to the Russian and Kazakhstan governments for all the help he gave us? It might help his family. He did save our lives, after all.'

'That should be relatively easy compared with the other stuff that needs doing.'

'I'd also like you to send a commendation for my colleague Greg Palmer.'

'Thank you very much for that, Brad,' said Palmer. 'I appreciate it, considering how I acted.'

'Mike,' Willis said, 'one member of the group is American. Can you send a couple of heavies over to take him back to the US?'

'That will give me great pleasure,' Reilly said grimly. He cleared his throat. 'What are everybody's plans for the rest of the day?'

'I have a shift booked on one of the telescopes on Mauna Kea in Hawaii tomorrow night. I'll be flying out this evening,' volunteered Palmer.

'Good luck with the rarefied air up there,' Willis said. 'You won't have had much time to acclimatise.'

'I've managed it before. It gets easier the more often you do it, as you will be well aware, Brad. The opportunity came at short notice, and my time allocation request had been in for some time. Even more importantly, after that, I will make a quick trip to Langley, Virginia, because I have arranged to go for dinner with a very Special Agent – Charlie Dexter.'

'Congratulations, Greg. So you haven't been lazy while you've been injured. Sophie and I are having dinner in the hotel with our associate here in Kazakhstan. We wish we could invite you guys, but we'll be thinking of you.'

They signed off, and the conference ended.

Sophie said, 'I didn't know we were going for dinner with Grigori?'

'Well, you don't have to go if you don't want to. You can always fly back to a Prêt a Manger in London and get some sandwiches, but I've ordered some candles and our favourite wine for after Grigori leaves.'

'Let's go for dinner.' Sophie smiled and kissed him on the cheek. 'We can pretend we're in the Savoy.'

CHAPTER 53

Sophie, Willis and Grigori spent the next few days either in the bar or in the pool. Unfortunately, the time finally came to leave. Grigori's jet had been repaired and was waiting for him in Baikonur. As for the refinery, although it was still smoking, it was under control. All flights out of and into Atyraū were taking place as usual. Grigori had offered Willis and Sophie a lift back to Baikonur, and they had accepted. Grigori's rented Dassault Falcon would be a little crowded. There were only eight seats, but, as Grigori had pointed out, what remained of the Atyraū 'team' would have to rough it on the floor. They had left the American in Atyraū, where his own people could take care of him.

By noon, they were ready to leave. There was still the solemn task of bringing Boris Korolev's body on board. That was soon completed, and the door closed, ready for take-off. They sat at the bar, and Sabit fed them with drinks and snacks. Willis had got used to Sabit's appearance, and he no longer reminded him of Borat. He was a friendly man, and they chatted from time to time throughout the flight.

'We should keep in touch,' said Grigori. 'We have worked well together, and we've been watching each other's backs very well.'

'I would like that,' Willis said, 'but I can't imagine when that might be. I don't expect to be in Kazakhstan or Russia anytime soon.'

'Still, let's exchange details. You never can tell.'

'Who will collect the seven – or should I say six? There's one less now since we left the American behind.'

'They will stay on board with me until I leave Baikonur and get into Russian air space. I have permission to land at a military airport not far from Moscow. They will take them from there. I couldn't care less what happens to them from then.'

The six men sat aft and well behind the main seats. Their arms and feet were tied, so every second man had one arm free, and he could offer food and drink to his partner.

'How the mighty have fallen,' Grigori said. 'A week ago, they were living in the lap of luxury and looking forward to a life of plenty. Look at them now.'

'I've arranged for two heavy CIA agents to pick up the American from Atyraū,' Willis said.

'That won't be a problem,' Grigori replied. 'We must keep the wheels of diplomacy turning.'

The alcohol was mellowing Willis's mood. This had been one of the most complicated assignments he had been on. He had made a few new friends besides Grigori – there was Palmer and, of course, Baker. They could be of use in the future: having doors opened for you in the USA was invaluable. This time tomorrow, he would be back in London. He glanced at Sophie and made a mental note to book a nice restaurant for them when they arrived.

Sabit announced they were approaching Baikonur Cosmodrome. The vast grassy steppes vanished from the port window as the jet circled and prepared to land. A sharp crosswind was driving the plane to starboard. The pilot aimed the craft's nose into the wind, and it crabbed its way down until it was feet from the runway. At the last minute, he straightened up and executed a perfect landing. Only the slightest squeal from the wheels was audible as the wide-bodied jet touched down on the concrete. Minutes later, it was alongside the hangar, and they were ready to alight.

The door opened. A military salute, followed by an equally loud blast from an army band, filled the cabin. A standard was flying a red and yellow flag that Willis assumed was Boris's regimental colours. The lively music stopped, and the band struck up a slow tune: Chopin's funeral march, from Piano Sonata No. 2. It was the default choice for the former USSR. Willis and Grigori stepped back from the door and took their seats again. Six soldiers came on board, carried Boris's coffin down the steps and loaded it into a waiting military carrier. Willis and Grigori glanced at each other; their faces wore a similar respectful expression. Willis's head drooped, and he closed his eyes to hide his tears. Korolev had been a good friend, and Willis would miss his mistranslated proverbs and quaint sayings.

A stream of other soldiers came on board to escort the prisoners to their secure location.

The evening continued with much drinking and discussion about the life of Boris Korolev. Grigori translated some of the stories and anecdotes for Willis. Boris had been quite a soldier: he had clearly been much respected by his men. His great-uncle would have been proud of him.

The next morning, Willis felt as if his head was going to drop off. His brain was rattling around inside his skull as if it were several sizes too small for the space it occupied. Grigori was no better. Willis assumed that Grigori would have developed some resistance to the local vodka; that wasn't the case. Sophie was the only one who was wholly compos mentis, but she said she wasn't in the mood to hand out sympathy; they deserved everything their heads were handing out to them.

They had missed breakfast and were sitting down to an early lunch when they heard a commotion from a large hangar on their left.

The prisoners were loose inside the hangar. They had managed to acquire a couple of rifles from soldiers who were presumably under the weather from the previous night's activities and not concentrating on their duties. There would be hell to pay for this. Soldiers surrounded the prisoners, but there was nowhere for them to go. They had taken a young private hostage. Klaus Fauler held the hostage in front of his body, using him as a shield. He had a gun he had purloined from an inattentive Russian soldier. It was a standoff; neither side could gain ground. They would need to wait until something gave.

Willis's pulse sped up. Sweat poured down his face and pooled around his shirt collar. His blue shirt grew darker as it soaked up the salty liquid. In a flash, he was off. As he ran, he snatched a pistol from a soldier. He raced into the hangar and ran along by the wall until he was level with Klaus. Klaus was holding a gun above the young soldier's head. Klaus was left-handed. The hand holding the gun was in clear view. Willis edged forward, then stopped. He raised the pistol, took a deep breath and fired. The gun spun out of Klaus's hand and clattered as it bounced on the hangar's concrete floor. Willis ran up to Karl and pulled the youngster free. Klaus and Willis were at least a hundred feet from the others. Willis was sweating more. The gun was slipping in his hand. He came face to face with Klaus. Willis's face was beetroot red and glistening. His eyes stung from the salt of his sweat. He aimed and shot Klaus in both knees. The crack of bones breaking filled the hangar. Klaus fell to the floor in agony as blood spurted out from both legs.

Klaus was pleading with Willis. 'No, please. Don't. I'm sorry. I didn't intend for anyone to get hurt. Please. Don't.'

Willis stopped and took stock. Not for long. He emptied the remaining three bullets into Klaus's abdomen.

'That's for Boris Korolev.' He stood over him, spitting the words into his ear. 'I am told that abdominal wounds are a slow, painful way to die. That's how Korolev died. I hope you suffer in hell.'

The remaining prisoners had come out from behind their crates and were standing with their hands held high.

Willis threw the now empty pistol at Klaus, who was writhing in pain. Willis dropped to his knees, and darkness overwhelmed him.

***

When Willis regained consciousness, he was lying on a hard army bed. He could see the shadow of a figure standing over him. Her voice was soft, and she kept repeating, 'Brad, it wasn't your fault. It wasn't your fault.' The image of Carole dissolved as Willis came to. He could now make out two dark figures standing over him. He could hear sounds, but they were muffled and indistinct. The sound that came first was Sophie's voice.

'Brad, Brad?'

The silhouettes became real people, and Sophie's and Grigori's forms dissolved into view.

'I'm sorry.' Willis was speaking, but his voice was coming from outside his body. It felt at least four feet away. 'I'm sorry,' he repeated.

It was coming closer now. It was above his face.

Another voice spoke. 'It's okay, Brad. You're a bit of a local hero here.' It was Grigori.

'I'm sorry,' Willis repeated yet again. 'He was your cousin. I'm so sorry. I wanted to kill him to avenge Boris, but he was your cousin.'

'He was no cousin of mine.' Grigori's voice was strong. 'He was a crook. He was responsible for killing or maiming so many innocent people. As you said, Brad, may he rot in hell.'

Brad was relieved, but Grigori's comments only helped a little. He had lost control again. He would get killed or kill the wrong person one of these days. It had to stop.

Grigori was saying something. 'Come with me to St Pete's for a week, and we will try to fix your PTSD. I recognised it immediately. We've had some good results in St Petersburg. I'll see if we can get you sorted.'

'Thank you.'

'I'm not sure if I want to fix you completely.' Grigori gave a throaty laugh. 'If you hadn't landed the Falcon after that jet attack, we'd all be dead.' There was a smile on Grigori's face as he walked away and left Sophie sitting by Brad's bed.

'You gave me quite a fright.' She took his hand and squeezed it.

'Now you've seen me at my worst, twice. I am evil. I am vindictive and aggressive. It has to stop.'

'You're not evil. It's just a disorder – it can be fixed. I'll stay here with you until after you visit St Petersburg.' She bent down and kissed him on the cheek. She stroked his hair back from his forehead. Willis closed his eyes and fell asleep.

CHAPTER 54

'Well, this is it.' Grigori was clearly proud of his home town.

'St Petersburg is beautiful.' Sophie was staring at the Church of the Spilled Blood. Its multi-coloured onion domes were bathed in the cool rays of the winter sun. From its position low on the horizon, the sun illuminated the three largest domes, displaying the church in all its glory.

'We have nothing as magnificent as this where I come from.' She took Willis's hand and squeezed it. They were standing leaning on the low wall at the side of the Griboyedov Canal. The canal flowed past the church on its left, completing the picture-postcard view of the panorama that stretched out in front of them. Grigori had informed them that 'Spilled blood' referred to the assassination of Alexander II in 1881. The Romanov imperial family had funded the church, to the tune of 4.5 million roubles, as a tribute to him.

'Your appointment at the Central Clinic is not until seven this evening,' said Grigori. 'I've managed to get you a late slot after the clinic closed. The professor owes me a favour.' He smiled mischievously.

'I'm not comfortable with this.' Willis wasn't keen on the idea of someone messing with his head, but he knew it was worth a try. 'But I'll give it a shot.' Somehow, he had to get his impulses under control.

They walked into the magnificent building. Inside, 7,500 square metres of mosaics decorated the church's walls and ceiling. Their bright colours filled visitors with awe, and a spectrum of hues and shades attacked their senses.

'Wow,' Sophie whispered as she admired the beauty of the central dome and the mosaic of Christ Pantocrator. His large dark eyes stared down at her, unblinking, unmoving. She shuddered and moved on to admire the circular mosaic pattern in the centre of the floor. Willis and Sophie were happy: they felt comfortable together.

'You two must make the most of your time together. Once treatment is underway, it will be more difficult to see each other.' Grigori's tone was serious, but then he smiled. 'Don't worry – it will all be worth it. We will be able to meet for dinner in the evenings once Brad's sessions are over.'

They spent the rest of the afternoon exploring, laughing and enjoying themselves. They felt carefree and at peace. They ate early in preparation for Brad's appointment at seven.

They arrived at the clinic in plenty of time. It was just as well, as it took over twenty minutes to register. Willis had to fill out a long form detailing his past medical history. Fortunately, most of the sections were blank as he had so little to report. The clinic was modern. Its walls were painted off-white and covered with bright, modern paintings of indeterminate objects. Edvard Munch could well have produced the oil painting that hung on the main wall. A vandalised version of *The Scream* was the first thing that came to Willis's mind. Someone had taken a brush and smeared the face into a big yellow semi-circle.

It didn't take long for Professor Sidorov to arrive and introduce himself. 'I'm Alek, and you must be Dr Willis?' He held out his hand and welcomed Willis. 'Please follow me. This is a large clinic, and it takes a while to learn your way around.'

His English was excellent, and he had only the slightest accent. He was about five foot eight inches but broad. He wore a tiny pair of half-lensed glasses. His hair was combed over to hide a balding area above his high forehead. The professor began the meeting in a relaxed way. He ordered coffee and biscuits, and they chatted about their journey and how they liked St Petersburg.

'Right then, let's get this kicked off, Brad.' The professor pointed down a long corridor and led Brad away. He turned and spoke to Grigori and Sophie. 'The first session will take about an hour. You are welcome to wait. There's a cafeteria through those glass doors.' He waved his hand in its general direction. Grigori and Sophie took the hint, rose and headed in the direction indicated.

'I wish I could be with him,' said Sophie. 'He isn't feeling very comfortable about this at all.'

'He'll be fine,' Grigori reassured her. 'Let's have some coffee. The time will flash by.'

***

Willis expected to be invited to lie on a couch. That was his image of how a psychiatrist operated. But the reality was nothing like that – and anyway, he wasn't even sure if the professor was a psychiatrist. They simply sat and chatted. Professor Sidorov was interested in his flashbacks and asked Willis what he had identified as triggers for his attacks. They chatted for about half an hour, then Sidorov suggested that Willis close his eyes and try to recall the incident. Willis told Alek about the car accident and his wife's death. Willis was becoming agitated even discussing it, so the professor cut short the session and suggested they recommence the next day, but at 10 a.m. He said that he would like to try hypnotism on Willis. Did he agree? Reluctantly, Willis agreed.

'I look forward to meeting you again tomorrow.'

'I'll be here.'

***

'That wasn't bad,' Brad told Sophie and Grigori, 'but I've got a feeling it's just the beginning.'

They went back to their hotel and retired to the bar. Willis was putting a brave face on things, but he was clearly nervous about the next stages. He sat and played with his cognac but made no attempt to drink it. He didn't join in the conversation; his attention was focused somewhere else. If this was to work, Willis would have to give it a fair chance. That would mean agreeing with anything the professor requested of him, but still, he was having doubts.

'I need to share something with you, Brad.' Grigori moved closer. 'I was involved in the Second Chechen War in 2004. It was a shit place to be, but I had no choice in the matter. I was close to the front line, and many of my friends and comrades were either killed or maimed. On my second tour of duty, I caught shrapnel from a landmine. I was in a bad state, and the army retired me from active duty. That's how I got to know Professor Sidorov. I had severe PTSD – that's how I recognised it in you so quickly. The man is a near genius, and he fixed me. He can do the same for you. Just give him a chance.'

Brad looked up from his drink. 'Thanks, Grigori, that gives me some confidence. It's good of you to share that with me. It's like staring down a dark tunnel and not knowing what lurks at its far end.'

'I know the exact feeling, but persevere – it is always better to know. You are a scientist. You know that knowledge is always better.'

Willis nodded. Then he took a swig of his cognac. 'I think I'll have another of these.'

***

Willis's next two visits to Professor Sidorov followed the same pattern. The professor would try to hypnotise Willis, who would begin to go under, but later, when he got close to describing the accident, he would sweat, become agitated and sit up.

'This isn't working.' The professor sighed. 'We'll need to think of a different approach.'

Willis slouched in his chair, disheartened and exhausted.

'Tomorrow,' the professor said, 'I want your permission to try something different. I would like to try to sedate you before we proceed. May I do that?'

'I'll try anything, but won't that interfere with my recollection of the events?'

'It would if I used an ordinary sedative, but there is a special one I'd like your permission to try. Because it worked on your friend Grigori, I am confident that it will work on you. And he has given me permission to tell you about his treatment and that I used it on him. It will remove your anxiety but keep you alert enough to take part. Its effects are not fully known yet, and I can only use it once. It is the last resort. May I try it?'

Willis nodded slowly. He was unsure but was willing to try it.

'Tomorrow will be another early session. I will book you in for a two-hour slot.'

***

Willis didn't sleep well. He was worried that the treatment might be a waste of time, and he tossed and turned in bed.

This sedative had better be strong, he thought. He had discussed his conversation with Professor Sidorov with Sophie. Repeating it didn't make it sound more positive, but it was all or nothing. Tomorrow would be the day of reckoning. Until he had undergone all the treatment on offer, there was no way Willis could be sure that it would work, but hope was driving him to stay the course.

Willis's alarm went off at eight o'clock, but it needn't have bothered. He was wide awake and waiting for its irritating buzz. Sophie turned over and wanted to go back to sleep again. He showered, shaved, dressed and waited impatiently for Sophie to finish putting on her make-up. How strange it is, he philosophised. On important days in your life, other things appear so trivial – shaving, for example.

They finished breakfast and were at the clinic by nine thirty. The professor was already waiting. Willis vanished into the consulting room and prepared himself for what lay ahead, whatever that might be. The professor seemed to be in no hurry: he took the time to discuss what he was planning with Willis once again. 'I would like your permission to record the session. It will help me later with my assessment of your condition.'

Willis nodded.

When they were both clear about the route they were taking, the professor produced a hypodermic and carefully filled it with a pale yellow fluid. He strapped and wiped Willis's arm and felt for the best vein. The liquid took no more than five seconds to dissipate into his system.

Professor Sidorov went over to his desk and picked up a pen to fill in a form. As he did, he glanced over at Willis several times. Five minutes passed. Ten minutes passed.

While Willis was waiting, he bit his tongue and lip. Both felt normal. If this was a sedative, it was having little or no effect on what he sensed or felt.

'I don't feel any different.'

'I wouldn't expect you to. That's the strength of this sedative – you feel completely normal.'

After fifteen minutes, Professor Sidorov came and sat beside Willis. 'Still feeling normal?'

Willis nodded.

'Okay,' the professor said, 'let's see how we get on now. Close your eyes and empty your mind as much as possible.'

There was a long pause to let Willis relax and allow his mind to wander. Professor Sidorov put a CD on the player and set the volume control to the minimum level possible.

'Now, Brad, in your own time, I want you to describe the day of the accident to me. Go back to when you got into your car to drive home.'

Willis was speaking slowly. He described leaving the restaurant and having difficulty finding his car keys. When he got to the car, there had been a flyer under his wiper blade for a company that organised weddings. Willis was amazed by the amount of detail he remembered. He drove out of the restaurant's car park and onto the road back to the village. It was dark. When a car braked in front of him, its lights were painfully bright. It was incredible – the details he recalled impressed Willis. They continued along the road and passed the hardware store. The radio was off, and they were deep in conversation. Wasn't the restaurant lovely? Carole told him that the service and the waiters were excellent. Music was playing in the distance – playing loudly. He could make out the song. It was Neil Sedaka's 'Oh Carole'. Willis turned and smiled at Carole.

'It's our song.'

She smiled back and blew him a kiss. The road straightened. A red car was approaching, fast. It was a TR3. It was the last version manufactured in 1962 – a beautiful car. Its top was down, and the driver and passenger were waving their arms in time with the music. The car swung around the corner, wider and wider. It crossed the double white line in the centre of the road. The driver had lost control and was heading straight for them. Time slowed down as Willis heaved his car hard left. It was no use: it was still going to ram him.

It hit them.

The impact was powerful. Willis and Carole were thrown forward. Airbags and seatbelts lessened the impact; as Willis opened his eyes, he saw steam billowing out of his fractured radiator. He turned to look at Carole. The horror of the situation became real. Carole was staring into space. She was gone.

Willis screamed and waved his arms at the driver of the Triumph. A thin man with dark hair and a pencil-thin moustache was struggling with the steering wheel. An image of Clark Gable sprang to Willis's mind. The driver was revving his smoking engine and reversing away. Shit, he was running from the accident. The steam had cleared from the burst radiator. Willis could read the TR3's number plate. All of it. He could clearly read the six-digit number plate. The digits of the old-style plate were clear in his mind.

Willis sat bolt upright in his chair, taking the professor by surprise. He lurched back to avoid a possible collision.

'I saw the number plate – all of it.' Willis was grinning from ear to ear. 'I saw the bastard's number plate.' He stood and walked over to the professor's desk. He picked up a pen and notebook, and then he stopped. His face lost all of its enthusiasm.

'Damn. I can't remember it.'

The professor gave Willis a few minutes to compose himself. He needed to recover from his disappointment and the trauma caused by the interruption to his concentration.

'The good news is, I have plenty to work with. Two more sessions and I should have you well on your way.'

'But I saw the bloody number plate.'

'The drug I gave you has that side-effect; it blocks out memories of the finer details you experience.'

Willis slumped in his chair and held his head in his hands. Tears filled his eyes, and his gaze dropped. Disappointment was written all over his face.

'Let's stop for the day,' the professor said kindly. 'You've been through enough. But don't be despondent – we have made good progress.'

One thing was clear: the sedative had the ability to enhance Willis's memory and make him remember, in great detail, things that had previously been locked away and hidden. As soon as he had the opportunity, he would persuade the professor to try the drug on him one more time so he could remember other details about the accident.

***

The next two visits were fruitful, but Willis kept pushing the professor for another session using the drug. He kept refusing, emphasising the danger. They had, nevertheless, covered a lot of territory. They had gone over the accident again and again. Willis was tired of the constant repetition. Professor Sidorov sensed his frustration: that was the effect he wanted. Willis was making progress: one more session might do it.

The last session was longer than the others. Professor Sidorov gave Willis a grilling about his feelings and thoughts. They went through the details of the accident one more time. Willis provided the detail without thinking; it had become automatic and was completely devoid of emotion. The professor smiled, looking pleased. He was finally satisfied that he could record a definite improvement in how Willis was handling his memories.

'This will be our last meeting,' said the professor. 'You need to go back to your life and let things progress. It might not improve straight away – it will be a gradual process.'

'Thanks, Professor. I feel different. Although I can't put a finger on what it is, it feels better.'

'That's what I would expect at this stage. Take things slowly – you might still dream now and then, but the incidents should reduce. As long as things are improving, fine. If they get worse, I'm at the end of the phone. We can always Skype if necessary.' The professor rummaged in his untidy top drawer and produced a business card. 'Don't hesitate to let me know how you get on. I'd like to follow up on how you are doing for my notes in any case.'

'Thank you again, Professor.' Willis stood to leave.

'Wait a moment. I have something for you.' Alek opened his desk drawer and produced a thumb drive. 'What I didn't tell you is that I record everything in my sessions. I don't give copies of the sessions to clients, but in this case, I've made an exception. It's not a full session, but it's a few important seconds of one.' He pushed the drive into the player on his desk and adjusted the volume. Willis sat up straight when the recording began to play. His voice could be heard indistinctly in places.

Hell, I can read the number plate. His voice was low and indistinct. *MN? 3? On a 1962 TR3, and there's an antique AA badge on the radiator.* The recording went silent. That was the only part of the interview the professor had recorded. Willis's jaw dropped. Only the first two letters and the first number were intelligible. During the interview, his voice had lowered, and he had swallowed the rest of the details.

'I have made an exception in your case as this is evidence. You couldn't have it earlier in case it distracted you from your recovery. I hope you find whoever you are looking for.'

'Thank you. Thank you. Even a partial is useful. On a classic car, it will be easy to trace.'

The professor handed over the disc. Willis took his hand and gripped it in both of his, shaking it with enthusiasm. It was the kind of enthusiasm that followed an epiphany.

They walked out to reception, where Sophie and Grigori rose to meet Willis.

'I've had a very successful session.' He was grinning from ear to ear.

EPILOGUE

Sophie had been as good as her word. She had stayed with Willis throughout his treatment in St Petersburg. Only time would tell whether it had been successful or not. They were back in Madingley, at Willis's house. He walked over to the Welsh dresser and picked up a silver frame. It contained a picture of Carole. She was smiling in it. It was the smile Willis would always remember. Fond memories of their time together flooded into his mind. He reminisced about their honeymoon in Venice. He smiled as he remembered their gondola trip down the Grand Canal. They had travelled from San Marco Basilica all the way to the Santa Chiara Church before exploring the smaller back canals of the city. They were alone on the gondola, as Willis had privately hired it for the afternoon. Carole had lain, relaxed, in his arms throughout the four-hour trip. Every so often, she would turn and kiss him, sometimes on the cheek, sometimes on the lips. Those were fond memories indeed. Willis shook his head. He was experiencing no adverse reaction – no sweats or increase in his heart rate. Perhaps he could now get on with his life?

Perhaps he could learn to manage his grief? Perhaps the professor's treatment had worked, and he was cured? The professor had warned him not to expect miracles right away, but surely this was a good sign? He smiled and secretly crossed his fingers.

***

Their flight had landed early, and they had arrived at the house before noon. Willis collected the ingredients to make brunch. He had just put the bacon in the pan when Sophie put her arms around him.

'A penny for your thoughts. You were smiling. Care to share them?'

'It's nothing,' he lied. He wanted to keep his thoughts to himself for the time being.

'Okay, then tell me something else. What's all this about you and British intelligence, Brad? That sneaked up on me. I had no idea. Will that mean you'll hardly ever be at home?'

Willis switched the heat off under the pan and turned to give her his full attention. 'I was planning to tell you, and I meant to on several occasions, but I kept putting it off. It was one of the reasons I didn't get in touch with you after university. I was travelling a lot, and I spent several months in South America, then … you know what happened next. I was married. Then I wasn't. And it might complicate our relationship a little if I keep dashing about all over the place.'

'No more than when you were an astronomer.'

'I am still an astronomer. Being an astronomer makes it easier for me to travel across borders than most people. I have the cover of conferences, lectures and my research. I visit countries where there are big telescopes, and it fits in quite well with my work with the department. For example, I used my status to get into CERN on this trip, but Kazakhstan was another thing. I've never travelled with a forged passport before.'

'Don't any of your work colleagues ever suspect?'

'I sometimes have a bit of explaining to do because I sometimes miss appointments, as you can imagine, and I'm not always where I'm supposed to be. Other than that, it works quite well. My department chief is aware, which helps.' He grinned.

'I can only imagine.' Sophie smiled. 'I wish I could have travelled with you.'

'I owe my life to you. If you hadn't rung Korolev in twenty minutes rather than my suggestion of thirty minutes when I was in that storeroom, I'd be dead now.' He took her in his arms and kissed her.

Sophie broke his embrace and smiled again. 'Actually, I left it for thirty-five minutes. I couldn't bring myself to ring him before you had a chance to do whatever you were planning to do.'

'What? Oh! Keep smiling,' Willis said. He took her in his arms and kissed her again. 'Is this the first time you've been kissed by a spy?'

'Don't you guys call yourselves agents? Don't answer that.' She rolled her eyes.

'Why don't you move in with me in Madingley? It isn't far from the Institute of Astronomy in Cambridge, and this is my second home when I'm away from my telescopes.'

Sophie held him tighter. 'You could, of course, offer to come to Geneva instead. But Madingley might be nice. I'll give it a lot of consideration, but it won't be for a while. I have a job to finish. I ought to explain …'

'That would indeed be nice.' Willis suddenly gasped and struck his forehead. 'God! It's just dawned on me. What an idiot. The real name of the Golden Triangle's leader, Pythagoras, is Klaus Fauler. That's an anagram of Klaus Laufer. So, it was he who called me at the Institute of Astronomy and kicked everything off. He did it to get as much publicity for their scheme as quickly as possible. Anyway, how about some pizza?'

'Before we think of pizza, I have something to tell you,' Sophie said seriously. 'You might like to sit down. I've been putting off telling you about this, *and* you interrupted me as I tried to answer when you asked me about moving in with you at Madingley.' She took a breath. 'The holes Yeung forged in the photograph were probably false … or they might not have been. Sorry, that didn't make sense. Anyway, I asked for fresh photographs to be taken, and guess what? The latest photographs show the holes. The holes are real. The holes in the bloody magnet are real.'

Willis's mouth fell open.

'They're even smaller than the ones Yeung had fabricated – that is if he really did fabricate them. They are a lot smaller, but they are there nevertheless. Villiers's photographs might be genuine.'

'Does that mean that we might have a new energy source like the Russian mob proposed?'

'I hope so. It doesn't necessarily follow, but it does suggest a new particle or at least a new combination of particles. It took a lot of energy to create the holes in the core of the magnet.'

'That is amazing. Might the particles only get produced at a critical energy level in the detector?'

'Hmm, maybe,' said Sophie. 'You might have hit on the right answer. It would explain why we hadn't detected them before.'

'This will cause a run on the oil markets again if it gets out.'

'I doubt it. Many years of work will have to be done on the discovery before we can state anything for definite. You know how conservative we physicists are.'

'Well, you might get your Nobel Prize yet,' joked Willis.

'That's the rub,' said Sophie. 'There's so much to do in Geneva. I will need to be there for some time. There might be Nobel Prizes going in the future – not necessarily for me, but for members of my team. So, the bottom line is, I can't consider moving to Madingley with you – not for some time, at any rate.' Her eyes filled with tears.

While Willis had expected this reply, and although he knew he deserved it, he was still disappointed. But he knew he had treated Sophie terribly in the past by not staying in contact. Perhaps things would change when her research was completed, but he would need to pay her more attention in future.

'Well, that's let me down with a thump. But it's nothing more than I deserve. Maybe I was too impetuous, but I was hoping that you were thinking long-term. Maybe even Willis and Fenwick.'

'Fenwick and Willis would be more like it,' she said, wiping her cheeks.

'Or even Willis and Willis.' Willis gazed into her eyes.

'Are you suggesting what I think you are?' Sophie came close, put her arms around his neck and kissed him on the mouth.

Willis returned her kiss with even more passion. 'As soon as we can find the time, let's sit down and discuss all the options. We're both scientists, so we should be able to find a solution.'

There was a loud meow from by the back door. Willis opened it, and Ptolemy came rushing in. He ignored Willis and ran straight for Sophie. He jumped on her lap and stretched up to rub against her face.

'Well, I'll be… Even Ptolemy gives his approval. That's a first. He doesn't usually make friends that easily.'

'I can't right now.' Tears filled her eyes again. 'But I promise you I'll give it my fullest consideration. I'll be with you as soon as I can.'

By now, Ptolemy was purring loudly.

'Okay. I'll settle for some pizza if you fancy it?'

'Well, maybe one slice … just maybe…'

Willis was happy. He was very, very happy.

If you enjoyed this story, please consider leaving
a review on Amazon. Reviews help attract readers' attention
to books and promote sales.

Thank you

Contact the author:

tom.boles@tomboles.org

Follow Tom Boles on Bookbub:

https://www.bookbub.com/authors/tom-boles

ACKNOWLEDGEMENTS

I would like to thank my editor Jane Hammett for keeping me on the straight and narrow and for her encouragement and useful suggestions. My gratitude goes to my friends John and Linda McElroy, who provided help and suggestions in the early stage of writing. Many thanks to my many astronomer friends who double-checked my facts and read the manuscript.

About The Author

Tom Boles has discovered more supernovae than any other person in history. Tom is a Fellow of the Royal Astronomical Society and a past President of The British Astronomical Association. He was awarded the Merlin Medal and the Walter Goodacre Award for his contribution to astronomy. The International Astronomical Union named main-belt asteroid 7648, Tomboles, in his honour. He has published many scientific papers on supernovae and written numerous articles for popular astronomy magazines. He has made many television appearances, ranging from BBC's Tomorrow's World to The Sky at Night. During recent years, he has given Enrichment Lectures on astronomy aboard Cunard liners, mainly their flagship Queen Mary 2. During these trips, he has designed and presented shows using the ship's onboard planetarium, the only one at sea. His experience as an astronomer inspired this story. His first novel, DARK ENERGY, was published in June 2021. He lives in rural Suffolk, where he enjoys regular cloudless nights and dark skies, free from light pollution.

BOOKS BY THIS AUTHOR

SHADES of WHITE

The second book in the Brad Willis series

MI6 calls on Brad Willis to go to Antarctica to investigate powerful and dangerous radio surges. Their strength cannot be rationally explained. They are interfering with experiments and instrumentation. Laboratories have been damaged. People are dying.

Electrical supplies are mysteriously failing. Planes are dropping from the sky. Who is doing this? How are they doing this? Murder and sabotage impede his investigations. Brad Willis must stop them before the Antarctic base is locked down for the winter. If he fails, everyone on the base will freeze to death.

MURDER comes by LIMO

The third book in the Brad Willis series

Brad and Sophie trace the red Triumph sports car involved in the hit and run that caused his late wife's death. His investigations reveal many facts about Carole's life that neither Brad nor Carole knew. This leads him into a world of crime and deception, putting both his and Sophie's lives in danger. Soon, Brad is investigating crime at the highest levels of British society. An innocent man's future depends on Willis succeeding.

Printed in Great Britain
by Amazon

83956941R00193